He was dres
from a

The only thing missing

that Dorothea imagined all those cow-fellows wore.

"Where is he?" the man demanded as he pushed past Dorothea. "Get Bright out here! *Pronto!*"

"Sir," she said in her fiercest voice, "I demand that you leave my father's house at once—"

"Your father!" He let out a bark of a laugh and pierced her with his steely blue gaze. "Don't tell me the old bastard has a partner in crime!"

"I should say n— Crime?" Dorothea sputtered. "What on earth are you—"

There was a murderous gleam in his eyes. He was not a man to be taken lightly, and a shudder of apprehension skittered down Dorothea's back. The men she knew in Oxford were all civilized men.

Dorothea had no idea what to expect from *this* one....

* * *

Scoundrel's Daughter
Harlequin Historical #656—May 2003

Praise for Margo Maguire's latest titles

His Lady Fair
"You'll love this Cinderella story."
—*Rendezvous*

Dryden's Bride
"Exquisitely detailed...an entrancing tale that will enchant and envelop you as love conquers all."
—*Rendezvous*

The Bride of Windermere
"Packed with action...fast, humorous, and familiar...*The Bride of Windermere* will fit into your weekend just right."
—*Romantic Times*

Margo Maguire

SCOUNDREL'S DAUGHTER

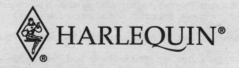

HARLEQUIN®

TORONTO • NEW YORK • LONDON
AMSTERDAM • PARIS • SYDNEY • HAMBURG
STOCKHOLM • ATHENS • TOKYO • MILAN • MADRID
PRAGUE • WARSAW • BUDAPEST • AUCKLAND

ISBN 0-373-29256-2

SCOUNDREL'S DAUGHTER

Copyright © 2003 by Margo Wider

Visit us at www.eHarlequin.com

Printed in U.S.A.

This book is dedicated to my daughter, Julia Maguire.

Prologue

Africa
December, 1882

It couldn't possibly get any hotter or more desperate, Jack Temple thought as the son of the Bahisi chief yanked the ropes tighter around his wrists. Jeering women and children had gathered around, and the village witch doctor pranced in circles around them, shaking a rattle made of lions' teeth in one hand, while he screeched incantations.

Distracted, the chief's son didn't notice when Jack turned his hands back to front before being tied. Jack managed to keep a small space between his hands so the twine would be easier to slip off. It was his only hope of getting himself and O'Neill out of this mess.

Christ, he was getting too old for this!

The warrior jerked Temple against a tall, wooden stump that stood upright in the center of the village and tied him to it. Sweat poured from his forehead, running into his eyes, and he was powerless to wipe it away.

Unfortunately, sweat was the least of his worries.

When the drums began their ominous beat and the warriors started dancing, Jack knew that trouble had just begun.

"Where in hell is Alastair Bright?" O'Neill muttered. Jack could feel the older man twisting his arms against the ropes that tied them to each other's backs. If Bright did not return and mount a rescue effort, O'Neill and Jack were certain to die. Miserably.

On the other hand, anything Bright managed would have to be nothing short of a miracle. They were outnumbered at least twenty to one, and that was counting only the men. Looking at the people gathering around him, Jack knew he wouldn't want to have to do battle against any of the women, either.

His eyes burned with the blistering heat while his head pounded with whatever drug they'd poured into him earlier in the day. His tongue felt thick, and it stuck to the roof of his mouth, to his teeth. Half-naked men and women swayed before him, their colorful figures becoming blurry as the drug took effect.

Even so, Jack's wits were still at least somewhat intact. He might be slow, but he wasn't dead yet, and he had no intention of departing the land of the living without a fight. Even as the Bahisi people waved their rattles and bangles threateningly before him, he actively worked to get free.

Twisting his hands to loosen his bonds, he forced himself to keep his focus, to ignore the witch doctor's pointed taunts and the sharp spears carried by each of the warriors.

"*Kizushi! Majiza! Wauaji!*" sputtered the prancing, brightly painted man. He was naked except for a bright red sash tied around his waist and wide armbands made of leopard fur. His legs and chest bore bright slashes of paint, intricate patterns of blue and white contrasting with his black skin.

"What's he saying?" O'Neill croaked. Jack's old friend never learned any of the local languages of the exotic places they traveled. He hired the bearers and sailors and managed to procure lodgings, food and medical services when necessary—always using a kind of pidgin-English that somehow got him by.

"He says the tribal gods are angry that the Kohamba figure was taken."

"Yes, but we don't have it, do we?" O'Neill said petulantly.

"No, Bright's got it," Jack replied.

"And it didn't belong to the Bahisi tribe anyway!" O'Neill's voice was an angry rasp. His words were beginning to slur, but they were still tinged with the indignation of an idealist.

"You want to clarify the situation for them, O'Neill?" Jack said through gritted teeth. "Tell them that we came into deepest, darkest Africa only to *photograph* the powerful Kohamba, but that one of our party decided to steal it?"

"Can't we?" O'Neill asked desperately. "After all, it was Alastair Bright who double-crossed us and took it. And the statue belongs to the Mongasa tribe, so—"

"So the Mongasas should be the ones to kill us?"

"Kill us?" O'Neill sounded even more panicky than before. "They m-mean to kill us?"

Jack loosened his tongue and tried, unsuccessfully, to moisten his lips. For all the miles they'd traveled together, O'Neill was painfully naive. "When all this hoopla is over—the drums, the chanting—they're going to torch the brush at our feet and burn us."

"*Christ,* sir!" O'Neill cried. "We've got to *do* something! How long will the dancing last?"

"I don't know," Jack replied. "But I'm working on these bindings around my wrists. You might want to do the same."

"Then what?" O'Neill asked and Jack could feel him struggling frantically to yank his hands free. "We're surrounded by an entire village of naked heathens! They have spears! And knives!"

"I don't have a plan yet," Jack replied with as much calm as he could muster. "Go easy on the bindings, O'Neill. Use your fingers and see if you can feel a rough edge on this stump that we can use to cut the ropes."

"All r-right, all right," O'Neill said, and Jack could feel the man's hands moving less frantically than before. He didn't think it would be possible to saw through the ropes in such a short amount of time, but the task would give O'Neill something to think about while Jack got his own bindings off.

And then what?

Jack squinted his eyes against the painful light and looked around him. Their situation was as hopeless as any he'd ever been in. If they managed to escape their bonds, they'd have to get out of the village. Once out of the village, they would be in jungle so deep, they'd be lucky if they traveled a mile without being attacked by wild animals or captured by another hostile tribe.

Damn Alastair Bright!

Jack should never have trusted him. The man called himself professor, but Jack now knew he was a charlatan—certainly he was no academic man of any reputation.

It seemed like years since Jack had met Bright in a

tavern on the isle of Unguja. Jack's instincts had warned against trusting the man, but he hadn't been able to get around the Englishman. Bright was the one who'd learned the location of the Mongasa tribe from a slave working on a Persian steamer out of Mombasa. Bright was the only white man who knew how to find the village of the Mongasa people, where the tribesmen most certainly kept the obsidian carving of their god, Kohamba.

Jack hadn't been able to resist going on the expedition deep into Njiri territory. Few white men had ever ventured so far into the jungle, and even fewer had returned. Enough, however, had spoken of the Kohamba Legend, to pique the intense interest of archaeologists and explorers all over the Western world. Jack Temple had not been immune.

"The ropes won't budge, sir," O'Neill said, his voice edgy with panic, but thickly drugged. "If you have any other ideas, you might share them with me now."

Jack was out of ideas beyond catching Alastair Bright and beating him to a pulp. When he got out of this mess, he was going to hunt the man down and flay him within an inch of his life. Then he was going to take the Kohamba from him and see it returned to the Mongasa tribe.

He shook his head to clear it. Planning his revenge against Bright was not going to break them out of their fetters, nor see them safely away from the village. He would have to try something drastic. Something completely unexpected.

The drums stopped and an eerie silence ensued. Jack could practically hear O'Neill's heart beating as loudly as the drums had pounded. Or was that his own heartbeat?

"Munga hasira kupanda Bahisi!" Jack yelled to the head man. It was an impulse, a delaying tactic, and nothing more.

"What did you say?" O'Neill croaked.

"I think I told him that the gods believe the Bahisi stole Kohamba from the Mongasa tribe."

"What? Now, they'll just kill us outright! We don't stand—"

"Kodi ukami gunduliwa tena yenu majana ka-rema," Jack shouted.

He had only the barest inkling of a plan, and a slim hope that he'd know what to do next—that is, if the Bahisi didn't decide to torch them immediately.

Four men approached, gathering around the stake. None of them spoke, but all eyed him suspiciously. One held up a gourd, painted and decorated with animal hair, and shook it. The others bared their glistening, white teeth. They were angry, but they were also afraid. They had probably never encountered a man like Jack before, and certainly never a red-haired fellow like O'Neill, with his ruddy face and bushy mutton-chops. Jack had to make the most of their ignorance.

He didn't dare move. He would not flinch, nor blink an eye. He hoped he had spoken the Njiri words correctly, telling these men that the gods would be angry with them for stealing Kohamba. That they would have drought and their women would be barren. He hoped his words might make them a little bit afraid of him—as if perhaps he had some power to call down the wrath of the gods.

There was a sudden, significant give in the bindings

around his wrist, and Jack worked at them as he spoke quietly and slowly to O'Neill, as if he were chanting. "I might have rattled the chief enough to get us out of these ropes. If they free us, keep quiet and let me do the talking. Act as if you know something they don't."

The quiet words were meaningless to the chief and his sons, but Jack wanted O'Neill to be prepared for anything. "Are you making any progress?" Jack asked.

"Maybe," O'Neill replied. "I've got one hand entirely free. But I don't know if I can stand up unassisted."

The Bahisi tribesmen stepped away, eyeing Jack suspiciously. The gourd-rattling continued, but the drums remained silent and Jack thought the warriors didn't look as confident, or as belligerent, as they had only a minute before.

Still, Jack had to remember his perceptions were probably skewed by the drugs in his system. These men might be wielding machetes and he would not know it.

"How's your head, O'Neill?" he asked. Something snapped and he felt the rope give way. Both hands were loose. He kept them still, holding on to the rope so it wouldn't slip down and gain the warriors' notice.

"I—I'm not sure," O'Neill replied. "I feel like someone's taken an ax to it, sir."

"I'm going to untie you. But stay where you are," Jack said. "Lean against the stump for balance."

One of the Bahisi tribesmen ventured closer to the prisoners. Hissing through his teeth, he squinted his eyes and gave Jack a sidelong glance. Jack wasn't sure whether he was supposed to be frightened or impressed. Standing stock-still, he furiously tried to wrap his mind around a plan.

A wild shriek pierced his ears, and the tribesmen scuttled away. Fighting waves of dizziness, Jack took advantage of the moment, turned and grabbed O'Neill's hands. He tore at the ropes until the man was free, then propelled him toward the closest hut. They had difficulty walking, but continued on out of sheer force of will. Reaching the cover of the hut, Jack turned and saw that their captors were trying to repel an all-out attack. Spears flew, and grass huts were in flames.

Jack could not be certain, but it looked like the Mongasa warriors had come.

Chapter One

London
Late spring, 1883

The crush of the crowd and all the disgusting smells of London assailed Dorothea Bright as she rode toward her father's house atop a wagon carrying her belongings. She lifted a clean linen handkerchief to her nose and sniffed daintily. No wonder her mother had chosen to live in Oxford. Honoria Bright would never have allowed Dorothea, with her delicate constitution, to live in such a horrible place.

The train ride had been noisome, her fellow travelers rank and offensive. Dorothea could not understand how anyone would tolerate traveling by rail more than once in a lifetime.

She would never have come to London, but circumstances had dictated the move. Her dear mother had recently passed on, and their house in Oxford was to be occupied now by its rightful owner, a distant cousin, the earl of Groton. Dorothea tried not to harbor any resentment against the earl, who had allowed Honoria and Dorothea to reside in the Oxfordshire house for nearly twenty years, ever since their ignoble abandonment by Alastair Bright.

For those twenty years past, Dorothea had seen neither hide nor hair of her father. She knew little more of him than his credentials as a scholar and his reputation for wanderlust. The latter was responsible for her parents' estrangement. Honoria could not abide a husband who was away more than he was present, and therefore she did without any husband at all.

Mother and daughter fared very well in Oxford. As long as Dorothea avoided any upset, she did not suffer the shortness of breath and palpitations of the heart that had resulted from a terrible illness when she was a child.

Honoria was well respected in town. And Dorothea, by virtue of her surprising head for ancient languages, became a highly regarded consultant to several of the professors of antiquity at the university. She earned a respectable allowance through these endeavors, along with the esteem of Albert Bloomsby, a young master whose primary academic interest was in the written languages of ancient India. Dorothea happened to be quite expert in Avestan, Pali and Pakrit, and Albert made use of her fluency in these ancient languages whenever he came across a particularly sticky translation.

He'd been a suitor of sorts, as well, though his aptitude for courtship rivaled his talents at translations of ancient texts.

Still, Dorothea had been surprised when he had not offered for her hand upon her mother's death. Surely he had known that she had nowhere to go, no other family to help her. None but her father, whom she had not seen in twenty years and could easily have gone another twenty before meeting again. Dorothea would have been the perfect wife for an aspiring academician—intelligent, poised, well-bred. She was, after all, the granddaughter of an earl. Surely Albert knew he would not do better.

Unless he had somehow learned of her heart condition. Her mother had always warned her never to discuss her condition, or she'd find herself left out of the few activities that were allowed. So Dorothea had learned early on, to keep her little sufferings to herself. As long as she did not engage in any activity that taxed her weakened heart, she remained mostly free of symptoms.

Sighing, she straightened her sagging spine and gave her attention to the buildings she passed, to the overcrowded omnibuses and to the men digging at the roadways. Activity and industry was everywhere she turned. She felt tired, but not overly so. It felt strangely good, in fact, to exert herself, even to this small extent. Of course she'd never done such things in Oxford, or she'd have caught a terrible scolding from her mother.

''Comin' up to it, ma'am,'' said the driver. ''On yer left.''

They reached a neighborhood of residential buildings, and it seemed decent enough to Dorothea. The streets were clean and the houses neat and tidy. Road traffic was not quite so heavy here. Porter Street seemed an acceptable location for her father's home.

Dorothea straightened her jacket of dark blue, then brushed the worst of the dust from her skirt of the same material. She wished she'd had proper mourning attire, but there hadn't been enough money to purchase anything new. She hoped her father would not notice its wilted condition. Not that she cared what he thought, exactly, but he hadn't laid eyes on her since she was five years old. She would not have him thinking she look anything less than the perfectly bred lady her mother had reared.

Refastening the pins in her elaborately decorated straw hat, she smoothed back the loose tendrils of hair that had escaped her prim topknot. She centered the small blue bow at her collar, and pinched a bit of color into her cheeks.

The wagon came to a jarring stop in front of a red-brick house with a black door, nearly throwing Dorothea off the bench and onto the floor. Regaining her balance, she came to her feet and stood unsteadily in the wagon bed with her trunk of clothes and several boxes of books and notes.

Intending to speak sharply to the driver, she discovered him engaged in loud conversation with a man who'd come out from the house. It took Dorothea only a moment to understand that the two men were arguing.

She cleared her throat loudly, then placed her gloved hands on her hips and began to tap one foot. Surely they did not mean to leave her up there. Her driver should notice she was incapable of jumping down and come to her assistance.

But he did not. The argument continued, with both men gesturing toward the wagon bed, the man from the house shaking his head, crossing his arms over his chest.

"I beg your pardon," Dorothea said.

A carriage drove past with a clatter, and a fruit seller with a cart full of apples called out to gain attention for his wares. With all the noise it created, the two arguing men did not hear her.

"I beg your pardon!" she called, much louder this time, mortified at the necessity of raising her voice in such a crass manner.

The driver and the man from the house stopped, then turned and gaped at her.

"My good man," she said firmly, "be so kind as to help me down. I believe I can clear up this misunderstanding."

The driver and the other man each took one of Dorothea's hands and assisted her from the wagon. When she was upon solid ground, she turned to the gentleman from the house. "Are you the butler here, sir?"

He laughed. "Couldn't rightly say that I am, miss," he said. "But I, er, I am at your service."

"Well," she said, straightening her shoulders and tidying her jacket once again, "then you can tell me if this is the Bright residence?"

"Aye, that it is," the man replied. "Though Professor Bright is not at home."

Dorothea frowned at this news. She'd sent a letter to her father when it had become clear that she had no choice but to come to him in London and had received a reply from his solicitor, giving her travel instructions. It was unthinkable that her father was not here to greet her, though it changed nothing.

She stepped out of the street and turned to the driver. "Everything is to be unloaded and carried into the house. I'll direct you once you come inside and—"

"But, miss—"

"—and show you where everything is to go."

"But there's no—"

"Please be careful with those boxes," she said as she made her way toward the front door of the house. "Some of those documents are irreplaceable."

The two men watched her trim figure retreat into the house, each muttering to himself.

It was dark in the front hall, and Dorothea went immediately to the drawing room at the front of the house and pulled open the heavy drapes. The room was sparsely furnished, and filthy crates were stacked in every corner. Turning on her heel, she moved through the first floor of the house and found conditions to be much the same in every room. A few pieces of furniture, and boxes and crates everywhere. It was as if her father were in the process of moving either in or out.

"Miss!" the manservant said, coming up behind her in the kitchen. "This is highly irregular! Your father is not—"

"Your name, my good man?" Dorothea demanded as she turned to look up at him.

"Creighton, miss," he replied.

"Is my father at the museum, Creighton?" Dorothea asked. She did not care for the man's appearance and sensed that he was only as good a servant as he had to be.

"No, miss," the man replied, slipping a finger into his collar and pulling it away from his neck. "Your father has not yet returned from his African expedition."

Dorothea's mind went blank for an instant. The solicitor had not mentioned that her father was on one of his trips, nor had he indicated that Alastair Bright might not be at home when she arrived. She experienced a moment of indecision, but quickly recovered herself.

"Never mind," she said, taking the tone her mother always used when she wanted to show that she was in charge. Dorothea certainly didn't feel that way now, but she would never allow her father's servant to know that. "I'll just settle in, and we can rearrange my things after my father returns."

The driver, along with a burly adolescent hired off the street, shuffled in with her trunk and dropped it on the floor in the hall. "Where d'you want this, ma'am?"

Dorothea took over a small room on the second floor of the house. In it, she found an old trunk and some blankets, a broken-down chair and a cracked mirror in a frame. For lack of a maidservant to do the work, she dusted and scrubbed every corner of the room and pulled the musty curtains off the windows. Finding herself fatigued and a bit short of breath, she rested for a while, then got back to work, taking it at a much slower pace. She got rid of the broken furnishings and had a few intact pieces brought in from elsewhere in the house.

Creighton found a rusty metal cot in the attic and dragged it into the room, taking its mattress to the garden to beat the dust out of it. Once Dorothea had made up the bed and put her clothing away, she took a look around and decided the room would do. She would need a desk in order to keep her work organized, for she had every intention of continuing to do translations for the professors at Oxford, as well as for any new connections she might make here in London.

Her father might even have contacts at the museum who would be interested in her skills.

A sudden crash that seemed to vibrate the entire house startled Dorothea out of her room. Loud pounding followed the noise, along with a man's deep voice, raised in anger.

"Bright, you son of a bitch!" the man shouted in a distinctly American accent. "Open this door before I break it down!"

Startled, Dorothea hurried down the stairs before she had a chance to settle her nerves and gather her wits. She made it to the door before Creighton and pulled it open.

The tall man on the other side of the threshold was dressed like some ruffian from a Wild West show. His head of dark, uncombed hair was uncovered, and he held no hat in his hands. His shirt was dingy and half-open, Dorothea realized with alarm. And there was no collar in evidence.

Holding up a pair of disreputably filthy trousers were equally dirty suspenders. The only thing missing was a pair of ornate six-shooters that Dorothea imagined all those cow-fellows wore.

"Where is he?" the man demanded. "Get Bright out here! *Pronto.*"

"P-Professor Bright is not at home, sir," she said, closing the door partway to prevent the man from entering the house. "Now if you'll kindly..." She couldn't very well ask a ruffian of his ilk for a card. Surely he wouldn't have one. "If you'll give me your name, I'll tell him you called."

"Not bloody likely," the man said. "I'll wait."

Pushing past her, he strode into the drawing room, tracking dust in his wake. Without regard to the state of his clothes, or his boots, the American came to a stop in front of the modest fireplace. He crossed his arms over his chest and stood motionless.

Powerless to stop him, Dorothea followed the brash American.

"Sir," she said in her fiercest voice. "I demand that you leave my father's house at once—"

"Your father!" He let out a bark of a laugh and pierced her with his steely blue gaze. "Don't tell me the old bastard has a partner in crime!"

"I should say n— Crime?" Dorothea sputtered. "What on earth are you—" Her mother would never have dignified such a statement with a response. Clearly, the only thing possible was to make the man leave. She strode back to the front entry with the reasonable expectation that the big American would follow. But when she turned round, he had not budged. His tall frame still dominated the drawing room.

He was a big man, and Dorothea guessed he would be considered well made, with broad shoulders and muscular limbs. His face might not be so unattractive if ever he bothered to shave the layer of disreputable black whiskers that shadowed his square jaw.

There was a murderous gleam in his eyes and an expression of pure ruthless anger on his face. He was not a man to be taken lightly, and a shudder of apprehension skittered down Dorothea's back. The men she knew—her male neighbors in Oxford and the professors at the university—were all civilized men.

Dorothea had no idea what to expect from this one.

"I must insist," she said, gathering whatever bravado she could muster, "that you leave this house at once."

"Not until I meet with your...*father*," he said. His

coldly appraising eyes raked over her, and Dorothea felt the heat of a blush start at her neck and work its way up. She had not given a single thought to her own dusty, unkempt appearance, but decided there was no course but to brazen it out with as much dignity as she could rally and hope that Creighton would appear and make the American go away.

For six months, Jack's raging anger had not abated. It had festered and grown until he had become fully capable of breaking the crooked little Englishman in half with his bare hands. Alastair Bright had masterfully lured Temple's research party deep into Mongasa territory for the sole intention of stealing the tribe's precious Kohamba.

While Jack's purpose had been only to photograph the figure and offer gifts to the Mongasa chief while he spent a few weeks studying the tribe, Bright had managed to filch the sacred statue, causing an uproar. Jack's party had split up and escaped, only to fall into the hands of other, equally primitive tribes. It had been many weeks before his team had been reunited. Luckily, all five of the men had survived, no thanks to Alastair Bright.

But Gauge O'Neill had fallen ill during their escape through the jungle. He'd contracted malaria and was down with the sickness all during their long journey to England. Even now, O'Neill lay in his bed in a nearby rented room, thrashing with fever, dehydration and joint pains.

And Bright would pay for that most of all.

In frustration, Jack slid his hands across his face and rubbed his eyes. He could not believe Bright had managed to elude him again. When Jack and his party had finally been reunited in Unguja, they'd sailed north, putting in at every port where their paths might cross Bright's. Jack had come close to catching the wily fellow twice: once in Mogadishu and again in Cairo.

Somehow, the swindling professor managed to stay at least one step ahead of Jack.

"He'll have to come here sometime, won't he?" Jack said. She didn't look anything like her old man other than her diminutive height. Her features might have been downright pretty if they hadn't been screwed into a haughty, disdainful expression. Soft tendrils of auburn hair that curled around her face made her look as if a man's hands had just been running through it.

Jack stopped short. Her hair was a mess, and so were her clothes. *Had she just arrived from the docks, too?* Was she covering up for her father to allow him a chance to get away again?

Not this time!

He made a cursory examination of the boxes nearby, then stormed out of the drawing room and searched the entire main floor, throwing doors open and exploring every nook and cranny. Finding no trace of anyone else on the first floor, he trudged up the stairs while Miss Bright followed, protesting his intrusion with every step. He shook off her dainty hands as if they were a child's and continued opening doors. At the back of the house, he discovered one door, locked against him.

"*Bright!*" he roared at the closed door.

"My good man, I cannot allow—"

"Open it, or I'll kick it in!" he bellowed.

He heard no sounds coming from behind the door,

but that didn't mean anything. The weasel was probably hiding in a closet.

"Sir! You cannot mean—"

Before giving it another thought, Jack raised one
booted foot and kicked the door open.

The room was illuminated by a bank of windows
along the back wall. And the space itself contained
Bright's collection of artifacts. He took a few steps
into the room.

Jack heard a horrified gasp behind him and glanced
back at Bright's daughter. Her face had lost all its
color and she looked like she was going to faint. When
her eyes rolled back, he grabbed her by the waist and
lowered her to the polished wooden floor.

What the hell? Surely the woman had seen her father's collection of ancient erotica? He had to admit
the articles were stunning…perhaps Bright kept the
door locked to keep his daughter sheltered from such
graphic works.

Jack tapped her lightly on the face, but when she
did not come around, he realized more drastic measures were needed. He pulled her jacket open, then
unfastened the buttons at her throat.

A faint pulse fluttered there, and looking at it gave
Jack an odd sensation. "Damnable corsets…" he muttered. "How in hell is she supposed to breathe?"

He opened a few more buttons, then reached in and
unhooked the front fastenings of her corset. Thus
freed, her breasts nearly overflowed the thin shift that
rested between her skin and the rigid corset as she took
a sudden deep breath.

Her eyes opened.

"Are you out of your mind, woman?" he demanded.

Dazed green eyes looked up at him in puzzlement.
"Lacing yourself up so you can't breathe doesn't
make a hell of a lot of sense to me." He shook his
head and left her where she lay on the polished
wooden floor.

He would never have left another woman in such a
sorry state, but she was... He took a deep breath and
canceled the mental picture she made from his mind.
She was Bright's daughter, and that's all he needed to
know about her.

Ignoring the faint sounds made by the woman behind him, Jack walked through the collection of carvings and drawings that were assembled on various tables and pedestals throughout the room. He took a
moment to appreciate the frescos and fragments of ancient Indian erotic bas relief.

He had to give Bright credit. The man had amassed
a superb collection that had to be worth a fortune. And
no doubt, he had buyers from all over the world who
paid him handsomely for such things.

An ebony phallus from Siam, exquisite in its detail.
A primitive stone sheela-na-gig from Ireland smiled
lasciviously at him as she exposed her most private
parts to all who cared to see. A scene from the *Kama
Sutra* played out on the wall above the desk.

Another shocked gasp from behind, and Jack knew
Miss Bright had just realized what he'd done to her.
Or perhaps she'd just gotten a good, close look at one
of her father's pieces. Finding amusement somewhere
amid his anger, he managed to hide it and continued
to walk around Alastair Bright's collection while the
man's daughter made a hasty departure from the room.

Jack knew more about old carvings than women's
fashions, but he recognized a travesty when he saw

one. It was an utter crime to hide such magnificent assets behind a whale-bone corset, but clearly, Miss Bright had intentionally done so.

Jack could not imagine why.

Chapter Two

With indignation puffing out her chest, it was difficult for Dorothea to return her bosom to its confines, the way her mother had taught her. There was a slight tremor in her fingers, which did not help, but she was determined to master her embarrassment, right her attire and confront the barbarian who had invaded her father's house.

Except that she did not want to go into that room again.

She could not bring herself to think of those… obscene likenesses and their connection with Alastair. Why would such awful things be in her father's house? Everywhere her eyes landed was yet another indecent piece—a carving or a painting. He even had some rude bas-relief sections hanging on the walls. Surely there was some reasonable explanation why a reputable scholar of antiquities would possess such a collection.

Dorothea straightened her bodice and brushed at her skirt, then paced the hall outside that awful chamber, waiting for the American to come out.

Such unsatisfactory events would never have occurred if her mother were alive. Honoria Bright did not allow chaos or disorder in her presence. Yet here Dorothea was, on her own for merely half a day, and confusion reigned. What was wrong with her?

And where was Creighton? Her father's odious manservant had apparently decided to disappear at exactly the right moment. *He* should be the one to deal with this brash intruder. What did her father pay the man for, if not to keep street riffraff from entering the house? If ever a servant was in need of a reprimand, it was Creighton, and Dorothea was determined to see that he got it.

She clasped her hands in front of her and moistened her lips. She paced the length of the upstairs hall. Creighton was not here. Dorothea was on her own. Her mother would not have shrunk from the challenge of removing an intruder from her house. No, Honoria would have set her face in a disapproving expression, taken firm hold of the man's arm and physically ushered him out of the house. And, by heaven, no one would have dreamed of crossing her.

Seeing no alternative but to confront the American in those coarse surroundings, Dorothea braced herself and marched back in.

He was in a crouched position, putting him eye level with the most lewd carving Dorothea had ever seen. That the man could look at it so brazenly—actually *touch* it—brought a flaming heat to her cheeks and a palpitation to her breast. She felt slightly faint again, but used every ounce of her willpower to master it.

"Very nicely done," the man said quietly. "Anatomically perfect. Wouldn't you agree?" When he turned his eyes to her, they were alight with an expression she did not understand.

Dorothea started to speak, but no sound came out. She clapped her mouth shut, then turned around abruptly, nearly knocking a marble carving off its stand. She grabbed it, and refusing to be flustered, turned back to face the intruder. Nothing he said or did made any difference whatsoever. He did not belong here, and she was going to see to it that he left.

"I insist that you leave this house at once, sir," she said firmly.

He stood up to his full height and met Dorothea's direct gaze. When he crossed his arms against his broad chest and gave her a sidelong glance, Dorothea forced herself to refrain from doing the same. She resisted the urge to put her hands over the part of her that he'd exposed, that still *felt* exposed under his icy gaze. Unconsciously, she allowed her free hand to slide up her bodice, making certain all her buttons were properly closed. To her chagrin, they were not. She swallowed and tried not to think of how much he'd seen.

"I'm not going anywhere until your conniving little poltroon of a father returns," he said, oblivious to her discomfiture.

"But he...I..." His height was imposing, and he suddenly felt more dangerous than anyone she'd ever encountered before. She was alone in the house, in a room that contained figures and paintings of men and women engaged in all sorts of licentious activities. They were assured to arouse the most base aspect of his masculine nature. Even *she* felt an odd tingle, merely from looking at the figure he'd just had his hands on...

A hot flush heated her bosom, then crept up her neck and into her cheeks when she considered what he'd seen. What she'd seen. What they'd looked at *together*.

Dorothea began to tap her foot angrily. This was absurd. This was her father's house, and *he* was the invader here. She had every right to order him out of the house.

"I will call for a constable if you do not leave immediately," she said, drawing herself up to her full height. "Get out."

Jack almost laughed aloud at the sight the little termagant made. He didn't doubt that she'd have another episode of the vapors if she knew how she appeared, with her hair dribbling down around her face, her bodice askew and her bustle listing to one side. The icing on the cake was the fifteen-inch marble phallus she wielded in her right hand, using it to point toward the door.

He wondered if she'd faint all over again when she realized what she held in her hand.

Though she was mighty entertaining, Jack had a purpose here, and he would not be deflected from it. Ignoring Bright's daughter, he turned away and opened the man's heavy oak desk.

"I *will* call the constable!"

Invoices, bills of sale, travel tickets, were all piled haphazardly under the rolltop. Jack sifted through them, searching for the one object that would even the score. Ignoring the persistent tapping on his shoulder, he pulled open drawers and thumbed through their contents. When he reached the last drawer and found it locked, he knew he'd located whatever was most precious to Alastair Bright.

It would not be the Kohamba. Bright would have had a ready buyer for that piece, somewhere in Cairo or possibly Venice. The little man must have made a fortune off the unsuspecting Mongasa tribe.

"This is your last chance, you…you…"

He didn't bother to listen to whatever indelicate name she would call him, but gave the locked drawer a good yank.

"Damn!" he muttered when it didn't give. He pulled it, shook it and tried to pry it open with a sharp letter-opener. But it wouldn't budge.

Reaching into his boot, Jack pulled out the two-shot derringer he always carried, even though O'Neill said it was a woman's gun. Ignoring the squeal of shock behind him, he shot the lock off the drawer, then tore into its contents. It took only a second to find what he was looking for—a map.

One night during the recent ill-fated expedition into Mongasa country, Bright had imbibed a bit too freely of the medicinal whiskey they'd brought along. Inebriated—for that was the only way his tongue would have been so recklessly loose—he'd boasted of an amazing discovery. He had recently taken possession of a map that led to the Edessa Cloth—an ancient towel that was said to have been used to wipe the face of Christ as he walked to Golgotha.

Jack knew that the Mandylion, as the cloth was called, was of little interest to Bright, whose tastes ran to ancient erotica. If the swindler found the cloth himself, he would sell it to the highest bidder. As a result, the cloth's scientific, religious and historic value would be lost forever.

Jack Temple was not going to let that happen. He was no mercenary explorer caring only for the fame or financial rewards of his discoveries. No, he enjoyed the hunt as much as the discovery. He was a man with a well-developed sense of history and an interest in the foreign cultures and theories unearthed by his findings. And his academic credentials were solid, too.

He unfolded the map and quickly verified that it was what he was looking for. Now, all he had to do was find the key to the map, and he would be able to search for the Mandylion himself.

"Put that back!" Miss Bright demanded.

"Not on your life, lady," he replied, turning around to face her. For the first time since entering this house, he felt confident, exhilarated. He might have grabbed the woman and kissed her, if she hadn't been poking his chest with the oversize, marble phallus.

"This map is payment for the havoc your father wreaked on my expedition."

"Now, see here—"

He looked pointedly at his chest, and when she glanced down and saw what she held in her hand, she squealed and dropped it. The marble piece shattered.

"That was a fairly commonplace linga from ancient India," he said, suppressing a smile at her shocked expression. "First century A.D. Probably worth two or three thousand pounds to the right buyer."

Dorothea could not believe the nightmare her life had become. Her mother had been in her grave less than a fortnight, and here Dorothea was, facing one disaster after another.

"Where is the key?"

Still gazing down at the green marble pieces in horror, Dorothea did not understand his question. She barely *heard* the question. Her life had become a fiasco that she could not control, and now the man asked about a key when he'd already shot the lock off the drawer.

He was a madman, and the best she could do was to escape him. She hurried from the room and went down the stairs. Perhaps if she got to the street, she could call for help. But before she reached the front door, he was there in front of her, holding the ragged map in one hand.

"All right, enough of this," he said. His anger seemed to have returned, and Dorothea started to back away. He grabbed her arms, preventing her retreat. "Where is your father?"

She did not respond.

"Don't bother trying to protect him," Jack added. "If it takes dragging you along to— Now there's an idea."

"What?" she whispered. Her mouth had gone dry and she could barely speak.

"Taking you with me," he said, turning her and putting a firm hold upon one arm. "Come on."

When the American tried to get her out the door, she dug in her heels and refused to go one step further.

"Unhand me or I will scream!" she cried, though she did not know how she would manage it. She was frighteningly short of breath.

"Don't be ridiculous," he said, ushering her outside. "I'm only taking you to the docks and you can show me where he's hiding. Then I'll let you go."

"I don't know—"

"Yeah, sure," he said, "you don't know where he is."

"But I—"

"We'll start at the docks," the man interrupted.

And before she had a chance to protest, he put his hands around her waist and hoisted her up onto a huge tan horse. She landed face first in the horse's thick mane. She tried to right herself and slide down the opposite side, but the man mounted behind her before she could move. He put one hand around her waist, pulled her tight against him and rode off, oblivious to her pounding heart or the faintness in her head.

"Where's the key?" Jack asked again. He started to sweat and not from the heat of the day. He hadn't anticipated how it would feel to have Miss Bright's body pressed tightly against his own. It was his first tactical mistake.

There wouldn't be another.

"What key?" she replied, as if she truly didn't know. "You destroyed the lock with your nasty little gun, sir. What need would you have of a key at this point?"

"Very convincing, Miss Bright," he said, glad of her saucy response. It made her all the more resistible. A scoundrel's daughter was bad enough, but one with an insolent mouth was even worse.

She had to know that the Mandylion map was useless without its key. At least, that's what Bright had bragged six months before, swaying drunkenly in camp. Some sort of code had been used in making the map, and the key was necessary for deciphering it. Somehow, Bright had acquired the key and hidden it separately from the map. Perhaps it was still in the house.

Jack had given himself a bit of insurance against that. He'd unlatched one of the windows in Bright's collection room, so he'd be able to gain entrance to the house later if he didn't catch up with the man at the wharf. Jack wanted the satisfaction of seeing

Bright's face when Jack told Bright he no longer possessed the Mandylion map.

"I don't know where my father is *or* the key that you seek, sir," she said. "So there is no point in taking me any further. I insist you return me to my father's house at once."

She held herself away from him, as if he had some disgusting disease she might catch. But she sounded a little bit breathless—as if his proximity had an effect on her feminine sensibilities. He could not resist moving in close and putting his lips to her ear to speak. "While we're down here, you can show me your ship."

Ducking her head away from his mouth and smoothing back the hair he'd disturbed with his breath did not mask the slight tremor that went through her body. He found it very interesting that the straight-laced old maid was not immune to him. Maybe he'd be able to use that attraction to get the information he needed.

They rode in silence toward the wharf where he had disembarked from his ship just an hour before. Jack had no doubt that Bright's daughter would have screamed and kicked to get away from him if such a public display had not been considered scandalous.

He had her pegged as a very prim and proper miss—notwithstanding the condition of her clothes or her reaction to him. Travel was tough on a body and worse on the wardrobe. He was sure that, like him, she had just arrived in port and had not had the chance to clean up. With luck, her father was still on their ship, perhaps overseeing the unloading of all his illegal artifacts.

Jack had to hand it to her. She was doing a fine job

of protecting her father—not that it was going to do
him any good. Jack had every reason to believe he
could track the culprit down very soon, and when he
did... Well, he hadn't decided exactly what he was
going to do to the little man.

"If you intended to tear my arm to shreds, you're
doing a fair job of it, ma'am," he said, sliding his arm
away from her sharp fingernails. She grabbed on to his
shirt and held on as if her life depended on it. He got
the impression that she'd never ridden horseback before, but quickly dismissed the notion. She couldn't
be the daughter of Alastair Bright, world traveler, and
not have ridden a horse. Hell, she'd probably straddled
her share of camels, too.

"You have no right to force me to accompany you
this way, sir," she said. Her voice was tighter and
more prudish than ever. It made him want to remind
her that he'd had his hands down her blouse less than
twenty minutes ago.

He refrained.

"Just so you know, I plan to keep you until you tell
me where your father is."

"But I don't know where he is," she replied, "as
I've told you before! Now take me back to the house."

He gave a sarcastic laugh. "Not until you tell me
the name of your ship."

"You are the most bullheaded, obstinate person I've
ever met," she said, scorching him in such crisp English he was surprised his skin didn't blister. She
pulled away and turned slightly to face him. "I re-
peat—I have never—"

"Don't bother to lie about this, too," he said, using
his own tactics on her. He pulled her back against him
and breathed into her ear once again. "I don't suppose

you have a Christian name, Miss Bright? Something a little less…''

''Formal?'' she asked, jerking away. *''No.''*

He laughed. ''Mine's Jack Temple. Of New York.''

''Do you make a practice of accosting women in their homes, Mr. Temple,'' she said with acerbity, ''or is this something you do only when abroad?''

He grinned for the first time in months. ''Only when the woman's father is a no-good, swindling thief, ma'am.''

Jack smelled the river before he saw it and knew they were near. He steered the horse toward the quay where most of the passenger ships were moored and rode up to a hitching post.

''Which ship?'' he asked as he dismounted. He took her in hand and lifted her down.

''How many ways can I tell you that I do not know!''

''Then you'll just come along with me and we'll check them all.''

Pulling her arm from his grasp, she hissed, ''I will not, sir! I have no intention of tramping around this disgusting old dockyard with you!''

''Then you'd better tell—'' Jack caught a glimpse of Paco Fleming, Bright's giant henchman who rarely left the old rogue's side. He was Jack's best chance at discovering where Bright was hiding. ''Wait here!''

He sprinted off toward the man, but the tall, bald island man caught sight of him and fled. Jack kept on his trail, running between crates of cargo and ships' stores, dodging wagons and people as he went.

Fleming disappeared a time or two, but Jack did not lose heart. He was fast on his feet, much faster than the bulky Fleming could ever be.

He knew that leaving Bright's daughter on her own was problematic, but he hadn't seen any alternative. He wouldn't have left her if he hadn't thought she was reasonably safe on the dock. With so many people coming and going, certainly nothing untoward would happen to her.

He caught sight of Fleming's shiny brown head, towering above everyone he passed, as he turned into a street with a warehouse at its end. A cartload of luggage crossed Jack's path at that moment, and he lost his momentum. By the time he'd gotten around it and the crowd of men that accompanied it, he'd lost Fleming.

He ran to the street where the islander had turned and followed, but the man was nowhere to be seen on the sparsely populated street.

Jack went inside warehouses and checked alleyways. He scoured the adjoining streets. He questioned pedestrians and dockworkers—anyone who might have seen Bright's henchman pass. But he had no luck. He'd lost Fleming.

Looking around to get his bearings, he realized he was at least a mile from where he'd left Bright's daughter. Instinct told him that Fleming was the more likely path to Bright, but Jack had no choice but to return to the man's daughter—uncooperative as she was.

He didn't use his speed to get back to her, but trotted at a more leisurely pace, taking note of every ship and all the cargoes, especially the ones in the vicinity where he'd first seen Fleming. He might be able to deduce which ship Bright had been on and return to question the crew after he returned the woman to her father's house.

Feeling more confident now than he had when he'd first stepped into the streets of London, he covered the last few yards to the place where he'd left Miss Bright. Through the crowd on the quay, he saw the buckskin mare he'd hired from a nearby livery and headed toward it.

At least the trip down here hadn't been a complete waste, and after he questioned the woman again, he was certain he could get her to tell him the name of her father's ship. Not that her help was so essential now, but it would speed the process of tracking her father down. All he needed was that name and he'd be able to learn where his cargo had been delivered. He would then have the bas—

The woman was nowhere in sight. Jack looked at the horse again and saw that his packs were still intact, a miraculous thing for London.

But the woman was gone.

Chapter Three

This was not good. Jack had abducted the woman and now she was missing. What could have happened? Had someone else taken her?

"You!" he called to a group of young boys tossing stones into the river nearby. "Did you see a young lady standing here next to this horse a few minutes ago?"

"Why should I tell you, Yank?" was the leader's insolent reply. The boy's friends gathered around him.

Instead of tossing them into the river one by one as he was inclined to do, Jack reached into his pocket and pulled out a coin. "Tell me what you saw, and it's yours."

Without hesitation, the smallest boy spoke up. "Pretty lady, but she was all mussed up," he said. "Wearing a blue dress and a white shirt, like. Dark hair. No hat. No gloves."

"That's her," Jack said. "Where did she go?"

"Walked away." The boy turned and pointed toward a street that led away from the quay. "Down there."

Jack flipped the coin to the boy. He mounted the

mare, then headed in the direction the boy had indicated, keeping an eye out for Miss Bright, with her bare head, wearing the disheveled, dark traveling suit.

Taking the most direct route to Bright's house, he saw no sign of her. He wandered up and down the adjoining lanes, searching. When he had no luck on the street, he stopped in several shops along the way, places where a lady might spend the time of day, even though he sensed this was a woman who would care that she was not properly dressed for such an outing. But he had no luck. No one had seen her.

Jack was just about to look for a constable when he remembered who he was dealing with. This was Alastair Bright's daughter, a woman who must have traveled the world with her father. She was probably as comfortable in Singapore as she was in Tangiers. He guessed London would pose no problem for her.

Dorothea wasn't sure where she had taken the wrong turn, but she was lost. And London was a very frightening place for one who had never ventured outside Oxford's boundaries. Though she had started out smartly dressed this morning, she now looked like a street urchin—or worse. She didn't see a single omnibus, and there wasn't a hackney anywhere that would stop for her. Not that she could blame them. She looked as if she'd climbed out of a dustbin.

Remembering the general direction of her father's house, she trudged along on foot, taking care to avoid any well-dressed pedestrians in her path. Hatless, gloveless and with her clothes in such terrible disarray, she was in no condition to meet or speak to anyone. She would die before presenting herself in such a state.

Dorothea's mother had always shown the highest

degree of propriety and expected nothing less of her daughter. Though she had divorced her husband many years ago, it had happened before their move to the house in Oxford, and Honoria Bright had never seen fit to enlighten her neighbors on her true marital status. Everyone assumed she was a widow, which suited Honoria.

Even Dorothea had forgotten she had a father, until the occasion of her mother's untimely death nearly three weeks before.

Dorothea and her mother had lived near the university in a comfortable home that was owned by Dorothea's maternal grandfather, the earl of Groton. Dorothea had never known exactly how much she and her mother depended upon Grandfather for his largesse, until he died at Christmas time, leaving all his cash, investments and properties to his heir.

The new earl was a distant cousin, who wanted possession of his Oxford house. Honoria had managed to put off moving until she could arrange some other suitable lodgings, but she had become ill and died. When Dorothea and the solicitor had gone through Honoria's papers, they found that she'd had very few prospects for any new accommodations and even fewer means to pay for such.

Dorothea earned some money through her talent for ancient languages, translating old manuscripts for a few of the professors at the university, but certainly not enough to live on. She did not know what her mother had been thinking, how she had expected them to survive. Perhaps it was worry about their future that had caused her to sicken and die.

That thought saddened Dorothea immeasurably. If

only her mother had confided in her, discussed the problems they faced, she might never have fallen ill.

The bright afternoon sunshine gave way to clouds, and suddenly it was dusk and Dorothea still did not know where she was. She felt as weary as she'd ever been, and her heart was heavy in her chest. But she moved on, searching hopelessly for her father's house.

Soon, the women she passed on the street seemed more shabbily dressed than the ones she'd seen earlier, and the buildings were run-down. Dogs barked and children played in dusty streets, and Dorothea began to feel some alarm—not only that she did not know where she was, but she began to have some concern for her safety.

And she was a bit short of breath. She would have to stop and rest soon.

This was all Mr. Temple's doing. If the burly American had not abducted her from her father's house, she would now be standing in her father's kitchen, perhaps overseeing the inefficient Creighton as he prepared for tea. She would not be wandering the streets of London alone and unprotected as darkness fell.

She had to admit that if she had waited for Jack Temple on the wharf as he'd told her, she might have ridden safely back to her father's house—at least as safely as a woman could be, sitting in such improper proximity to his…body.

Once again, Dorothea felt heat rise to her cheeks when she considered the sensations that had run through her during their short ride. She had never felt anything like them before. Not even when Albert Bloomsby had come to call and kissed her hand in greeting had she felt anything compared to the disturbance Mr. Temple had caused.

Though now was not a good time to analyze the emotions that careened through her, she could not forget the rough texture of the arm that had been draped around her midriff as they rode together. She'd felt strong muscle, tough sinew and thick veins, as well as a generous pelt of hair. Dorothea stumbled over a crack in the cobbles, but righted herself before falling.

Leaving the relative safety of Mr. Temple's company had been foolish, though Dorothea thought that staying with him might have been worse. Clearly, the man believed terrible things of her father, and Dorothea was not about to put her person under his protection. Lord knew it had already suffered several indignities at his hands, not the least of which had occurred during her fainting episode.

The very idea that he had undressed her—had exposed her body to his gaze—was mortifying. She doubted she could ever face him again. Not that such an occasion would ever arise. She would be certain never to answer the door herself, and she would give specific orders to Creighton that Mr. Temple was not to be admitted to the house. That should take care of it.

She would do these things *if* she ever got back to her father's house on Porter Street. It was nearly dark now, and, as much as she disliked having to ask for help, she saw no choice but to begin searching for a constable or some other likely person who might assist her. She was absurdly lost and needed directions—or an escort—to her father's house.

"Eh, miss," said an adolescent girl, teasing a kitten with a length of string. "Don't suppose y'could spare a penny for cream for m'kitten?"

"I'm sorry," Dorothea said, "but I haven't any money. I left without—"

"What happened to yer clothes?" the girl asked, leaving the kitten to its own devices. She was obviously much more intrigued by Dorothea than she was by the furry feline. "Y'look like y've been run down in the street!"

"I just moved to a new house, and I was unpacking," Dorothy said, embarrassed anew by her appearance. It was just one more indignity she'd suffered at Jack Temple's hands. "Then I…left…and I've lost my way back. I don't suppose you'd know where Porter Street is?"

"Oh, aye, miss," the girl said. "It's just two streets down." She pointed the way, then told Dorothea that she probably wanted to turn left once she reached the correct street. "That's where them fine houses are, miss."

"You've been very helpful," Dorothea said, truly grateful, and regretting that she had nothing to give the girl. "Do you live here?"

"Aye, miss," she replied. "With my mum and brother."

"What is your name?"

"Kate, miss."

"You are a very kind young lady, Kate," Dorothea said. "Would you mind very much if I sat here a bit to rest?'

"All the same to me," Kate said.

In spite of the impropriety of doing such a thing, Dorothea sat down next to the girl and watched as she resumed her game with the kitten. Then she reached into her jacket and discovered she did have a bit of money.

"I haven't a penny, Kate," Dorothea said, handing the child a pound note, "but will this do?"

Jack kept to the shrubs across from Bright's house, waiting for the man to appear. There were no lights in any of the front rooms, and he wondered where the old man's daughter might be. He could not imagine that she had taken to her bed so early.

He squelched that thought the minute it entered his head. He did not need to visualize Miss Bright with her lush curves unfettered under her nightclothes, her wild hair spread out beneath her, her fiery green eyes dormant under closed lids. While he sat crouched in the gathering gloom of night, he did not care to recall the delicate scent of lavender that emanated from all that glorious hair or the softness of her skin.

She was Bright's daughter, and that was reason enough to avoid her and to refrain from having any preposterously wicked thoughts about the straightlaced old maid.

Jack scratched his head. He should never have dragged her down to the wharf with him, but he had to admit he'd enjoyed his encounter with the woman far too much to let her go so quickly. He really regretted that she'd been gone when he'd returned.

It didn't matter now. Jack had no business with the swindler's daughter. He only wanted to get his hands on Bright and force him to turn over the key to the Mandylion map. Once Jack had it, and he found the cloth, he would have his vengeance for Bright's treachery in Africa.

Jack doubted the key would be in the house, but he decided that if Bright didn't show up soon, he was going to go inside and search the place. It wouldn't hurt to know what else the old man was hiding in there.

"What the...?"

A haggard figure limped through the darkness toward the front door of Bright's house.

The daughter! Jack felt a sharp pang of guilt. By the light of the streetlamps, he saw that she carried one broken shoe in her hand. Her hair was down around her shoulders, and her clothes were badly disheveled. *She was only now returning from the wharf.*

He rubbed a hand across his unshaven face and muttered a curse. He should have known better than to take the woman with him, and to trust her to wait where he'd left her. She might be Bright's daughter, but she'd obviously had some difficulty in returning home.

Jack stemmed his guilt and forced himself to remain where he was. It was not necessary for him to charge up to the house and see for himself that she was all right. She might be small, but she was ferocious as hell, and there wasn't a derelict in London who would get the better of her.

Unless perhaps her corset was laced too tight.

Damn. That was a thought he really wished he'd squelched. He narrowed his eyes and watched from a distance, only to reassure himself that she truly was all right. He was responsible for taking her down to the dock and it would not have settled well with him if she had come to harm, even if she *was* Alastair Bright's daughter.

She went inside. After a moment, there was a faint light in the drawing room. Then nothing. No other lights, no one in the house to greet her.

That seemed odd. Wasn't there a housekeeper or

caretaker who maintained Bright's house while he was away? Surely he did not allow his daughter to inhabit the house alone. Yet there'd been no sign of anyone at home—besides Miss Bright—when he'd barged in earlier.

Well, this suited his purposes even better. A nearly empty house would be much easier to climb into. Obviously, Bright and his daughter had arrived home unexpectedly. If the old man didn't return home within the next few minutes, Jack would go through the unlocked window in the collection room, and look for the key to the map. Once he had it, he could begin his search for the ancient cloth and wreak havoc on Bright's plans to sell the thing to the highest bidder.

Ever since Jack's temper had cooled, he had known it would be better not to confront Bright. If he could manage to find the key without the old man, it would suit him better than getting it from Bright himself. That way, Jack could leave on his own in search of the Mandylion, and it would take some time—weeks, perhaps—for Bright to discover where the map had led him.

He touched his back pocket and felt the fastened button that secured the map within. He wasn't going to let this map out of his possession until he had the Mandylion in his hands.

But he would need the key. Besides being hundreds of years old, the map's markings were written in ancient Arabic, admittedly not one of Jack's best languages. He hoped the key would be written in Greek, or maybe Latin, but he wasn't counting on it.

It didn't matter. He would find someone who could do an accurate translation and follow the instructions to the letter. He hoped he would not have to check on every Mandylion rumor and legend that had circulated for centuries. Jack had heard stories about the cloth for years, but hadn't really believed them until Bright had boasted of the map.

Now, with the map, Jack would not have to investigate each of the rumors, which mostly centered in Yorkshire. He could just follow the instructions given in the key, and go directly to the Mandylion's location.

He almost laughed aloud. He practically had the cloth in hand. All it would take was a quick translation of the Arabic and the Mandylion was as good as his.

But he would have to work quickly. As soon as Bright learned that Jack had taken the Mandylion map, the old man would mount his own campaign to unearth the legendary cloth. Jack would have to cover his tracks in order to keep Bright from discovering where the map and key led.

The light in the drawing room faded, and Jack waited. He assumed Miss Bright would take herself off to bed soon, and he would then climb into the second-story window that he'd unlocked earlier in the day and gain access to the house. With the woman asleep in her bed, he would have free rein to search the place.

When sufficient time had elapsed, Jack left his hiding place and circled around to the back of the house. He had no doubt that he'd find a way to climb up to the window he'd unlocked earlier. Moving stealthily, he tested the short wooden fence that bordered the garden and found that it moved with only a slight squeak—not enough to disturb anyone.

Keeping low to avoid being seen by a neighbor, he edged his way along the house and saw a light coming from one of the back rooms. The windows were partway open, but curtains fluttered there, so he could not see inside. Beyond the lit window was the second-floor row of sash windows that covered the wall of Bright's collection room.

He looked around. No one was near, no one had spotted him, but he heard a soft voice coming from Bright's house. He listened closer. It was a woman's voice, singing quietly. A slight breeze ruffled his hair and disturbed the curtains at Bright's window. He looked inside.

She was sitting in a metal bathtub in the middle of the kitchen. With her body angled away from him, Jack could see only her back and part of her profile, but he had no doubt who she was.

The curtain fluttered closed again and he shook his head to clear it. Naked, she looked nothing like the overstarched spinster he'd met that afternoon. Her voice was soft and voluptuous, unlike that of the prim fusspot who'd been laced so tight she could hardly breathe. Yet he recognized the curve of her shoulder, the delicacy of her neck, the rich auburn color of her hair.

When he got another glimpse of her, she was washing her outstretched arms with a wet cloth. She drew the cloth across the back of her neck, then out of sight, and Jack had to close his eyes and try to slow the pulse pounding in his ears.

Still singing softly, she placed her hands on the sides of the tub and began to raise herself up.

The curtain settled over the window again, blocking his view, but not the sound of her voice, and the water sloshing in the tub. He did not need to see her to picture her in his mind, standing there naked, dripping wet. She would be reaching for a towel just now, rubbing it down her arms, across those extraordinary breasts, and lower, to her belly, her legs…

Snapping his mind shut to any more images of Miss Bright, he stepped over to the house, squelching the fire that boiled his blood at the mere sight of her. He took a deep breath, wiped a hand across his mouth and looked for a way to climb.

It was not difficult. There was a ladder lying length-wise against a nearby shed and Jack carried it to the house. He propped it up on the wall and began to climb, certain that he knew exactly which window he needed to enter. He pushed at the sash and the window gave an inch—just enough for him to slip his fingers inside and push it up the rest of the way in silence.

He climbed in through the window and lit a match. Once he located an oil lamp, he lit it and started searching the room. He was sure that Bright hadn't taken the map key with him on his African trip—he would not have risked losing it during such a danger-ous journey. He may have locked it up somewhere else, but Jack believed it was very likely to be some-where in this house. Perhaps not in this room, but after a great deal of thought, Jack was certain that Bright wouldn't trust anyone else enough to keep it safe for him.

He wasn't a very trustworthy character—why would he believe he could trust anyone else?

The stone and wood-carved genitals, the satyrs and the pictures of various methods of copulation were still here, of course. Old clay pots, depicting cartoonish figures engaged in libidinous activities, stood next to the rolltop desk that Jack had already violated once today. He tipped each pot over, in search of the document, but discovered nothing more than a few pen-and-ink drawings of Japanese origin.

Jack let out a slow breath of appreciation. He had to give Alastair Bright credit for his single-minded collection, though Jack's own tastes ran to the more mundane. He enjoyed flesh-and-blood women—not artistic representations of what men and women might do together. Still, he doubted there was a more extensive collection of ancient erotica anywhere.

He explored the room thoroughly, not missing a single crack or crevice, finding no hidden drawers or secret compartments—nothing of interest beyond the obvious.

Still certain that the key was somewhere in the house, Jack opened the hall door slightly and paused to listen for Miss Bright's singing. Everything was quiet now. He waited another couple of minutes, then exited the collection room. He turned down the lamp to give minimal light and went in search of the master bedroom.

Moving down the second-floor hall, he took care to make no noise. He slipped into the front room and closed the door behind him. A large bed, covered in deep blue brocade, was the centerpiece. Turning the flame of the lamp up again, he saw that there was one wardrobe and a small writing desk in the room. A battered trunk lay in one corner of a small alcove, and a pair of worn men's boots lay on the floor beside it.

After looking in every possible hiding place without success, Jack dropped to his knees and ran his hands across the surface of the rug that covered most of the floor.

When he reached the head of the bed, he found it. The ridges of something hidden underneath.

Pulling the lamp closer, he flipped up the edge of the rug and discovered a flat, metal receptacle. Pulling the edges apart, he opened it and discovered a large sheet of vellum, exactly like the sheet on which the Mandylion map was drawn. On quick inspection, it looked like the same ink, the same colors and the same style of writing as the map. It had to be the key—the ancient document that would lead him to the precious cloth.

Jack stood up and set the lamp on the desk and frowned while he studied it. There were several diagrams on it, as well as a few primitive drawings. There were numbers, along with a great deal of medieval script.

Unfortunately, it seemed to be mostly Arabic, and Jack had difficulty making out any of the words. Now he knew for certain that he'd have to find a translator.

That would have to wait. For now, he had to get back to see how O'Neill fared and make plans to travel north to York. He wanted to get a head start on Bright and put his hands on the Mandylion before Alastair managed to do it.

"Oh!"

Jack whipped around to see Miss Bright, standing in the doorway of her father's bedchamber. Wearing a thin wrapper that delineated the very curves he'd fought to forget, she appeared shocked. Confused.

And more than just a little bit angry.

Chapter Four

Dorothea was speechless. While she'd bathed in the kitchen, this rogue had been rifling through her father's belongings and helping himself to whatever he wanted. He'd probably taken a sackful of those disgusting figures and was now looking for money.

"Miss Bright," he said. There was a self-satisfied gleam in his eyes that was just as vexing as his burglary. He tapped a flat metal case against the palm of his hand. "Now that I've found what I needed, I'll be on my—"

"I think not, sir," she said angrily, blocking his exit from the room. "To my knowledge, common thieves are not let loose here in London any more than they are in any other city in the world."

"The common thief in this house isn't me, Miss Bright," he said. "If it's anyone, it's your father."

Dorothea snapped her mouth shut in outrage. How dare he insult her father, a highly respected explorer and archaeologist. She had heard her father's credentials enumerated by her mother. Just because her parents were incompatible did not mean Honoria had no respect for Alastair's professional qualities. True, she had not spoken of him often, but Honoria had made Dorothea aware of what she needed to know of her father.

According to Honoria, the British Museum owed a huge debt to Professor Bright for his contributions to their collections of ancient art, and certainly other museums had benefited from her father's daring explorations. To call Alastair Bright a thief would be to malign *all* explorers and excavators of ancient sites.

"How dare you!"

"Easily," he replied as his wicked grin faded. "I call it like I see it."

"Then perhaps your vision is impaired!"

"Not likely," he said as he moved around the bed to stand in front of her. He was like a mountain, huge and indomitable. His presence dominated the room, and Dorothea fiercely resisted the urge to step back. "Your father sabotaged my expedition in Tanganyika. He stole the most prized possession of the Mongasa tribe, and—"

"And I'm to take your word for that?" she asked caustically, crossing her arms over her chest.

"What you do is your business," he said. He moved to push past her, but Dorothea did not let him by.

"On the contrary, Mr. Temple," she said, ignoring the scent of the outdoors that he carried with him. "What you have in your hand is my business."

The man had the audacity to laugh in her face. His teeth lined up white and straight behind lips that were turned up in ridicule, rather than humor. "Right. A moldy old map, written in ancient Arabic is your business." He moved again, but Dorothea's hand shot out to grab the metal case in his hands. She only succeeded in knocking it to the floor.

They both bent down to retrieve it, bumping their heads together. A yellowed and withered length of old vellum fell from the metal case and Dorothea snatched it.

"Hand it over," he said menacingly.

Turning her back to Mr. Temple, she held it toward the light. *"To his most gracious excellency—"* she read.

"Give me that!" he demanded, reaching around her. Dorothea turned to avoid him, but he managed to slip one hand around her waist and yank her against him while he grabbed for the vellum.

"—the, umm, priest? No, the abbot...of—"

"One more chance to do the right thing, lady," he growled. "Then I take hold of this sash and you'll be wishing you'd handed it over."

With a gasp of outrage, Dorothea realized he had hold of the tie that held her wrapper together at her waist. She'd been in such a rush to investigate the noise in her father's bedchamber, that she hadn't taken time to dress properly. She was standing half-naked in this man's presence, and she was entirely at his mercy.

In a huff, she handed the document to him while she held her dressing gown together, in case he had other ideas. She tried to move, but he did not allow her to step away. Anxious to preserve some modicum of dignity, she did not struggle, certain that he would release her shortly.

"What do you know of this?"

"Of what?" she asked haughtily.

"The text...the writing." Still behind her, he shook the vellum once in front of her face.

"It looks like a letter," she replied.

"You can read it?" he asked, his voice incredulous. "You know Arabic?"

With his hold loosened, she pulled away, then turned to face him, drawing herself up to her full height and attempting to appear composed. When she spoke again, she used the exact tone her mother always used to express contempt, wondering if Honoria had ever felt the same kind of uneasiness that ran through Dorothea now. "I know a great number of things, Mr. Temple. The Arabic language is one of them."

"Wouldn't you know," he muttered. "Have you already translated this for him?" he asked her.

"This conversation is over, sir," she said, forcing her voice to remain steady. She was in the most compromising situation she could ever have imagined, with a man more dangerous than any she'd ever known. Her damp body was naked but for a thin wrapper, and she could not imagine the state of her hair. She did not know whether prudence dictated that she flee from him and lock herself in her room or force the issue and make him leave.

He was still dressed in the same clothes he'd worn earlier, only now they were even more disreputable. His awful whiskers hadn't gotten any shorter, and he appeared more threatening than ever.

But Dorothea had never known her mother to back down, no matter what the circumstances. And her will had always prevailed. "I'll thank you to return the letter to me and leave this house. Immediately," she said, holding out one hand to receive the document.

"What does he know of the map?" Temple demanded, refusing to budge from his place directly in front of her. "Has he figured it out yet?"

"I have no idea what you're talking about," she replied. She let go of her wrapper to push him out of the room, but when it started to fall open, she realized that he'd untied the sash. Heat blossomed on her cheeks and she quickly turned away from him, scrambling to repair the damage.

She heard a chuckle behind her and as her temper flared again, she realized that anger would not serve her now. She needed to unnerve the barbarian as badly as he had shaken her and wished she had a little gun that she could pull from her sleeve the way he'd taken his from his boot that afternoon.

"What are his plans?" he probed.

"Even if I knew, I certainly would not tell you," she said.

When Dorothea was as decently covered as possible under the circumstances, she turned to face him, tamping down her embarrassment. Not only was she half-naked, she was completely ineffective against this ruffian. It would be up to her father to deal with him when he returned. She could do no more, and she yearned to escape to the privacy of her room. "Now, if you'll—"

"Not until you tell me what you know," he said menacingly. With arms as thick as railroad ties crossed over his chest, he positioned himself in front of the door so she was unable to leave. "Does he have copies of the map? Can he get to the Mandylion without the map and key? Has he got a good translator for—?"

"I've never heard such nonsense," she said, startled by the rapid spate of questions. "What is this Mandylion and why—"

He barked a laugh. "You are very good."

Uncertain of his meaning, she continued. "—and why do you care what my father does with it?"

He shook his head in what appeared to be disbelief. "Besides being a thief, your father is a charlatan who will sell the Mandylion to the highest bidder."

"Well… Is there some reason why he should not?"

"My God, woman," he nearly shouted. "It's *the Mandylion!* The legendary cloth that was used to wipe the face of Christ when He walked to His death. The cloth that's said to bear the imprint of His face."

She did not wish to appear uninformed or stupid, but she had never heard of such a cloth. If it existed, as Mr. Temple believed, it would certainly be a priceless relic. Surely her father would not sell it indiscriminately. He was far too conscientious a scholar to do that.

"And the map that leads to the Mandylion was in my father's desk today?"

His eyes narrowed and he gave a slow nod as he scrutinized her.

"I cannot believe your audacity in coming here and maligning my father to my face," she said quietly, trying another tack. If her father found this Mandylion and turned it over to the British Museum, his reputation would be infinitely enhanced. A man like Jack Temple could never again accuse him of being a fraud.

"Your father sabotaged my expedition into Mongasa territory six months ago because of his greed," Temple said, and Dorothea heard the grimness in his voice. "We nearly lost our lives."

Certain that he was exaggerating, Dorothea held out her hand again, for the vellum he still held. She had an idea—though she really needed to think it through a bit more—that if she were the one to find the Mandylion, she could give it to her father and he could present it to the museum.

If only she knew where Alastair was, she would not have to go to such lengths. She could question him and discover exactly what he knew of the cloth, where he intended to look for it and what he intended to do with it once he found it, for surely he had a plan.

But according to Creighton, her father was not yet returned from his African expedition. Dorothea hadn't asked for details, assuming he would return home soon, so she did not actually know how long it would be before he arrived. One glance at the formidable man standing in the doorway, and Dorothea was certain that Mr. Temple would not wait and deal fairly with Alastair. The American would take the map and its key and do all he could to discredit her father.

Dorothea was not going to allow that to happen.

Reluctantly, Jack put the document into her outstretched hand.

She turned toward the light, obviously unaware that her robe was molded to every curve of her body. Damned if she wasn't the worst distraction he'd suffered since being tied to the stump in the middle of the Bahisi village. And while his senses were flooded with the delicate floral scent of her, all her attention was focused on the key, which she unfolded and studied.

Jack took a step closer. Looking over her shoulder as she scrutinized the document, he breathed deeply and reminded himself that this woman was *Bright's daughter.* He forced his attention away from the alluring curve of her neck and the pulse that beat there. He ignored the urge to pull out the pins that held her hair in place and touch the soft curls with his fingers. Instead, he looked at the swirling script on the page in her hands.

The text, which was not written in an orderly fashion, was surrounded on all four sides by intricate ink drawings. Jack could not tell if the elaborate border was part of the key or if it had been added just for the sake of decoration, in the medieval style. On closer inspection, he realized there were several Arabic characters interspersed in the design. Greek and Latin words were interlaced in the pattern, too.

"To his most gracious excellency, the Abbot of Rievaulx," she read.

"Right," he grumbled. "So you said already."

"The next line is Greek," she said, though she made no attempt to read it.

"Herein lies the precious cloth," Jack translated with ease. The Greek and Latin words posed no problem for him. And with Bright's daughter to take care of the Arabic... Damn! This was it! Between them, they'd have the whole thing worked out in a few minutes and he could leave for York on the night train, if that's where the clues led him. "What does the next line say?"

She turned her head and looked over her shoulder at him. "Did you know the abbot of Rievaulx had something to do with this?"

"I only know that the map was found in York, near Rievaulx," he replied. "But I haven't had a chance to study it yet."

"So you don't know where the Mandylion is located."

"No," he said, "although York makes the most sense."

"York?" Her tone was incredulous and he couldn't blame her. "The city? Or the entire—"

"I don't know," he said, feeling testy. "That's why I need the map. *And* the key. What does the next part say?"

"What will you do if you find the Mandylion?"

Jack did not bother to reply. What he did with the Mandylion was not her concern. He just needed her skill with Arabic, and he'd be on his way.

Impatiently, he tapped the vellum in her hands. "Can you read this?" he asked.

She looked back at the faded script on the vellum. After a long pause, she said, "I'm...not exactly certain of the words."

"What do you mean?" he demanded. As he took the document from her hands, she whirled to face him. "I thought Arabic was one of *the many things you know.*"

Ignoring his sarcasm, she replied, "Well, the words *blessed* and *fibers* are there..."

"And what else?" he asked. His words were slow and deliberate, his voice low and menacing.

"It's a poem...or a song, I think," she replied.

"Go on."

"Well, the Arabic is quite archaic," she said, "and it won't sound very poetic when I translate it."

"Just give me the general idea," he said, his patience waning.

Her eyes were shadowed and inscrutable, but when she straightened her shoulders and tilted her head slightly, Jack knew there was going to be trouble.

"I...I think I'll have to sleep on it."

"What?" he roared.

"There is no need to shout, Mr. Temple," she said, flinching at his outburst.

"You know perfectly well—"

"I should say not," she said peevishly. "It will take a bit of time and study before I can be certain that my translation is an accurate one."

He wanted to take her by the shoulders and shake her. "I'm leaving for York *tonight,* and I need to know what this says."

"Then you'll have to take me with you," she said, and it seemed to Jack that she had surprised herself. It was an audacious thing for a priss like her to even consider. He decided to take her bluff.

"Pack your things, then."

"Wh-what?"

"Pack. Now." He took her arm and led her out of Bright's room, then ushered her down the hall. "I take it your room is here somewhere?"

She yanked her arm away. "I've only just arrived in London, and I—"

"Exactly what I figured," he said, pleased to know that his theory had been correct. She *had* just gotten off a ship. "It'll be simple since you probably haven't unpacked yet. You're coming with me."

"But—"

"You're the one who suggested it," he said, not entirely bothered by the fact that Miss Bright would be traveling with him. She was the most prickly female he'd ever known. But she was also one of the most interesting.

Chapter Five

Jack might have dozed comfortably in the rumbling car of the train. He might have relished his discovery of the Mandylion map and that he had gotten it away from Bright and his associate, Fleming, but one factor in all this bothered him.

Miss Bright. Miss *Dorothea* Bright, as he'd discovered just before leaving her house.

The lady sat on the bench beside him, her head lolling on his shoulder as she slept soundly. A feather from her overly decorated hat tickled his ear occasionally, and he brushed at it unconsciously as he considered what she was doing here.

Obviously, she had her own plans. Her hostility toward him could not be mistaken, and he knew without a doubt that she would not help him find the Mandylion to the exclusion of her father. Whatever she did, he felt certain that she would be acting in her father's best interests.

Jack doubted she would give him a faulty translation of the Arabic lines on the map and in the key. She would not want to waste her time following him as he hunted down fraudulent clues. No, she would probably try to cause delays until her father could join her. If that didn't work, she would go after the Mandylion with him. He figured she planned to get the upper hand somehow—maybe by withholding the last line of Arabic—so that she could find the Mandylion first and give it to Alastair.

It actually wasn't a bad plan, he thought, absently moving her hat feather from his ear. And she probably thought she'd be able to contact her father and let him know of their progress somewhere along the way.

But Jack had a better plan. He wasn't going to let her out of his sight until he had the Mandylion in his own hands. He allowed himself a small smile of satisfaction before he dozed. Ah, yes, the next few days were going to be mighty uncomfortable for Dorrie Bright.

It was near dawn when Dorothea awoke. She couldn't remember ever having felt as exhausted as when they'd settled into their seats on the train the night before. Feeling the vibration of the railcar beneath her, she opened her eyes and realized she had fallen asleep on Jack Temple's shoulder. Mortified, she hoped he had also slept, and had not noticed her compromising position.

She did not move. Taking stock of her entire situation, she realized she was practically draped over the man. Her hat had fallen halfway over her face, and she had drooled on his shoulder.

And what was worse, her hands were loosely settled in his lap. The wool of his pants leg was soft and warm, but the muscle beneath was hard. Hard and taut.

Dorothea swallowed. Bracing herself for the worst,

she tipped her head and looked up at Mr. Temple, hoping to God that he was asleep.

His eyes were open, and he was gazing at her.

She sat up abruptly, unsure what to do first, whether to straighten her clothes, tip her hat back into place or wipe her mouth. What was the proper protocol for awakening in the morning with a man she hardly knew?

"Sleep well?" he asked.

She put her hand to her mouth and tried to think of something to say. He had cleaned himself up the previous night—shaving and changing clothes in her father's kitchen—while she had dressed and packed. And now that he didn't appear quite so barbaric, she found herself actually intimidated by the man.

He stood and stretched, then leaned over her to look out the window. Dorothea held her breath as his powerful body hovered over hers. Now that he appeared so much more civilized, she should have felt more at ease. She should have been able to relax her guard. Yet she felt that during the next few days, her wits were going to be sorely tested.

When he returned to his place beside her and sat down, she did not miss the wry smile that turned up his lips.

"You can...freshen up back there," he said, nodding toward the rear of the car.

Grateful to have a safe retreat, she threw him a scathing look and stepped over the brute, who hadn't the courtesy to move out of her way. She practically straddled his knees before escaping, which was no small feat, considering the slim skirt she wore.

Barbarian that he was, Jack Temple seemed to enjoy

her predicament and didn't even turn away when her bosom was at his eye level.

With no small degree of vexation, Dorothea ignored the palpitations in her chest and left Jack Temple long enough to repair what damage had been done overnight. When she was presentable again, she returned to her seat only to find him gone.

The train was still moving, so it was obvious that he had not gone far. Glad for an extension of her reprieve, she thought about the days ahead and how she would manage to gain the upper hand.

She had not yet seen the map, only the battered vellum they'd looked at together in her father's bedchamber. She did not know if they'd come to York only because Rievaulx was located here or if the map indicated something more specific.

It was certain she would have to get her hands on the map. How she would manage it was another question. As far as she knew, Mr. Temple kept it in one of his pockets at all times.

She pictured herself slipping her hand into his back pocket, but her imagination would allow her to go no further. Already, she'd suffered any number of humiliations because of him. Blushing hotly, she vowed not to subject herself to any further indignities where Mr. Temple was concerned. She would soon figure some way to trick him out of the map.

And then she would find the Mandylion for her father.

"We're just about to pull into the station," Jack said when he returned to his seat next to Dorothea. Her stomach grumbled loudly and he grinned at her, enjoying her discomfiture. Her appearance was quite captivating when she was not scowling at him. And with that fresh flush on her cheeks, she was nothing short of beautiful. He wondered what had her so flustered now.

Perhaps it was the memory of the way her hands had been curled on his thighs when she'd slept. *That* was something no proper miss would ever have allowed, but he'd certainly enjoyed it. His body reacted predictably when he thought of those delicate fingers resting in forbidden places and he wondered... Better not to wonder any further. The only thing he wanted from Dorrie Bright was her knowledge of Arabic.

''We'll get something to eat at our hotel,'' he said, as much to distract himself as to tease Dorothea for the noises her stomach had made without her consent.

''And then what?'' she asked primly.

''We'll rest awhile, then go and see what we can learn at Rievaulx.''

''But the monastery is gone,'' she said. ''How will you go about finding the cloth?''

''I have the map.''

''But it does not tell you what you need to know,'' she countered, ''or else you'd never have bothered looking for the key.''

''Speaking of which,'' he said, taking it out of the breast pocket of his coat, ''did you get enough rest to decide what the rest of this line might be?''

He kept the vellum on his lap, forcing her to lean toward him, almost as close as when she'd slept against him during the train ride. It was either that, or she'd have to pick up the vellum from his lap. Either way, he hoped she'd be thrown off balance.

''Um...''

''Blessed fibers?'' he prodded.

She glanced up at him then, her green eyes sparkling, and he knew. She was leading him on.

"Or is your knowledge of Arabic as limited as mine?"

She looked down at the vellum. *"Its stained and blessed fibers,"* she read. "The next line is Latin."

"A testament of the comfort it brought," Jack translated.

"To one we hold divine."

Which said, exactly what, Jack wondered. He considered the lines they'd translated together.

Herein lies the precious cloth,
Its stained and blessed fibers
A testament of the comfort it brought
To one we hold divine.

The lines sure didn't give any clues to the meaning of the tightly folded map in his back pocket. Both documents contained words, or lines, in several languages. It was as if the writer wanted to make sure that no single person would be able to do a full translation, and therefore, find the Mandylion.

Jack frowned. Was this document the key?

He considered asking Dorothea her opinion, then decided that whatever answer she gave, he was not likely to trust it. She had her own motives for coming to York with him, and it sure wasn't to help Jack Temple.

On the actual map, he'd recognized the word *Eboracum,* the Roman name for York. Using that as a base, he'd looked north and found a cross marking Rievaulx Abbey, then several other markings between the abbey, the town and the coast. Jack just didn't know what these markings meant.

He could approximate the distances and explore the areas represented by all the symbols, but this was a medieval map. Distances and land configurations didn't mean the same thing to people five hundred years ago, especially when they were drawing maps. It was possible that he'd need to consult a medieval historian, but with luck, someone here in town would be able to help him.

The train came to a stop, and in a short time, Jack got them into a cab and on their way to the Ainwick Arms Hotel, a reputable place where he'd stayed when he'd visited York some years before. When they arrived, he made sure that Dorothea was seated in a comfortable chair in the lobby with a cup of hot tea, before he registered for a single room in the name of Mr. and Mrs. John Adams.

He saw no need to upset her before it was absolutely necessary, and certainly not in public. But he was not only going to keep her with him tonight, he was not going to advertise his own name so that Bright could locate him, just by asking for Jack Temple.

Taking the room key, he turned their luggage over to a porter, then joined Dorothea. "Shall we go have some breakfast?" he asked cordially. He knew there would be some histrionics when she learned about their room and wanted to have a meal first.

He escorted her into the dining room, where several tables were engaged. Most of the other patrons were men who appeared to be discussing business, although a few tables were occupied by couples who seemed completely absorbed in one another. Jack figured they must be newlyweds—they were the only men he knew who looked at their women like such saps.

Jack didn't mind looking at Dorothea. Not at all. Her skin was about as pretty as any he'd ever seen, smooth and flawless, from the faint blush of her cheeks to the hint of a cleft in her chin. Her cool green eyes intrigued him. Framed by thick dark lashes, they sizzled with anger or became razor sharp when her brain was at work. But it was their expression when she'd awakened, when they'd been as soft as wet moss, that he could not forget.

As he looked at her lips, full and pink and inviting, she brushed at her chin. "Do I have something on my face?" she asked without guile.

Jack shook his head and put that sweet image of her aside. No point in him looking like a sap, too.

Breakfast could not have been more uncomfortable for Dorothea. With Mr. Temple's undivided attention on her, she was hardly able to choke down her muffin and egg. No one had ever disconcerted her so.

"What do you expect to find at Rievaulx?" she asked. She finished her tea and dabbed daintily at her mouth. Then she set her napkin on the table next to her plate and placed her hands in her lap. She'd been surprised to discover that Mr. Temple understood table etiquette. For a barbarian, his manners rivaled her own, and she disliked having to admit it. She had looked for every possible reason to continue thinking of him as a rude and uncouth colonial.

But, since their arrival at the hotel, he was proving her wrong.

"I'm not sure," he replied, leaning back in his chair. He didn't take his eyes off her, and Dorothea resisted the urge to squirm in her seat. His steely gaze never failed to make her heart pound, and she would have avoided looking directly at him, except that she refused to be cowed by him. She reminded herself that Jack Temple was the one who had stolen her father's property, *he* was the one in the wrong here, and Dorothea was going to see that her father got his due.

"Do you think there will be someone whom you can question about the map?"

"Possibly, although it's not likely."

"Then I fail to see what the point is," she said.

A small smile softened his lips and Dorothea was chagrined to note that a long dimple creased his cheek. He looked so much less disreputable with those awful whiskers gone, but no less dangerous. Dorothea didn't allow herself to consider what that meant but went on questioning him.

"What does the map say? Can you read all of it, or will I have to help you translate?"

"Tell you what," he said. "I'm beat. Why don't we get a couple hours' sleep, then we'll look over the map together. If you see anything you recognize, we'll go after it."

He stood and helped her from her chair, just as a true gentleman would, although Dorothea could barely give him credit for that. She needed to remember that he was the enemy, as courteous as he might pretend to be.

"What do you mean, if I recognize anything? Is the writing Arabic? Do you think I'll—"

"No," he said. "It's a typical medieval map. It's formed in a circle, with the main point of interest at the center."

As he placed his hand at her lower back and guided

her up the main staircase, Dorothea couldn't help but imagine herself being led upstairs by a devoted husband—like the ones she'd seen in the dining room. Those young men had looked so devotedly at their wives… Surely, those couples were newlyweds enjoying their wedding trip.

They would spend the day together, touring the countryside, having picnics or driving out to the seaside. And at night, they'd return to their room together and spend it in each other's arms.

At least, that was what Dorothea thought, although her mother hadn't spoken much about marriage. The most Honoria had said was that the wedded state was something for which Dorothea—and all respectable women—should strive, to gain security and stability in her old age.

Dorothea definitely wanted security and stability, and if only Albert Bloomsby had proposed before she'd left Oxford, she would have happily become his wife.

But here she was, being escorted by a coarse and barbarous American, rather than sitting quietly in her father's London home awaiting word from Albert. She sighed.

Mr. Temple pulled a key from his waistcoat and pushed open the door to her room. It was lovely. She quickly took in the restful shades of blue and gray in which the room was decorated and the large bed that dominated the space. She would be comfortable here for the length of their stay, and while Jack Temple was sleeping in his own room, she would slip away to find a telegraph office and send a wire to London. Certainly Creighton would see that Alastair received the message as soon as he arrived home.

She turned to close the door just as Jack Temple's shabby valise caught her eye. A nasty jolt of suspicion shot through her. What was that valise doing here?

Turning to confront him, he shut the door behind him.

He nodded at her with a self-satisfied smirk on his face. "That's right," he said. "It's just you and me, Dorrie. Together."

Chapter Six

"**Y**ou're not going to faint, are you?" Jack asked, alarmed by Dorothea's sudden pallor.

Color quickly flooded her cheeks and she placed her hands on her hips, showing her figure to great advantage. Jack decided it was in his best interests to ignore it for the moment.

"Of course I'm not going to faint," she said, reaching to place one hand on the doorknob. "But I'm going to have you removed from my room. The very idea!"

"Uh-uh," he said, covering her hand with his own. "We stick together through this whole expedition or all bets are off, Dorrie."

"Why, I—"

"Planned to summon the old man, didn't you?"

"Certainly not!" she cried. "I—I only want m-my privacy. It is entirely improper for me to be here with you. Like this."

"Like what?" Jack said, moving closer. His face was only inches from hers, and, as he anticipated, she did not retreat a single inch.

"Alone."

"What do you think is going to happen?" He was but a breath away. He had intended only to tease her, but she was so close he could almost count her eyelashes. He could see a few faint freckles dusting the bridge of her nose and smell whatever floral scent she'd dabbed behind her ears.

He wanted to taste her.

He wanted to touch the smooth, soft skin of her face and breathe in the scent of her hair.

Luckily, he remembered exactly who he was dealing with, before he did something stupid. "Nothing," he said, answering his own question. "That's what's going to happen. Absolutely nothing."

She released the breath she'd seemed to be holding. A small frown creased her brow, and Jack stepped away. He decided to take pity on her. "Take the bed. Have a rest. I'll be back in a while."

When Jack left the room, he started down the stairs, planning on a long walk to clear his head. He must be insane to entertain the kind of thoughts that had crossed his mind while gazing into Dorothea Bright's eyes. No doubt her father used her as a very effective distraction whenever he negotiated terms. There wasn't a man on earth who could avoid being distracted by her.

Jack didn't know how he was going to stick with her for the entire time they were in York. He'd have to…

Jack stopped at the foot of the staircase. What a fool! He'd almost been tricked into leaving her alone. A woman of her intelligence wouldn't have the slightest difficulty slipping away to get a telegraph message to her father. And when Alastair Bright arrived, Jack would have to take drastic measures to keep the man from sabotaging him again.

Jack wanted the Mandylion discovered and publicized before Bright had a chance to get his greedy hands on it. And the sweetest revenge was that he was going to use the old man's daughter to do it.

He hurried back up the stairs, unwilling to give Dorothea the slightest opportunity to slip past him. There was a small sitting room at the end of the hall, and he decided to stay there and have a smoke while he waited for Dorothea to get settled. Then he was going to join her in their room, grab one of the blankets from the bed and bunk down on the floor in front of the door.

He needed an hour's rest, too.

Dorothea did not know how long she stood with her back to the door, her hand at her breast, her heart pounding. She was short of breath, too, but Dorothea did not think it was due to her condition. Jack Temple had an entirely too unsettling effect upon her, and she was going to have to guard against it. She would present no more opportunities for him to intimidate her in any way—including that most recent episode.

Now that he'd left her alone and she could think clearly, she decided to approach the hotel desk and ask someone to send a message to her father. It was entirely unfair of Mr. Temple to have stolen the Mandylion map and to get so far ahead of her father in his explorations. She did not think any of her translations had helped him so far, but there was more— much more—Arabic written on that document. She hadn't really studied it, but it was entirely possible that it would point exactly to the spot where the Mandylion was hidden.

Dorothea opened the door a crack and looked to the left. All clear.

"Looking for me?" Temple asked.

Dorothea slammed the door shut and slipped her hand down to the lock, but there was no key. She couldn't keep him out. And when a suspicious metal click sounded loud in her ears, she knew she couldn't get out, either. He had locked her in.

"Mr. Temple!" she called, her voice a harsh whisper. She would not make a scene in this respectable hotel, but she certainly would not allow him to jail her! "Open this door."

"Aw, honey," he drawled. He was playacting! "Don't be mad. I'll just give you a few minutes to settle down, and I'll be back. Go ahead and…get ready."

"I'll get ready all right," she muttered angrily, stepping away from the door. No doubt he'd uttered his words for the benefit of anyone who might overhear. Dorothea certainly wasn't going to heed them. She would sit up in the boudoir chair by the window and wait for him to reappear. Then they would have it out. She would not be held prisoner by that barbarian.

No, she would turn the tables on him. She would make certain that he couldn't come back into the room. Pulling the chair to the door, she tipped it, placing the back under the doorknob as she'd done years ago with a childhood playmate. When she was satisfied that she had effectively locked him out, Dorothea took the pins out of her hair and shook it loose. She undressed down to her chemise, then crawled into bed and fell asleep.

Her last thought was that her mother would certainly never approve of lying abed in the middle of the morning.

Jack turned the key in the lock and pushed the door. Dorothea had obviously placed something in front of it so that he wouldn't be able to enter, but it posed no real problem. He eased the door forward and the blockade slid along with it, allowing him entrance.

Since he was prepared for an angry outburst from Dorothea, he was surprised to find her sleeping soundly under the blankets. He grinned. This trip was proving to be a lot more interesting than if he'd traveled alone.

He took off his jacket and tie, then moved the chair over to the window where it belonged. Unbuttoning the back pocket of his trousers, he pulled out the map and smoothed it over his lap to study it in the bright sunlight.

It was a typical medieval map. Distances and landmarks were exaggerated or ignored. Latin and Greek script filled the margins, and a cursory look at the writing had given Jack no better understanding of the sites shown on the map. In the center was York, and if Jack was not mistaken, the old town was drawn much too close to the eastern coast. And it was way too large.

He reached into his jacket pocket and pulled out the other document. There had to be some connection between the two, but Jack could not see it, though the two documents were clearly drawn by the same hand. What did these lines in Greek, Latin and Arabic mean?

Dorothea sighed deeply in her sleep, drawing Jack's attention. He hadn't wanted to look at her, especially not now, as she turned to her side. The blanket pulled away from her shoulders, leaving too much of her soft skin naked to his gaze.

She really must have thought the room was secure against him, or she would never have undressed so completely. He wished she hadn't. He'd already seen more than he would ever be able to forget. Had that only been yesterday when she'd fainted in Alastair's collection room?

It seemed as if she'd been with him forever.

Chagrined by the thought, Jack jerked his attention back to the map and key. His only reason for keeping Dorothea Bright with him was to prevent her from sabotaging his attempts to recover the Mandylion. The fact that she could translate the Arabic lines was a gift, one that could be had from a number of other sources.

Jack had to admit, though, that he didn't want to involve anyone else in his search for the Mandylion, especially not another antiquities scholar. Things always got much too complicated when a gaggle of academics got involved. Since this was such a limited expedition, Jack hadn't even brought his own team with him. His men were taking a well-deserved holiday to recover from their disaster in Tanganyika. Gauge O'Neill was recuperating from his last bout with fever, and the rest of them were enjoying the delights London had to offer.

Looking over at Dorothea, Jack knew he wasn't missing anything by leaving them.

Refusing to allow her to distract him again, he began translating the place names on the map. He was familiar with some of the locations, since he had visited York many years before with his mentor, Charlie MacElroy. Most of the places, however, were unfamiliar. *Foston, Wharram Percy, Elmswell, Wetwang.* Jack wondered if these places still existed and what significance they held to the mapmaker.

To the north was Rievaulx, and just below the abbey was the image of a face. Could it be one of the Templar faces?

Jack rubbed his hand across his own face. He was tired. More than that, he was exhausted. He'd had very little sleep in the past few days, and none at all the night before. He needed to rest before he taxed his brain trying to remember everything he'd ever known about the Templar Knights and their connection to the Mandylion.

He folded the map and key, put them into his pocket and eased down on the bed beside Dorothea.

Jack had planned on doing the gentlemanly thing by taking the floor, but as long as Dorothea was asleep, she would never know he'd lain right next to her. Besides, all they were doing was sleeping. Nothing else, even if he *did* enjoy the view as he drifted off.

His sleep was not restful. Turbulent dreams of a sheela-na-gig and a Celtic warrior intruded. Jack was the warrior, and damn if Dorothea Bright wasn't the sheela, bare and exposed, just like the ancient female figure. But this sheela was beautiful. And she was beautifully proportioned of flesh and blood, not carved in stone with exaggerated anatomical parts like the one he'd seen displayed in Alastair Bright's collection.

Jack saw himself sweep her into his arms and carry her away on his stallion, riding hard, until they were both breathless. Holding her naked body close to his, he could smell lavender in her hair, feel the weight of her hips against his huge mahogany phallus.

Jack groaned in his sleep, the sensations of the dream all too real, the images from Bright's graphic collection fresh in his mind. Stone figures engaging in illicit acts flooded his mind, while he rode on with his sheela until they were alone in misty, green hills. She slid off the stallion and ran from him, laughing, taunting. Her breasts were bare, and when her hair swirled around her shoulders, the pale, soft globes were hidden from his view.

He could not keep up with her. Each time he reached her, she gained some distance. Every pore of his body ached to touch her. Her sweet, seductive laughter filled the air, and Jack's body pulsed with need.

A muffled shriek pierced his consciousness and he sat up abruptly. Still half-asleep and more than half-aroused, he was momentarily disoriented.

''*Out!*'' came the voice again. This time, it was accompanied by a shove, and Jack came more fully awake.

''What is it?'' he asked. ''What's the matter?''

''You're in my bed!'' Dorothea hissed.

''Good of you to tell me,'' he muttered, looking into flaming green eyes. ''Especially when I was in the middle of the most…the most amazing dream….''

Her eyes widened, and the fists holding the blanket over her breasts tightened. Her neck and shoulders remained enticingly bare, and her hair cascaded down her back, over her shoulders. Jack couldn't keep his eyes from roving over her, taking in every attribute, even though the sight of her prevented him from getting his unruly reflexes under control. And on the heels of that damn dream, it was nearly impossible to tamp down the intensity of his arousal.

Dorothea gave him another push, but he was immovable. He grabbed her wrist to keep her from shoving him again. She blushed, and he pulled her toward him.

"We need to get something straight, right now," he said quietly. "I'm not going to give you the leeway you need to contact your father. That means we're going to be together. A lot."

"But I will not al—"

"You and I are going to find the Mandylion," he said, keeping his voice low but without menace, "without any interference from your sneaking, greedy father. We'll take equal credit for the find, but you're going to have to cooperate with me, or I'll cut you out of the deal."

Dorothea moistened her lips, and Jack found himself breaking eye contact to watch her tongue move slowly, seductively across her lips. Instantly, he knew it was a mistake. Drawing on every ounce of willpower to keep from laying her down on the mattress and using his own tongue on her mouth, Jack turned away and took a deep breath.

"If you try to lock me out of this room again," he said, dropping her wrist, "I'll find myself another epigraphist, and you'll have nothing."

He swung his legs off the bed. Picking up his coat from the chair where he'd put it, he grabbed his tie and left the room.

Dorothea practically flew into her clothes the minute Jack Temple closed the door behind him. She'd thought him merely unnerving before. Now he was downright frightening.

Or perhaps she was more frightened by her reaction to him.

Dorothea stopped buttoning her blouse before she was half finished, and put her hands on her cheeks to cool them. Had Jack Temple had his arms around her while they slept? Had he fondled her breast and nuzzled her neck before she'd bolted up in bed?

She swallowed. It had seemed like part of a dream, but now Dorothea was unsure whether or not his touch had been real. One thing was certain, though. She had never felt anything quite so exquisite in her life, had never imagined that a man's touch could feel so… She didn't know what to call it. Exciting…arousing.

In all her talks about marriage, Dorothea's mother had never spoken of such feelings, had never hinted that there was any pleasure to be had from the mere touch of a man's hand, the heat of his body. How was it possible that Honoria had not known?

Dorothea finished dressing, then pinned up her hair and put on her hat. There was no time to think of these things now, not when Jack Temple was about to leave and search for the Mandylion on his own. Besides, Mr. Temple was not the kind of man suitable for any respectable woman. Along with being a crude American, his way of life was exactly the same as her father's, and it had driven her mother away. And with Dorothea's weak heart, she would never be able to travel to exotic, foreign excavation sites, even if she wanted to.

She pulled open the door and hurried outside, colliding with the man who'd occupied her thoughts. He grabbed her by her upper arms and kept her from los-

ing her footing. And he did not release her immediately, as a gentleman should.

A shiver of excitement raced through her at his
touch, and in that moment she knew she had not been
dreaming. He'd held her close while he slept, and
more. Her breasts tingled with an awareness of how it
felt for them to be cupped in his hand, fondled by his
fingers.

''Better get your jacket if you're cold,'' he said
gruffly.

''But I'm—'' He'd obviously felt her tremor.
Rather than own up to it or the reason for it, she agreed
with him and went back into the room to retrieve her
jacket.

''Where are we going?'' Dorothea asked.

Jack had wanted to keep her in the dark as long as
possible, but now that they were riding in an open
buggy on a country lane south of the city, he didn't
see how he could avoid letting her in on his plan, what
there was of it.

''Just getting the lay of the land,'' he said.

She tilted her head to look at him. ''Does the map
give any indication of where the Mandylion might be
hidden?''

''Not exactly,'' he said. He transferred the reins to
one hand and reached into his breast pocket. Pulling
out the packet that contained the map and the key, he
handed them to Dorothea.

While she studied the documents, Jack studied her,
keeping only one eye on the lane.

She was all buttoned up again—as prim and proper
as she could possibly be, with her hair tightly tucked
under her silly hat and her long jacket concealing all

her soft, luxurious curves. But Jack knew what lay concealed, and he wasn't likely to forget.

"Is this a Templar head?" she asked, pointing to one of the drawings that Jack had been wondering about ever since he'd found the map in Bright's desk.

"What do you know of the Templar heads?"

"Not a lot," she replied. "Only that the Templar Knights worshipped a man's head. This looks similar to a drawing I once saw of the heads at Temple-coombe."

Jack was impressed. Not many people knew about the Knights of the Temple beyond the rumors of their secretive affairs. The organization had started out early in the twelfth century with the blessings of the Church and the Pope and ended in disgrace less than two hundred years later. "Anyone who believes the Templars worshipped a stone head is wrong."

"Then why is the head a recurring motif in their churches?"

"Because of the—"

"Mandylion?" she asked. "The heads are representations of the face on the Mandylion?"

"Exactly," he said. He gave her a grudging smile. For one who'd said she knew nothing of the holy cloth, she certainly came to the right conclusion. "Most scholars believe the Mandylion is actually the Shroud of Turin."

"But you, in your infinite wisdom…"

He laughed outright and had the pleasure of eliciting a spark of humor in her eyes. "I have another theory. One, I would add, that's shared by a number of learned men."

"Which is?" she asked, leaning slightly toward him.

"We know that the cloth found its way to Edessa some time after the death of Christ. It eventually traveled from Edessa to Constantinople and was lost when the city was sacked by Crusaders in 1204."

"I could never understand that—Christians going off and raiding a non-Islamic city."

"Greed is a powerful motivator."

"I suppose," she replied, and Jack was struck by her lack of guile. It was almost as if she did not know of her father's mercenary approach to the treasures of antiquity.

"There is documentation that Templar Knights were involved in the raid on Constantinople," he continued. "So it's entirely feasible that the cloth fell into Templar hands."

"But why didn't the Templars make it known to the rest of Christendom?"

"They were a secretive bunch," Jack explained. "There are theories about what they were doing in the Holy Land—tunneling under Temple Mount for Solomon's treasure, for example. Whatever they were doing, they did not want the rest of the world to know it."

"So you're saying that the Shroud, which, if I remember correctly, turned up in France after the Templars were disbanded, is not the same cloth that was known to be in Edessa?"

"Right again," he said, admiring the sharpness of her intellect. "I think there were two entirely different cloths. The shroud that is now in Turin and the Mandylion."

Dorothea didn't comment, but Jack could see that her mind was working to assimilate all that he'd said. She had to know that her father wouldn't have collected and perhaps paid a handsome sum for the Mandylion map unless he believed it to be a valuable artifact.

While Dorothea studied the map, they drove in silence, and Jack wondered if he would be able to locate any of the places that were marked or if they'd disappeared over time. They were in the general vicinity of one of the heads, but Jack didn't see anything of significance in the landscape.

"I don't see how you can tell what's what on this map," she finally said. "The mapmaker put York in the center, with the coast drawn at the bottom. Rievaulx Abbey is to the right of York, which is actually directly north." She turned the map to reorient the four directions. "Hmmm. It appears that everything is laid out correctly, I suppose, if you turn it this way. But York seems much too close to the coast."

"That's what I thought," he said.

"There's a cross marked on a site a few miles south of York—probably around here somewhere. It could signify any church," she said, glancing up at him.

"True," he replied, "but why would it be specifically marked on this map?"

Dorothea did not answer, but returned her attention to the map. "There are heads—Templar heads?— drawn in three different places. Two are right next to the two crosses, and the third is directly below York— or rather, *east* of York—near the coast."

"And there are several other markings. Villages. And these—" he pointed to the drawings of crenellated walls "—I would guess are castles."

"But there are so many."

Jack winked at her. "That's what makes my line of work so interesting."

"You mean to search them all?"

"No. I mean for you to finish translating the key and then maybe we can narrow down the hunt."

"Mr. Temple, I—"

"Jack," he said, turning again to meet her eyes. "I never stand on formalities when I'm on expedition, Dorrie."

"M-Mr.—" She licked her lips again, causing a blast of heat to shoot through him. "Um, Jack, I don't see how you can possibly believe I would help you work against my own father."

He had an answer for her, but words escaped him. They were alone in the country, with only the birds and a few cows for company. Though it had turned cloudy and cool, it was a beautiful day, and Dorrie Bright was sitting close to him. Her lips were full and moist, but she looked as tightly laced as ever. He wondered if she would allow him to put his arm around her if she became chilled.

Or perhaps kiss her.

He put *that* thought out of his head. "The man's a thief and a scoundrel." Kissing her was nothing but a fantasy, the result of that ridiculous dream he'd had while lying on the bed with her.

"So you've said time and again, but you've never given me one reason to believe you."

"Did I tell you about my expedition to Tanganyika?"

She crossed her arms over her chest and looked straight ahead. "No."

"I had thousands of dollars' worth of photographic equipment," he said. "We'd planned to study the Mongasa tribe, deep in the interior, and take photographs. Nothing more."

"Very admirable, I'm sure. But not entirely un-profitable for you."

"Of course not. But your father stole the tribal fer-tility god—the Kohamba," he said. "He took it one morning before dawn and slipped out of the Mongasa village, leaving my team to take the blame for its dis-appearance."

She said nothing, but he saw the muscles in her throat move as she swallowed hard.

"The situation got very ugly, very quickly. In the end, it was an absolute miracle that we all got out."

"If what you say is true—"

"Every word," he said.

"No," she countered. "I can't believe it. Why would he go off to Africa on some dangerous expe-dition when he had the Mandylion map right here? And the Mandylion itself probably right here in York-shire?"

"Because the price he could get for the Kohamba would be astronomical."

She turned to look at him. "But won't he get a handsome price for the Mandylion?"

Jack shook his head and glanced up at the sky. Rain was coming. He would have to raise the hood of the carriage if they were going to stay dry. "The Mandy-lion isn't a sure thing. It's a legend."

Her expression turned quizzical. "Do you mean you're going to all this trouble to chase a legend?"

"No," he said as he brought the buggy to a halt. "*We* are."

Chapter Seven

In spite of his accusations against her father, Dorothea was impressed by the speed and efficiency with which Jack raised the top of the buggy. Too demure to watch him openly, she observed covertly while he reached back to free the canvas top, then fit it on its frame, sheltering them from the rain. She felt her cheeks flame when his jacket pulled away and her face was even with his well-formed behind.

He drove the buggy under a canopy of trees to help shelter them from the downpour, then turned to her.

"You'd better move in or you'll be soaked."

He was right. Her left arm was getting wet, but just as she moved over, Jack placed his arm across the back of the seat.

"Let's be careful with those," he said, indicating the documents that she held in her lap.

She started to fold them, but he stopped her.

"Seems like a good time to try and decipher the rest of the lines," he said, leaving his hand over hers. It was rough and hard, unlike her own.

His face was close to hers, and, for a moment, Dorothea forgot to breathe. His eyes met hers, then drifted down to her mouth. Every time he did that, her lips tingled expectantly. She couldn't help but part them on a sigh, and when he tipped his head down and brought his mouth to hers, she could not resist meeting his touch.

Her heart fluttered, but not from weakness. She felt as if it had been set free, rather than fettered by the malady that had kept her so quiescent for most of her twenty-five years.

His arms went around her and he pulled her close, all while his mouth moved seductively over hers. Dorothea felt her bones begin to melt as one of his hands slid down her back. She did not care when he removed her hat and didn't feel him take down her hair. But it was loose around her shoulders, and when he threaded his fingers through it, she shivered.

The rain poured down around them, but Dorothea felt warm, cocooned in the buggy within the shelter of his arms. Nothing mattered but his hands at her waist, his tongue touching hers. Shards of heat shot through her when she leaned into him, pooling in the tips of her breasts and low in her belly.

One of his hands slid up to cup her breast and Dorothea's breath faltered. His lips trailed hot kisses from her ear to the niche at the base of her neck. Her fingers threaded their way through the dense hair at his nape and she felt him shudder with pleasure. She'd thought it an innocent touch, but his reaction made her realize that it wasn't.

Moving her thumbs, she brushed them across his ears, eliciting a groan. She touched her lips to the sensitive spot and got a reaction that excited her nearly as much as his kisses. Emboldened, she traced the shape of his ear with her tongue and his breath rasped in his throat.

Suddenly, his lips were on hers again, his tongue sweeping in and possessing her mouth. Sensation pulsed through Dorothea, hot and thick and relentless. She placed her hands on his chest, slipping them under his coat. His muscles bunched at her touch, and she felt his strength again. Still, he was wonderfully gentle with her, even as he lowered her to the padded bench and worked at her buttons.

A sound in the distance startled the horse and the buggy jerked. Jack muttered something under his breath and grabbed the reins, leaving Dorothea for the moment. It was long enough for her to come to her senses. With color heating her face, she realized where she was and what she was doing. Her mother had not raised her to engage in such shameful behavior in a buggy with a man she'd known barely one day.

She sat up abruptly and righted her clothes while Jack wrestled with the horse. Thunder rumbled in the distance and the storm seemed to be worsening.

''We'd better get to some real shelter,'' he said. He pulled off his jacket and rolled it up, stowing it under the seat of the buggy. Then he turned the horse and headed back in the direction from which they'd come. Dorothea started to look for hairpins and quickly found enough to repair her hair. She pinned her hat in place, and, regaining as much dignity as possible under the circumstances, she straightened her collar and cuffs.

Jack turned, looked at her and frowned. Dorothea allowed her eyes to skitter away. She did not know what to say to him or how to act after such indelicate behavior. Luckily, finding adequate cover from the storm occupied him and he drove the buggy back down the lane toward an old barn they'd passed earlier.

Lightning streaked the sky nearby, and thunder crashed in their ears just as the barn came into sight. The buggy didn't entirely protect them from the rain, so they were already wet when Jack tossed Dorothea the reins and jumped down to go open the barn door. As soon as it was open, Dorothea drove the horse, following Jack inside.

He was soaked to the skin, his shirt and trousers plastered to his body.

While he shoved the barn door closed, Dorothea observed the play of thick muscles beneath the transparent cloth of his shirt. When he turned, she could see the shadow of dark hair upon his chest.

She was blushing again. Jack surely enjoyed that flush of color on her cheeks, even though he knew it meant that she was embarrassed. Though what she had to be embarrassed about now was beyond him. Probably just the thought of what had transpired before the downpour was enough to raise her color.

Hell, he'd be surprised if his own color wasn't high. He couldn't remember the last time he'd felt such a frenzied need to kiss a woman…to touch her and hold her. It was only because of those damn artifacts at Bright's house and that dream he'd had.

Fortunately, the storm had kicked up right when it did, because Jack had no intention of getting involved with Dorrie Bright. And by her expression, he could tell that she wasn't all that happy about what had happened, either.

It would be best if they both forgot it.

He unbuttoned his shirt and slipped down his suspenders. Taking off the shirt, he wrung it out, then raised the suspenders again.

"Would you hand me my jacket?" he asked, approaching Dorothea in the buggy.

It was bad form to be undressed in mixed company, but he hadn't seen any other course. He'd known he was going to get soaked, so he'd spared his jacket in order to have something dry to put on. But by the look on Dorothea's face, anyone would have guessed he'd lost his trousers.

"It's under the seat," he prodded.

She seemed to hear him that time and quickly bent down to retrieve the coat. He slipped it on and noticed that it was only slightly damp, and the map and key were safely in the breast pocket where he'd stashed them. Reaching up to help her down from the buggy, he was relieved that Dorothea had decided to ignore what had happened, too.

He stepped away from her. In the gloom of the barn, he located an oil lamp and lit it. Glancing around, he noticed there wasn't much inside, other than a few wooden crates stacked in one corner. Jack pulled a couple of them down and brushed them off with the edge of his hand.

There was room enough for two to sit, but Jack didn't want to risk being quite so close to her now. The trip back to York was going to be bad enough, and he didn't want to think about the coming night. He'd gotten himself into a fine mess.

When Dorothea walked toward him, he gestured for her to sit down, then took a step back.

"Maybe we should look at the map now," she said.

Agreeing that it was as good a diversion as any, he

took the documents out of his pocket and handed one to her. Spreading it over her lap, she studied it silently. Jack walked over to the barn door and pulled it open.

The rain was still pouring down. They were going to be stuck here for a while.

"These medieval maps are awful puzzles," she grumbled. "How was anyone supposed to follow them?"

"This one's better than most," he remarked from a distance. "At least York is marked."

"Um, yes. Eboracum."

A curly tendril of her hair slipped down unnoticed as she looked at the map, and Jack could almost feel its softness, smell its delicate fragrance. A part of him could easily imagine burying his face in her hair and filling his hands with her lush breasts.

"What makes you think that the cloth you seek is not the Shroud of Turin?"

"Pure instinct," he said. He closed the barn door and walked part of the way back to her. "I have a feeling that after the order was disbanded, there were still Templar Knights who continued on in secret. No doubt they appreciated having the Turin cloth turn up and take the attention from their Mandylion. The Templars liked their secrets."

"Wasn't there some connection between the Templars and the man who first displayed the shroud? What evidence is there to make you think there's more than one cloth?"

"One is the burial shroud," he explained, impressed by her logical reasoning, "which has been at Turin since the late sixteenth century. The Mandylion is a much smaller cloth and would only have a facial imprint. At least, that's how the legend goes."

"And you suppose the imprint on the cloth is the model for the Templar heads in the churches?"

"Why not?"

She considered his words thoughtfully, then pointed at the map. "Where do you suppose the Mandylion is located? At one of these sites where the head is drawn?"

"I was hoping the key would tell me," he replied, unfolding it. He joined Dorothea and laid the key on the crate next to her. "But all we're translating is some sort of poem."

"And a rather lame one, at that."

"Hm."

"What are you thinking?"

"Nothing really," Jack said, suddenly wondering if the poem didn't hold any clues at all. Had the key been intended to throw interest away from the map itself? "How about another look at these lines?"

Dorothea bent her head again and translated, *"Take care and guard this,* er, *chart."*

"Map," he said. "Maps were often called charts in medieval times."

She nodded and translated the next line from Greek. *"While we at home."* She glanced up at him. *"Defend?"*

"Or *protect.* Maybe *preserve.* But you've got the gist of it."

"I don't think this is a key to the map," she said. She bit her lip, then tapped her finger against it. "It seems more likely a letter that accompanied the map when it was sent to, well, to Rievaulx for safekeeping."

"You may be right," Jack agreed. "There sure

aren't any indications of what the markings on the map mean.''

Dorothea bent over the vellum and translated the next line. *"Our Savior's beloved face."*

''*Beneath our heart's domain,*'' Jack said, finishing it. He looked up and met Dorothea's eyes.

''Well, it looks as though your efforts to steal the key from my father's room were in vain,'' she said, standing up and walking away from him.

It was entirely possible that she was correct. Except that if he hadn't been confronted by her in the house, he'd have traveled to York alone and missed the hours in her company. He would definitely have missed that kiss in the buggy.

Jack didn't think he'd forget that any time soon.

The ride back to town was slow, due to the ruts and deep puddles in the lane. They'd left the barn during a lull in the storm, but the clouds had opened again when they were just outside the city walls, and a fierce wind made the meager protection of the buggy ineffectual. When they arrived at the Ainwick Arms, they were both cold and bedraggled. Dorothea's clothes were soaked and wrinkled, and Jack was still bare-chested under his jacket.

Dorothea was too miserable, cold and weary to think anything of it, other than how lovely Jack Temple's roughly hewn chest had looked when he'd first removed his shirt. With suspenders looped at his sides, his trousers had hung loosely, just below his waist. A distinct line of hair ran from the thick pelt across his chest, down his taut belly and into his trousers. With that sight fresh in her mind, she had had some difficulty discussing the Mandylion intelligently with him.

Well, that and the kiss.

How she had allowed herself to indulge in such behavior, she would never know. But it would not happen again. Not only had she been raised better than to behave like the lowest of loose women, but Jack Temple was her father's enemy. She could not allow herself to forget that the man had broken into her father's house and stolen his property—the map to the Mandylion.

Jack was ruthless and unscrupulous. He'd told her himself that he was an adventurer—a man who lived on the road and the high seas and off the profits he made from the artifacts he discovered. Well, perhaps he hadn't said quite as much, but Dorothea easily concluded it from what she knew of him. She had to remember that he was only keeping her with him to prevent her from alerting her father to his activities. She had no doubt that he could easily find another translator if she proved to be too much trouble.

Shivering with cold, Dorothea trudged up the steps to her hotel room, too weary to think of the mess her life had become. Nothing had prepared her for the last twenty-four hours, and she did not have the energy to ponder it now. She only wanted to get out of her wet things and crawl into bed.

Going on ahead of Jack, she hardly heard him ask the hotel clerk for a meal to be sent up to their room. She was short of breath by the time she reached the top and positively quivering with cold.

"Hey, your lips are blue," Jack said when he caught up to her. He unlocked the door and pushed it open for her. "You've got to get warm and dry."

She managed to get her hat off, but her hands were trembling so badly that she could not unfasten the buttons of her jacket. Jack shoved her hands away and did it for her. When he saw that her hands were still shaking, he cupped them in his own hands and blew warm breath onto them.

"Can you finish?" he asked. He'd never seen anyone get so chilled from a little rain.

"Of course," she said, though he doubted it.

He turned away to give her a moment's privacy and located his valise. Laying it flat, he opened it and took out a sweater. After removing his wet jacket, he pulled the precious sheets of vellum from the pocket and checked to see that they were undamaged. When he saw that they were still dry, he slid them into the bottom of his valise, then slipped the sweater over his head. When he turned around again, he saw that Dorothea was still struggling with her buttons.

He was amazed that she was so willing to get her clothes off in his presence, but he knew that she was just as anxious as he was to get out of the wet things.

"Having some trouble, Dorrie?" he asked.

She did not reply but continued to fumble with the buttons.

Jack moved her hands away and went to work, in spite of her protests. "I've already seen this much," he said as he slipped the buttons through the fabric. "And we've got to get you warmed up so you can stop all this shaking."

"I a-am p-perfectly f-fine," she objected through chattering teeth, though she allowed Jack to continue.

"Once I've got these damn things undone," he said, "you can get into your warmest gown and into bed. That ought to do it." He wouldn't let her know how the sight of her soft skin inflamed him or how her scent tantalized him.

The fact that they were sharing a hotel room meant nothing. He was going to bed down on the floor after they ate and forget the way her sweet mouth tasted, the way her ripe breast felt in his hand.

Jack helped her dig a soft flannel night rail from her bag, then turned his back while she finished undressing. After a few minutes, he heard the bed creak and knew that she'd climbed in.

One of the hotel's clerks arrived with a tray laden with plates of warmed food and a pot of tea. "I'll take that," Jack said. He set it on a table, then tossed the boy a coin and shut the door behind him. "Hungry?" he asked Dorothea.

"N-not particularly," came her muffled voice from under the blankets and quilt.

"Come on, Dorrie," he said to the quivering lump under the bed. "A cup of hot tea will help to warm you."

He poured the hot brew into a cup and took it to the bed. Sitting on the edge, he peeled the cover down her shoulder and looked at her. Frowning, he offered her the cup. She was as beautiful as ever, but he didn't like her pallor.

"You're not taking sick, are you?"

"Of c-course not," she replied, still shivering. She pushed herself up enough to take the cup and sip the tea. "I just can't seem to get warm."

"I don't think I've ever seen anyone take such a chill from a little rain."

"It was a-awfully c-cold out there," she said. "And not just a *little* rain."

He didn't disagree with that. It *had* been cold, but not enough to freeze a person to her bones. Jack got Dorothea to eat a little bit of the food on the tray and finished the rest himself. He considered taking the quilt in order to bed down on the floor but didn't want to take any of Dorothea's warmth from her.

The thought of shucking his clothes and crawling in with her to share his heat warmed him considerably. But Jack didn't think Dorrie would appreciate that. That kiss they'd shared had been an aberration, and he knew she wouldn't allow another one.

"Mr. Temple?"

"Jack."

"Um, J-jack?"

He was sure the hotel would have extra blankets. He would just go down to the desk and ask for one. "What is it, Dorrie?"

"Would you d-do me a favor?" she asked.

She was out of her clothes and miserable. It was safe to leave her here for a few minutes—she wouldn't be going anywhere. He crossed to the door, put his hand on the knob and waited.

"W-would you come to bed with me?"

Chapter Eight

"Dorrie?" His voice was incredulous.

"I'm f-freezing, Jack," Dorothea said. She despised the shakiness in her voice, the weakness of her heart that made her so vulnerable to something as simple as a rainstorm. "P-perhaps if you lie b-beside me, your b-b-body will help to warm m-me."

He didn't respond, and she didn't hear him moving, either. He was probably appalled by her request but didn't know how to refuse it. What decent woman would ask a man into her bed?

Her teeth continued to chatter and her heart beat erratically, but a minute later, she heard him moving in the room. The next thing she knew, the mattress had dipped, the blankets shifted and his body was sliding toward hers.

He pulled her back against him, his chest and lap nestling her back and buttocks. One hard arm encircled her waist. His warm breath tickled her ear. Dorothea knew she should be avoiding any physical contact with this man, not encouraging it.

But the heat from his body was marvelous. It seeped through her skin and into her bones. Soon her trembling slowed and her jaw relaxed. She reveled in his heat. She enjoyed the caress of his hand on hers, a caress that sent shivers of warmth through her.

Dorothea burrowed into him without thinking of any consequences, other than the spectacular warmth of his body. He was so solid, so hard behind her. The pure pleasure of that wall of heat was incomparable.

His legs shifted, and she realized they were as bare as her own below her gown. The hand at her waist moved, too, and Dorothea became aware of another kind of warmth shimmering through her body. She forced herself to ignore it, unwilling to consider the ramifications of being in bed with a naked man.

"Warmer now?" he breathed into her ear.

"Mmm, hmm," she replied, unsure what to say in these circumstances. Before she could think of anything coherent to say, he pulled her lower body into his own and moved against her.

"You are so soft, Dorrie," he said quietly. His hand slid down to her abdomen and pressed. "I could melt into you."

She made a low whimper. "Jack," she whispered. "I—"

A low, harsh breath escaped him. "Go to sleep, Dorrie," he said. "I'll keep you warm."

Jack sat with Dorothea at breakfast the following morning, watching her drink her tea while she studiously avoided his eyes. The less said about the night that passed, the better, but he had to get her talking if they were going to be able to continue working together.

He glanced out the window and said, "It's sunny

today. We can go up to Rievaulx and spend the day poking around.''

Dorothea turned to look out the window behind her and nodded.

''The local vicar will probably have records, maybe stories about the cloth,'' he said. ''We can see if there are any rumors I haven't heard—something we can connect with the translation.''

''I don't see what you hope to discover from rumors,'' she said.

He smiled. Her eyes were still a dark, sensuous green, even though she was buttoned up as tightly and properly as she could be. He would never have guessed that she was the same woman who had practically pleaded with him to join her in bed.

Not that she'd intended anything improper. She'd been cold and intensely miserable when he'd curled his body against hers.

But she had warmed up quickly.

Jack cleared his throat. ''If we finish at Rievaulx early enough, I'd like to ride from there to the place on the map marked by one of the faces.''

''Which one?'' she asked.

He did not take the map out of his pocket to show her, preferring to keep it private. ''The one southwest of Rievaulx.''

''Do you know where it is?''

''No,'' he replied, although he believed it was in the vicinity of the barn where they'd sought refuge from last night's storm. However, he did not want to mention last night. ''But if we head over that way, something might come up.''

''Like what?''

"Ruins of an old chapter house or church," he said. "Maybe a cemetery."

"How will you know when you find it?" she asked.

Jack shrugged. "I'll just track down whatever evidence I have and follow the legends and rumors. If I—" He nearly choked on his coffee when he saw Paco Fleming walk past the window.

"What is it?" Dorothea said. "What did you see?"

"Nothing," he replied. He sure as hell wasn't about to tell her that Fleming was in the area. She'd go after him immediately, in order to get to her father. "Just thought I saw someone I know."

She sipped her tea, seeming to lose interest in the momentary diversion. "I still don't see what you think you can get from listening to rumors. These maps must be five or six hundred years old. Any stories about the Mandylion would be horribly inaccurate by now."

"You're right about that," Jack said, keeping an eye on the street outside, "but it's all we have. We can filter out the obvious red herrings and follow the best leads."

When Dorothea shook her head and looked disgusted, Jack wondered if her father used some other technique. How did he go about finding all the valuable artifacts he peddled to his wealthy buyers? Jack knew firsthand that Bright didn't always have a reliable map. He'd found a man who'd actually been in Mongasa country and knew about the Kohamba before he'd attempted to go after it.

There was no question that Bright had a method that worked. Jack just hoped his own methods were as successful this time. And that he was able to keep Dorrie Bright from running to her father.

"Are you finished?" he asked.

She nodded.

"We might as well get started," he said. "Are all your things packed?"

"Why?" she asked. "I thought we were staying here for a few days."

"I changed my mind," Jack replied. He wasn't about to stay in York when Paco Fleming was closing in. Wherever Paco went, Alastair Bright could not be far behind. From previous visits, Jack knew there were small country inns all over Yorkshire, and he had every intention of finding one where it was unlikely they would be discovered.

He hired a carriage this time, one with better protection against any weather they might incur, even though Dorrie's bout with the chills had been anything but unpleasant—at least, for him. It took every bit of determination he possessed to keep from thinking about the night he'd spent with Dorrie wrapped in his arms.

They'd awakened in a tangle of arms and legs, with Jack as aroused as he'd ever been. Her gown had ridden up to her hips, leaving her lovely silken legs bare. She had to have felt his arousal, though she'd ignored it, turning away from him as he'd gotten out of the bed.

And he had once again reminded himself that she was Alastair Bright's daughter. If he turned his back on her long enough, she would certainly betray him.

They took the northern route out of town, toward the ruins of Rievaulx Abbey, easily avoiding the place where they'd shared the most amazing kiss of Jack's life.

He would have bet his best boots that Dorrie had never experienced anything like it, either.

The sun continued to shine, and it was a fine trip to the abbey, other than the awkward silence that hovered between them. Ever since they'd left the hotel, Dorothea had spoken only when absolutely necessary. Jack knew that her sense of propriety had been offended by the night's events, even though there had been no alternative way to keep her warm. Now that they were alone together, she was feeling awkward.

"I wonder if your father has buyers for all of the pieces in his collection," Jack said to taunt her out of her silence, "or if he likes to keep a few for...personal reasons."

His unexpected remark brought a blush to her cheeks and an expression of astonishment to her face. It was exactly what he'd hoped for. He didn't want to continue riding in uncomfortable silence.

"I have no idea," she said primly. "I never even knew all those...things...were there."

Jack could almost believe her. She seemed so earnest. So honest.

But he knew better. She was too intelligent to have lived there and not known what was in that room.

"My particular favorite was the *sheela-na-gig,*" he said, deciding to shock her into speaking to him. "Her face might have been ugly as sin, but all her parts were there. And quite spectacularly displayed, too."

"I've never seen such awful things," Dorrie countered. "The very idea of a female showing herself off in such— Oh!"

She covered her mouth with one gloved hand, dismayed to have been drawn into such a discussion. But Jack did not relent.

"He had a fair number of decent lingas—or *in*decent, as the case may be," he said with a grin. "I figure they'd be of greater interest to you…as a woman, I mean.''

"I am certainly *not* interested in such things!"

"You sure had a death grip on the marble one that you broke."

"This is a disgusting line of discussion, Mr. Temple," Dorrie said indignantly, "and I would appreciate it if you would desist."

"How can it be disgusting, Dorrie?" he asked, feigning innocence. "It's *your* father's collection, not mine."

"Then it's *his* business, not yours."

"All those images—drawings, pottery, figures," he said, as if to himself, "makes a man—"

"Mr. Temple!" Dorothea protested. "If you don't mind, I would appreciate a change of subject!"

"But Dorrie," he countered, "I was only talking about what most interests your own father. That collection is his very livelihood."

"Whatever it is, not one item holds any interest for me, and I'd prefer that you not speak of it again," she said.

"He's got some spectacular pieces," Jack teased. "Real works of art."

She shot him an icy green glare, and he chuckled.

They arrived at the village near the abbey in midafternoon. Jack drove the buggy onto the grounds and found them deserted. Ruins of the majestic buildings stood quietly and peacefully in the lush, green clearing. There was almost a hush over the site, a connection with the monks who once prayed and toiled here.

Dorrie was silent, her eyes betraying the awe she felt at the sight of these magnificent buildings, their stone shells mere shadows of their former glory. Jack felt the same way—he always did when he came upon a site of old, where men and women had lived and worked in antiquity. It was a passion he'd developed years before, under the tutelage of Professor Charlie MacElroy.

As a young student, Jack's first expedition had been to Italy, where he'd worked on the excavation site of a Roman city. The search for evidence of bygone times had never lost its allure. He had sat through lecture after lecture in various classrooms for only one purpose: to earn the credentials he needed to go out in the field and search for the treasures of the past, just like MacElroy.

"Was that the church?" Dorothea asked. She opened the door to the carriage.

"Yes," Jack said, jumping down. He moved quickly, circling around to Dorrie's side. He assisted her out of the carriage and took her arm as they walked into the ruins of the church.

For the daughter of a low-down swindler, she was surprisingly reverent standing here amid the broken-down bricks and mortar of the old building. She gazed up at the sky beyond the ruined roof and looked at the intricate stonework that remained. Jack felt her shudder. She ran her hands up her arms as if to ward off another chill.

"I can almost hear the monks' voices chanting," she whispered in the silence.

Jack guessed he could hear them, too.

He watched as she walked through the grass that grew unchecked all the way down the nave of the church. A breeze ruffled the feather on her hat, and she raised one arm to steady it. But her steps never faltered. She was completely enthralled by the site.

Jack forced himself to take his eyes off her. He had a purpose here, and it wasn't to ogle Dorothea Bright's trim figure.

He stepped out of the church. The ruins of several other buildings stood here, and Jack wondered if any clues about the Mandylion's location were among them. What should he look for? Some sign of a Templar face? The land upon which Rievaulx stood had once been a Templar holding, which gave a strong probability to finding something of use here.

Jack turned and looked at the other ruins. He wanted to look them over quickly and move on, because there was no doubt in his mind that Alastair Bright wouldn't be far behind. The old codger had seen the map so he had to have seen the marking for Rievaulx. That's why Fleming was in York, with Bright somewhere nearby. They'd be heading here before long.

"Dorrie!" he called. He wanted to keep her close in case they had to leave quickly.

She came out of the church and into the clearing. "I do not know why you persist in calling me that. My name is Dorothea, and no one has ever shortened it so tastelessly."

"Then it was long overdue," he said absently. He led her through all the buildings, stopping only long enough to look at the remains to see if there was any sign of a Templar presence. There were none.

"Come on, Dorrie," Jack urged when he found her standing under a vaulted arch. "We don't have a lot of time."

"Why not? There's plenty of daylight left, and I doubt I'll ever see anything as wonder—"

"We've got other places to go, things to do."

"Such as?"

"A room for the night."

"Two rooms," she countered.

"Not on your life," he replied, taking her hand and leading her through the cloister. No Templar heads here, either. "If you think I'm going to let you out of my sight so that you can run to your father——"

"Since I haven't any money, I don't know how you think I would manage the train fare back to London." She pulled her hand from Jack's and stumbled. He caught her with ease and walked on.

"I'm not taking any chances."

"Yes, well, *I'm* not sharing a room with you again."

Dorothea stomped her foot and steamed inwardly. As Jack locked them inside their room at the Boar's Head Inn and turned to face her, she wanted to slap him. He'd relied upon her sense of decorum to keep her quiet when he'd let the single room from the landlord. And he'd been correct. She'd been too stupefied to make a scene of any sort.

But she would make one now. Especially when he had the audacity to show her that utterly devilish grin of his and that rakish crease in his cheek. How was she supposed to forget how his lips had tasted, or how she had felt, warm and secure in his arms all night?

"How dare you!"

"I told you before——"

"You have the manners of a churl, sir," she rasped indignantly, "to place me in this situation against my will."

"Dorrie, will you——"

"I am not a strumpet, who will bed down with any man, a stranger——"

She backed away as he walked toward her.

"—a m-man who is an e-enemy of m-my—"

"This is strictly a business arrangement," he said impatiently. Shoving his suit jacket back, he put his hands on his hips and seemed ready to do verbal battle. "You and I will be sharing this room only because I can't trust you to keep from running off somewhere with the hope of reaching your father."

"We are miles from anywhere, in case you hadn't noticed," she snapped.

"Of course I noticed," he said, coming closer. Dorothea could feel the heat radiating off his body, heat that had enveloped her when he'd kissed her in the buggy, then later, all through the night. Pointedly, she ignored it. "That was my plan. We'll stay here tonight and in the morning, we'll see if we can locate the other spots marked on the map."

"I'd rather return to the Ainwick Arms," she retorted, even though, if they left immediately, it would be well after dark when they arrived in York.

Jack shook his head. "It's getting too late for travel. We'll take a walk if you like, then get a meal and have a good night's sleep before we follow the map tomorrow."

She felt her face heat at his words. If he thought he would spend another night in her bed, he was sadly mistaken. She did not care how cold the weather turned. She would see that he stayed in another room or, at the very least, spent the night on the floor.

"Come on, Dorrie," he said. His voice was deep and soft. Seductive. And she wondered if she would ever again be able to lie in a bed without remembering how it felt to be in his arms. "Be reasonable. You know it's not practical to go back tonight."

She felt the wall at her back, and then Jack was right in front of her, one hand resting on the wall beside her head. If he put the other hand there, she would be trapped. He could tip his head slightly and touch his lips to hers, and then she would be lost, for she did not really want to resist him.

Her eyelids lowered. She breathed deeply of his scent and inched away from the wall, hungry for the taste of his mouth on hers.

Dorothea could no longer deny that she wanted him to touch her as he had last night in the carriage. She ached to lower her corset and feel his hands on her breasts. She wanted to learn more of the things her mother had neglected to tell her.

"Let's get some supper," Jack said, dropping his hand and moving away. "I'm starved."

Chapter Nine

Strangely enough, their short walk before supper seemed to tire Dorrie. When they walked up the gradual incline that overlooked the abbey ruins, she seemed out of breath.

"Are you all right?" he asked.

"Of course," she replied indignantly, regulating her breathing so that it would not be quite so obvious.

It had to be that damn corset. If she wasn't laced up so tight, she'd be able to breathe properly. Jack wondered if there was any way to talk her out of wearing it.

"You can see the abbey from here," she said before Jack had a chance to wrap his mind around the idea of Dorrie without her corset.

Rievaulx was visible in the distance, and Jack wondered if Bright and Fleming had arrived and walked around the ruins after he and Dorrie left. If so, he hoped Alastair Bright's memory was faulty, and he'd have difficulty remembering exactly how the rest of the map was marked.

Jack wasn't too worried about Bright arriving at the Boar's Head Inn. He'd covered that possibility with a credible story for the innkeeper about tricks his friends might try to pull on himself and his new bride. The innkeeper had winked and told him not to worry. No pranksters would be allowed to ruin a honeymoon at the Boar's Head Inn.

Still, Jack intended to keep an eye out for Dorrie's father. The man had seen the Mandylion map, as well as the key, and he knew the general area where the cloth was likely to be found. He'd be prowling around Yorkshire, asking the same questions Jack was asking, though Jack hoped he was asking them first.

He wondered if Bright could read Arabic, then decided it didn't matter. He could find his own translator, just as Jack had done. And Jack took some satisfaction in the fact that he was using the translator Bright would have preferred.

As he watched Dorrie gaze into the distance, she shivered and ran her hands up her arms. Damned if the woman didn't take a chill at the least little breeze.

"Cold?" he asked, unbuttoning his coat to give to her.

Absently, she shook her head. "Just…just thinking about someone."

"Your father?"

"No," she said quietly. "Actually…my mother."

Jack had never heard anything of Alastair's wife. And Dorrie had never mentioned her before. He wondered where she was now, and how she felt about her husband's collection of lewd antiques.

"She died less than a month ago," Dorrie said. "Just took ill suddenly and never left her bed."

Jack did not know what to say. This was the last thing he expected to hear, and he felt a moment of shame knowing he'd dragged Dorrie out of her house while she was in mourning. She hadn't said anything, though she'd seemed a bit out of her element, stunned perhaps, when Jack had first encountered her at her father's house.

Damn, Alastair probably didn't even know his own wife was dead. Maybe he was still in London seeing to whatever details he'd need to deal with and had sent Fleming ahead to York. It was something to consider.

"I'm sorry, Dorrie," he said. "I didn't know."

She shrugged and continued looking toward the Rievaulx ruins. "It's all right. You couldn't have known."

Jack didn't think he'd have done anything differently even if he had known. He would still have brought her to York to help him translate the key and to keep her from helping her father.

But would he have kissed her in the buggy? Would he have entertained all manner of lascivious thoughts about her when he'd held her through the night? He would like to believe he was more noble than that, but he wasn't. Even now, when he knew she was grieving, he wanted her.

He'd needed all his powers of self-restraint to refrain from kissing her again in their room at the inn. She had not put up any serious resistance to his advances, and Jack knew he could have had her on the bed and under him within minutes of touching her lips. Luckily, his good sense had prevailed. He'd hurried her into her coat and down the stairs before anything could happen.

"My mother would have been appalled by this turn of events."

"You mean, traveling with me?"

She nodded. "And my...behavior. Anything but what she would have thought proper."

"Dorrie, I—"

"I just miss her so much," she said. The last word was caught on a sob that she quickly stifled. Her shoulders jerked and before Jack even thought about it, he'd turned her and pulled her into his arms.

She wept. At first he felt her trying to hold back, but when her tears came, they were accompanied by wracking sobs. Her hat fell off, but she didn't notice. Jack held her close as she poured out her grief and murmured quiet words to her. He didn't know what he was saying, only that he'd seen his mother do the same for his sisters when they were upset, and it always seemed to help.

Jack wasn't feeling particularly familial with Dorrie, though. He felt sympathetic and protective. He felt like a man taking care of his woman. He felt powerful and needed at the same time. And he felt her soft body against his.

Her crying subsided and she took a long, shuddering breath. "She was always so strong," Dorrie said. "Nothing like this would ever have happened to her."

"Dorrie," he said, rubbing her back. "You've done very well for yourself."

"You don't understand," she said. "My mother would never have allowed you to steal those things from my father's house, nor would she have let you drag her onto the Great Northern Rail—"

"I don't remember any dragging."

"—and force her to sleep in the same room with you."

He rubbed her back and stifled a chuckle. "You

were damn lucky to have me last night, sweetheart," he said.

"I'm sure I would have managed." She was prickly again.

"You didn't seem to think so when you were shivering your toenails off."

She pulled away from him. "I'll thank you not to refer to…to…body parts—"

He laughed. "When I start talking about body parts, honey, they sure won't be toenails."

Enjoying her shocked expression, he took her arm and started down the hill. "Dorrie, I'm sorry for your loss," he said, "and I regret that you ended up in the middle of this mess between your father and me."

She sniffed once, and he searched his pockets for a handkerchief.

"I will assure you that if we do find the Mandylion," he said, "it will be granted to a reputable museum and not sold as a black market treasure." As your father would do, he wanted to add, but decided against it. He didn't want to hear her defending Alastair.

"You're implying that my father will sell it if he finds it?"

"Dorrie, I don't want to imply anything," he said, finally locating his handkerchief and handing it to her. "I'm just telling you that when I find the Mandylion, it's going to the British Museum. The director of antiquities there can decide what's to be done with it after that."

Dorothea did not want to argue. She wanted to go to her room at the inn and let go the tears that were still welling up inside her. For days, she'd avoided thinking of her mother and how much she missed her, doing what was necessary to move out of the house in Oxford.

"Why don't we go back for supper?" Jack asked. "The innkeeper is a talkative fellow. I wonder if he knows anything about the Mandylion and its connection to Rievaulx."

Dorothea dabbed at her eyes, resentful of the fact that Jack was diverting her attention from her grief. "What do you think you'll find out?"

"I have no idea," Jack replied. "Sometimes local lore or legend has a basis in fact. Maybe the innkeeper can tell us some of the old stories about the abbey."

"Then what?"

"It depends on what he tells us," Jack said. "If he says there was an abbot in 1289 who had a secret treasure that he buried under the northeast pillar of the—"

"You don't think he'll say any such thing."

"Why not? I've heard stranger things in my travels," he said, "and I'll bet your father has heard even more, given the kind of objects he prefers to collect."

Dorothea felt as if her air had been choked off. She yanked her arm away from him. "I would appreciate it if you would not refer to my father's...collection... again," she said, loading as much dignity into her words as possible. "They are—I never—"

"Never saw any of that stuff before?"

"Of course not!"

"You mean your old man left that door locked all the time, and you never wondered what was in the room?"

"What my father does is his own business," she asserted.

Jack laughed, and she struck out ahead of him. She would let him laugh as long as he liked, but not within her hearing. She would return to the inn alone and close herself in her chamber until morning. And Mr. Jack Temple could fend for himself somewhere else until then.

She was out of breath again when she arrived in the inn yard, but she ignored the discomfort. She was sure the feeling of breathlessness would pass once she had a moment's rest.

"Ah, there you are, Missus," the innkeeper said when Dorothea entered the main room. "Supper is ready. I was wondering if you and your husband would be back in time."

Dorothea didn't bother to correct the man's perception of her relationship with Jack. Her incorrigible companion had registered them as man and wife, and it was much simpler to leave it that way. In fact, it gave her an odd thrill to be thought of as Jack Temple's wife, to have shared a bed with him, and she knew she should be ashamed of it.

"Mr. Atwater," Jack said in greeting. "Something smells good. Doesn't it, sweetheart?"

"I'm not particularly hungry this evening," she said, still annoyed with him and with herself.

Jack took her arm and made it impossible for her to leave him without making a scene. He ushered her into the common room, where a table had been laid for them. The innkeeper's wife and daughters were bringing out bowls and platters from the kitchen, and as the volume of food mounted, Dorothea wondered who else would be dining with them.

"Come in, come in! Sit!" called the older woman.

"Such a feast, Mrs. Atwater," Jack said, holding a

chair for Dorothea, but giving the woman his rapt attention. "All for us?"

"Nothing too good for our guests," the woman replied, beaming back at Jack and his captivating dimples. Dorothea did not care for the surge of wifely possessiveness that shot through her at the interchange. She needed to put some space between them, and soon.

"What part of America is your home, Mr. Adams?" Mrs. Atwater asked, calling him by the name he'd used when registering.

"New York," he replied as he handed serving dishes to Dorothea. His manners were impeccable, and he exuded charm.

"Do you have family there, then?" she asked.

Jack nodded, and Dorothea listened to his reply with interest. She knew next to nothing about him—other than the fact that he was an adventurer like her father. "My parents live in the city, along with my two sisters."

"Oh, you come from a small family, then?"

Jack winked. "Not if you count my three brothers," he said with a grin.

Mrs. Atwater poured ale in their mugs, while Dorothea tried to recover herself. She had not thought of him in the context of a family. He was a son. And a brother.

"And have you had a chance to visit New York, Mrs. Adams?" Mrs. Atwater asked.

Jack took her hand and spoke before she could reply. "Not yet, but she'll be coming home with me after our honeymoon." He turned and looked in her eyes, and it seemed to Dorothea that the room went silent. She could no longer hear the barking dog outside or the landlady's daughters chattering in the kitchen. The fire in the grate went silent.

There was only Jack, and he had her hand in his, his eyes on hers.

The smile slipped from his face as his gaze became more intense. Dorothea felt her blood pounding in her temples. Her corset felt tighter than usual, and her collar was choking her. Jack looked at her as if she were one of the courses set before him.

Dorothea should have been outraged, but she could not find any indignation in her. All she wanted was to feel Jack's arms around her, his lips on hers. She wanted to lie in the bed upstairs and feel his weight next to her, his warmth surrounding her.

And she wanted something more.

Jack tore his eyes away, to answer a question asked by the landlady. "No, this will be more than enough, Mrs. Atwater," he said, though his voice sounded odd to Dorothea. He released her hand and began to eat, avoiding her eyes.

Dorothea looked down at her plate and tried to make sense of what had just happened. Had she recognized the expression in his eyes? Did he want to kiss her as badly as she wanted him to?

She swallowed. This was so very improper. She could not allow him to kiss her. Albert Bloomsby had been limited to a mere touch of his lips on the back of her bare hand, and he'd been a frequent visitor. She and her mother had known him for years. Yet Dorothea had already given Jack Temple—a stranger—leave to kiss her intimately.

She needed to get control of herself and remember the lessons of propriety taught by her mother. Honoria would be aghast to know that her daughter was trav-

eling alone with a man. She would never have permitted such a thing.

But Dorothea did not regret her adventure. She had
seen and done more in the last three days than in her
entire life. It had been wonderfully liberating to forget
about her weak heart, to walk among the ruins of Rievaulx and up the hill beyond the inn. She had ridden
in an open buggy—something her mother had never
allowed—and was drinking ale with her supper!

She could not even consider how her mother would
have reacted to the knowledge that her daughter had
slept with a man.

Nothing about her life in Oxford could compare to
the last few days or to the sensations she experienced
when she was with Jack. Still, she knew she had to
guard against such foolishness. Jack Temple was a
wanderer like her father. Irresponsible, unreliable,
reckless. What would any sane woman want with a
man like him?

She refused to think of the dimple that appeared in
his cheek when he smiled. Or the strength of his arms
when he'd held her. She would not dwell on the comfort he'd given so freely when her grief had overcome
her.

No matter what some of his gentler qualities might
be, he was not a suitable man for her at all.

Dorothea ate a few bites while she dreaded the coming night. As exciting as her days had been, she did
not know how to manage Jack. It was entirely possible
that he would expect to share the bed with her.

Dorothea could not allow that again. It would never
have occurred last night, except for that terrible chill
she had taken in the rain. Tonight, she would insist

that he take his own room or remain here in the common room, finding rest any way he might for the night.

Concentrating on her meal, Dorothea wondered how she would enforce her decision. Surely Jack would not allow himself to be put out of the room so easily. He was in possession of the key, and he knew how to get around the chair propped under the knob, so she could not lock him out.

Up until now, Jack had relied upon Dorothea's sense of decorum to get her to comply with his will. What if she simply refused to behave? What would he do then?

This was an idea that was as frightening as it was compelling. To her knowledge, she had never acted inappropriately in her life. Her mother would not have tolerated it, and Dorothea didn't know if she could actually do it.

But what if she tried something now? What if she created such a scene that Jack Temple was forced to retreat?

She nearly laughed at the thought. Instead, she glanced up at him and watched for a moment while he put his energy into his supper. His jaw was square and solid, with the shadow of evening whiskers. A lock of his hair had fallen over his forehead, and her fingers itched to push it back.

She refrained and toughened her resolve to remain indifferent and distant.

"Are you finished?" Jack asked.

Dorothea was taken by surprise by his question. She had expected him to finish his meal quietly, then lead her to their room for the night. "Yes," she said.

"Why don't you go on up?" he asked, pushing

away from the table and helping Dorothea from her seat. "I'm going to get some air."

"B-but…"

He gave her a captivating smile. "I'll be up later."

Feeling duly dismissed, she watched as Jack left the room and tried to think of something to say.

"Your mister gone out for a smoke?" Mrs. Atwater asked, coming into the room with her daughters to clear up.

"He—"

"That's what my man does after supper," she continued, placing bowls and platters on a large tray. "Has his smoke and his whiskey before bed. I wouldn't be concerned, now. The girls have turned down your bed, so it's all ready for you. Just go on up."

Jack felt rather smug. He'd seen the light of mischief in Dorrie's eyes and managed to blindside her before she could act on whatever plan she'd concocted.

He'd sent her to their room, secure in the knowledge that she couldn't get to her father without riding back to York. There was no telephone here at the inn, nor were there any telegraph offices nearby. The Boar's Head Inn was about as isolated as it could possibly be.

Besides, Jack thought, she looked done in. It had been a long day, and he could see that she needed rest.

Jack inhaled tobacco smoke and stood in the yard alongside Mr. Atwater, who'd come out for the same reason. They walked to a low, wooden bench and sat down, looking at the clear, black sky. Jack decided to take the opportunity to ask questions about the abbey and any lore associated with it.

The landlord was a garrulous fellow and had many a story about the abbey. But there was nothing relevant to Jack's quest. Other than tales of a ghost or two over the centuries since the abbey's dissolution, there was no mention of anything of interest to Jack. No hidden treasure of any kind, no word of a sacred cloth hidden on the grounds.

He had no more information now than he did when they left York that morning. Jack wondered why Rievaulx had been so prominently marked on the map. Then he wondered if the other markings would be equally disappointing.

Even with no news of the cloth, Jack did not believe the trip here had been wasted. Though the Mandylion remained as elusive as ever, he'd spent the night and a full day with Dorrie, and there was nothing that could compare to the range of expressions on her face as she'd walked around the ruins. She'd been completely immersed in the peaceful setting, intrigued by the majestic columns and the flying buttresses that remained.

Jack didn't think he'd ever seen anything quite as beautiful as her eyes, bright and curious as she'd looked at all the stone staircases, the narrow passageways and the columned galleries. It had taken her breath away.

Experiencing it with her had taken *his* breath away.

He had to quit thinking about her before going up to their room, or he was going to find it impossible to avoid touching her. Though it had been nothing short of torture to hold her in his arms last night, he had a suspicion that a night without her was going to be worse.

Jack scraped his fingers through his hair and wondered how he had come to this: thinking about a woman—a prissy, bossy woman—every waking hour.

Dorothea Bright was not at all what he'd thought at first. He still didn't know quite who she was or what was going on under her bristly surface, but she posed a number of contradictions to his way of thinking. She acted as if she didn't know her father at all, but her knowledge of ancient languages was staggering. No one but Alastair Bright would have bothered teaching her all that.

And she seemed ridiculously naive about travel. Was it possible that she hadn't shared her father's quest for ancient artifacts, that she hadn't actually traveled with him?

Sometimes she seemed so puzzled by the smallest things. And worn out by such modest exercise as walking through the ruins today. He truly did not know what to make of her, but he decided that he was not going to figure her out tonight. Nor was he going to spend the night in that room with her. Sure, he'd considered seducing her to gain her allegiance, to turn her against Alastair. But he was not such a scoundrel that he would use a woman that way. Besides being too dishonest for his constitution, he couldn't bring himself to hurt Dorrie Bright.

And that *would* hurt her. She was not some pawn to be used in his revenge plot against Alastair, even if she was the man's daughter.

As Jack stretched out on a long sofa in the main room of the inn, he could not keep himself from remembering how it felt to have her lying next to him, tucked up in his arms. And he considered the possibility of lying with her every night for the rest of his life.

He pulled up the collar of his coat to ward off the sudden chill. Oh, yes. He was much safer here.

Dorothea propped both pillows behind her in order to ease her breathing. She hadn't felt so short of breath in years, and she remembered her mother's frequent admonitions to remain quiet and avoid overexertion.

Until now, she had always followed her mother's wishes. She'd heeded the warnings that overexertion would cause problems—that she would have trouble catching her breath, her heart would pound erratically and her ankles would swell. In truth, Dorothea guessed she hadn't actually believed her mother's dire predictions. She had not considered a walk through Rievaulx to be any more taxing than her walk from the London docks to her father's house. On the contrary, she had enjoyed it immensely and did not know how she would ever be able to return to her passive, quiescent existence after three days with Jack Temple. Three days of learning how it felt to be alive.

One full day to think about his kiss.

Dorothea hadn't realized how sheltered she'd been in her mother's home. They'd had a maid and a footman to attend to their needs, and Dorothea had hardly ever needed to leave the house. Of course she'd spent time in the garden when the weather permitted, but, in general, her mother insisted that Dorothea stay indoors and not exert herself in any way.

She'd had very few gentlemen callers. Honoria had discouraged such activities, leaving Dorothea with only a few contacts from the university. That was how she'd known Albert Bloomsby, the only young man who had satisfied Honoria's requirements in a suitor.

Thinking of him now, Albert seemed impossibly bland. Not just in appearance, for that was pleasing enough, Dorothea supposed, but in personality. Albert was dull. He was deferential to the point of being submissive. And he had been so solicitous of Dorothea's mother. Until now, she had not realized how annoying that had been.

There was no fire in Albert...no passion. *That* was what had always been missing in her life. There was no exhilaration or excitement, no amazement or awe and certainly there had been no outbursts of any kind of temper, either good or bad. Honoria had maintained a perfectly modulated household. She'd kept her daughter sheltered and protected from all the upsets of life.

It wasn't until Dorothea's move to London and Jack Temple's arrival in her father's house that she had ever had to fend for herself.

And, in spite of the physical weakness that plagued her now, Dorothea discovered she liked how it felt to be on her own. The small discomforts she suffered now would be nothing compared to what she would endure if she were forced to become sedentary again.

Inching up her gown to look at her feet, she was gratified to see that there was no swelling. At least, not yet. Then she glanced at the door and wondered when Jack would arrive. Somehow, she had to keep him from discovering her heart condition.

Because if he knew, Dorothea was sure he wouldn't let her accompany him any farther on his quest for the Mandylion.

Chapter Ten

Jack awoke at an ungodly early hour with a sore back and a crick in his neck. He sat up on the sofa, rubbed his aching muscles and realized no one was up and about yet. The sun hadn't risen and only the earliest robin had started to sing.

He figured Dorrie would sleep another couple of hours at least, giving him a chance to ride back to Rievaulx and wander around the ruins again. He wanted to explore some specific areas of the abbey.

He put his shoes on, grabbed his coat and headed for the door, then retraced his steps and returned to the registration desk. Locating a sheet of paper and a pencil, Jack wrote a quick note in case Dorrie came looking for him before he returned.

He slipped out of the inn, borrowed a saddle and a shovel, mounted his horse and headed for the abbey.

After talking to Atwater, Jack had a better idea of the layout of the monastery. He knew where the refectory and chapter house were and the layout of the cloister and dormitory. With so much rubble all over the ruins, he thought he might dig a bit and see if he could turn up anything in the vicinity of where the abbot's office would have been located.

If there were any clues to be had, that's where they would be found.

It did not take long to reach the site, and Jack dismounted to wander in the predawn light. He found himself wishing he'd waited for Dorrie.

He'd wandered many an excavation site in his years as an explorer, but had never felt such pure enjoyment in the search as he had yesterday afternoon. Dorrie's presence had magnified Jack's pleasure.

Still, she was her father's daughter, he reminded himself, and Jack had to be cautious about how much he revealed to her. No matter how much he enjoyed baiting her—hell, he enjoyed watching her do the smallest things—he was not about to let her get hold of the Mandylion before him. She would just turn it over to her father.

Not that he had any real worry on that score. As he'd noted before, she didn't seem to have the vaguest idea how to go about following the clues of the map and key. She'd been completely enthralled by the ruins, and if Jack were honest with himself, he felt the slightest bit guilty about coming back here without her.

It had come down to the two of them in this together, no matter what their separate motives happened to be.

With the shovel he'd appropriated from Atwater's stable, Jack started digging through debris. After an hour, he realized it would take weeks to get through the three hundred years' detritus that was scattered about. He wasn't going to find anything significant under the top layer.

He brushed off his hands and placed them on his hips. He didn't mind the hard, tedious work that was usually required to make grand discoveries. But this was pointless. He needed his team—men who had the skills to unearth anything worth keeping—in order to excavate the site properly.

He picked up the shirt and jacket he'd discarded and threw them on, but when he headed back to the inn, it was with anticipation, rather than disappointment.

When Dorothea awoke, she felt much better. Her breathing was fairly normal, and her appetite was back.

But there was no sign of Jack. It didn't look as if he'd even slept in the room, unless he'd spent the night on the floor without even a blanket to ward off the chill.

She should have felt grateful for the privacy he'd given her. She *did* feel grateful. She had certainly not missed him in her bed, sharing his heat, feeling the weight of his presence. She had spent many years alone and was content to spend many more.

Sliding out of bed, Dorothea went to the window, opening the curtains to a beautiful, golden morning. Lifting the sash, she leaned out, breathing deeply of the fresh air, and wondered what the day would bring.

Would they travel to another one of the sites marked on the map? And if they did, how would Jack know exactly where it was? Maps drawn in medieval times were notoriously inaccurate. Dorothea knew Jack would have to be guessing when he decided where they went next. But Dorothea decided she did not care what their destination was. She only wanted to join in on the search.

Smiling at the prospect of another exhilarating day, she went to stand before the commode and poured fresh water into the basin. Humming quietly to herself, she washed her hands and face.

Jack stuffed the map in his back pocket and quietly opened the door to Dorrie's room. It was well past midmorning, and though he'd allowed her to sleep this long, they had to get going soon. He had chosen the next site he wanted to visit, and it would take a few hours' travel to reach it.

He had looked in on her several times throughout the morning, only to find her sound asleep. This time, however, she was standing at the washstand, wearing a thin, white night rail that touched the floor. Her arms were bare and her hair was a luscious mass of shining mahogany waves that reached her waist. She had not heard him come in, so he had the pleasure of listening to her sweet voice humming a quiet tune, until she suddenly turned and caught sight of him.

''Jack!'' was her whispered cry.

She was buttoned up to the neck, but the gown did not conceal her curves from him. The cloth was thin, and the water she'd splashed down the front made it nearly transparent. The sight of her clad so simply was more erotic than any of the pieces in Alastair's collection, and even more revealing than what he'd seen through the kitchen window the night he'd broken into her father's house.

He knew he should beg her pardon and see himself out of the room. But he did not. His feet would not move.

But his eyes did. They looked their fill, appreciating every feminine inch of her, down to her toes, then back up her trim legs to the dark vee where they met. His glance grazed the peaks of her breasts before moving up to her neck and chin and to that full mouth that he ached to taste.

Her lips parted, and he was suddenly standing a hair's breadth away from her. He touched his mouth to hers, then slipped a hand around her waist to pull her close. When he felt her breath catch, he deepened the kiss, closing his eyes to all but the woman in his arms.

He had wanted this since the last time they'd kissed. He'd thought of it all afternoon while they'd first explored Rievaulx and again at supper when he'd gotten lost in her eyes.

Her taste was intoxicating, and the sensation of her body against his was even more arousing now than it had been when they'd shared a bed. He changed the angle of the kiss and felt her arms slide up his chest and over his shoulders. When her fingers dipped into the hair at his nape, an insatiable hunger ran through him.

His tongue invaded her mouth, sampling heaven as he used his hand to press her body against his. Her innocent response was as strong an aphrodisiac as the cantharides powder used by the ancient Greeks. He shuddered with arousal and slipped his hands lower, cupping her buttocks.

Soon, that was not enough. He had to feel bare skin beneath his hands.

Without breaking the kiss, Jack drew her night rail up until the length of it was bunched in his hand at her waist. Then he caressed the silky skin of her bottom, feeling every soft curve. He caught sight of her—

and of his hands stroking her—in the cheval mirror standing in the corner behind her.

Jack nearly came apart.

Her bottom was heart-shaped and smooth; her legs delicately shaped, tapering to trim knees and ankles. Jack could continue lifting the gown until he had her completely undressed, but he lingered there, caressing, his fingers seeking, arousing.

Dorrie moaned and rocked her hips against him. He groaned when he realized the situation had spun away from him. Breaking the kiss, he rested his forehead against hers and fought for control. He had two choices: either turn around and leave now or lay her on the bed and do exactly what their bodies were demanding of them.

He must be out of his mind.

"Dorrie," he rasped, letting the fabric of her gown slide back to the floor. "I...we...still have differences," he finally said. "Your father...the Mandylion..."

He watched her long lashes close over her eyes. She took a deep breath while he cursed himself for letting lust sneak up on him and rule his actions this morning. He'd been a far better man last night.

Dorothea could not have been more mortified. She had behaved no better than a common trollop, though Jack Temple had clearly shown he wanted no part of her.

She turned away abruptly so that he would not see the tears of embarrassment she was frantically blinking away.

"Dorrie."

"I'll be ready to leave in a quarter hour," she said,

keeping her voice as steady as possible. "I'll meet you downstairs."

He did not move, but neither did Dorothea, who was willing to wait him out. Once she was dressed, she would feel more composed. She would not have to dwell upon what had nearly happened here or Jack's rebuff.

In the meantime, she stood perfectly still while she waited to hear the sounds that accompanied his departure from the room. When he was gone, she crumpled to the bed and wept.

She had never felt so stupid, so worthless, in her life.

After a few minutes of tearful indulgence, Dorothea composed herself and got dressed, taking care to leave no part of her body—besides her hands and face—exposed. It had been quite enough to be naked to Jack Temple's perusal once this morning and to have been found wanting. It would not happen again.

There was no reason to become sidetracked from the task at hand. She was going to find a way to discover the Mandylion without Jack Temple. He was relying upon her to make the translations, and she could make up anything she pleased. She had never had occasion to lie before, but she was certain she could manage to do so with such an important prize. Then she would turn the Mandylion over to her father, and he would receive credit for the discovery.

Once she was laced tightly and buttoned up, she pinned on her hat and slipped on her gloves. Feeling as well girded as she could be, she descended the stairs and stepped into the room where they'd had supper the previous night.

"Good morning, Mrs. Adams," said a cheerful Mrs.

Atwater. "Your breakfast is ready. Your husband is hitching the horses to your carriage, and then, I expect you'll be on your way."

"Yes, I expect so," Dorothea said quietly, attempting to be as polite and friendly as the innkeeper's wife.

"Shall I have one of the boys gather your bags? Take them down to your carriage?"

"Yes, please," Dorothea replied.

She sat down to her breakfast and ate sparingly, dreading the moment when Jack would appear to collect her. She did not know how she would face the man after their disastrous encounter. How did a woman behave with a man who'd seen her naked...a man who then decided he didn't want her?

Dorothea swallowed thickly and pushed away from the table. The best thing was to get it over and done. Soon.

"Thank you, Mrs. Atwater," Dorothea said. "I don't have much appetite this morning."

The woman gave Dorothea a wink, then looked pointedly at her abdomen. "You must not be too far along," she said. "You're not showing at all."

Dorothea nearly choked at the implication that she was carrying Jack's child.

"Don't worry, deary," Mrs. Atwater added, "it doesn't last long—the sickness, I mean. And soon you'll have a young one to look after."

Unconsciously, Dorothea placed a hand on her midsection. The thought of Jack's child inside her... She did not know what to say.

She jumped when Jack stepped up behind her and placed his hands on her shoulders.

"You take care of the missus, now," Mrs. Atwater

said as Jack turned Dorothea and they started out of the room. "Don't be dragging her all over the countryside in her condition."

The only condition that had ever been ascribed to Dorothea had been her heart condition. An illness, not a joy. In a daze, she allowed Jack to lead her to the carriage. She mounted, seated herself and thought of possibilities she had never considered before.

Jack drove the carriage away from the inn, and when Dorothea glanced up to look at him, she found him gazing at her with an odd expression. She blushed. He was probably remembering…

"You all right?" he asked.

She gave a brusque nod. "Yes."

A child. The thought of bearing Jack's child was not as abhorrent as it might have been only yesterday. For the first time in her life, Dorothea imagined herself as a mother. First, she would have to become a wife, of course. She had every reason to believe that Albert Bloomsby would eventually come to London for her and ask for her hand. He was a most suitable candidate for marriage, even though he was a bit dull. And after they were wed, she and Albert would…engage in the sort of activity that led to procreation.

The trouble was that she could not imagine any kind of intimacy with Albert. His hands were pale and soft and would not feel anything like—

Jack's.

Dorothea took a deep breath. She mustn't let thoughts of Jack intrude. He was certainly not the kind of husband she would aspire to. On the contrary, he was the worst sort of man—obviously a womanizer and an adventurer, with no sense of hearth and home.

Still, his children would be beautiful.

"Take a look at this," Jack said, handing her what looked like a modern map. He kept his eyes on the path ahead and did not touch her.

Dorothea opened it, glad that he'd decided to disregard what had taken place in her chamber only an hour before. Now, if only she could do the same. "What are we looking for?"

"One of the Templar faces is directly south of York," he said, placing a finger on the spot, "along with a cross. I'm wondering what's there now."

Dorothea was unable to refrain from taking note of his hand. It was large and hard and seemed ever so capable. Fully aware of the unbridled sensations that hand could cause, she cleared her throat and gave her full attention to the map. "There's a town about fifteen miles south, but the face is between there and York."

"Anything else?"

Dorothea shook her head. "Not that I can see. Where's the Mandylion map?"

Jack leaned forward and reached into his back pocket. He pulled out the map and handed it to Dorothea, who opened it up and began comparing it to the modern map. "I don't see anything here that corresponds to the places marked by the Templar faces."

"That's why we have to go to each one and see what we can find."

"But how are we going to locate the exact spots?" she asked. "The geography is so skewed—"

"That's why I needed the key," Jack said. "Some part of it will begin to make sense eventually."

Dorothea had her doubts about that. "The poem indicates where the *map* is, not the Mandylion,'' she said.

''Right,'' Jack replied. ''So we know we're on the right track.''

''I don't see how,'' Dorothea said.

''We know that the map was given to the abbot of Rievaulx.''

''We knew that *before* we went to Rievaulx, Jack,'' Dorothea said, turning in her seat to face him.

''But I had to wander around the site,'' he said.

''Whatever for?''

''To see what kind of excavations had been done there.''

''How did that make a difference?'' she asked.

''I had to judge whether enough excavation had been done to unearth the map if it had been hidden there.''

''And what did you decide?''

''That anything of value must have been removed over the last three hundred years.''

Dorothea mulled that over. ''I fail to see how you're going to know when you find the place where the cloth is hidden,'' she said. ''I doubt very much that the spot will be marked with an *X*.''

Jack grinned and looked at her. ''That's what makes it interesting,'' he said. ''We search for clues, talk to people, look around the sites. Pretty soon we have an idea of what kind of place we're looking for.''

Dorothea shook her head. She did not see how he would ever find what he was looking for, not with this awful medieval map and a handful of clues. Still, she could not deny that she was enjoying her part in the search. Her adventure with Jack was so different from anything she'd ever done before. It was exciting, exhilarating and everything her mother would have objected to.

Even so, Dorothea could not regret all these new experiences. She had mixed feelings about the way Jack made her feel, but she could not say that she regretted any of it.

She smoothed the Mandylion map over her lap and looked at it again. *"Rumble, roar and crash away."*

"What?"

"The French words," she said, pointing to the old text written in a semicircle over the actual map.

Jack frowned. "I'd forgotten about that."

"It looks like a child's poem."

"Yeah," Jack agreed. "That's what I thought. Probably not significant."

Dorothea looked back at the text and translated the entire poem aloud.

"Rumble, roar, and crash away,
Our savage sea on a windy day.
Though wee and tiny you may be,
God's Angels will guard over thee.

"Rumble, roar, and crash away,
Wind and waves and autumn's haze.
Mama will always stay with thee,
'Til flowers come with summer bees.

"Rumble, roar, and crash away,
Stars and clouds and sunny rays,
Mama hugs and kisses thee,
For wee and tiny you may be."

"Right," Jack said. "A children's rhyme."

"But why was it transcribed onto the map?" Dorothea asked. "Surely it has to have some significance."

"Not necessarily," Jack replied. "It might have been a popular ditty in the twelfth or thirteenth centuries or whenever this was written."

Dorothea shook her head. Surely there was something they were missing. Was there a clue to the Mandylion's location hidden within this poem? Were there clues in the multilingual key?

"Where are we going now?"

"South," he said. "To the next cross. Right where you see the Templar face."

Dorothea looked at the place Jack indicated. It seemed to be just a few miles beyond York, but this map was so inaccurate, it was hard to tell exactly where they'd end up. "Will we stay at the Ainwick Arms before going on?" she asked.

"I'd rather not," he replied. "I remember a country inn south of the city."

"You've been to York before?"

"It's been several years, but yes. I was here with my mentor, Charlie MacElroy."

His *mentor?* Adventurers had mentors? Dorothea wondered if Mr. MacElroy had taught Jack to plunder graves and dig for treasure. She supposed someone had to have taught him Latin and ancient Greek.

If it had been Mr. MacElroy, then he had been very successful. Jack's command of those languages was perfect. And he had a fair command of medieval French.

To look at him, no one would ever think he'd entertained a single scholarly thought. He was a big and brash American, unlike any of the academics she knew at Oxford. He was certainly quite different from Albert Bloomsby.

"It's a long way to York," she said. "Couldn't we just stay at the Ainwick? It was quite pleasant there."

"Not on your life, honey," he said, twitching one eyebrow. "We're staying away from big cities where you might just find a telegraph office."

Anger surged through her veins at his statement of distrust. She had done nothing… Well, it was true that she'd had no opportunity to try contacting her father since leaving York. And she could not deny that the idea of sending a wire to him in London had crossed her mind.

She also had to admit that she had every intention of finding the Mandylion and giving it to her father. But Jack didn't know that. She had never given him any reason to suspect that.

She knew her father was not the villain Jack described. Surely Alastair would take the Mandylion to a university setting where it could be studied by scholars who would understand all the implications of such a discovery.

"Anywhere you choose will be fine, I'm sure," she said, though she didn't add that she intended to insist upon having her own room. She was not going to allow Jack any further intimacy. There was no point to it…no future at all.

They continued on in silence until early afternoon. Jack was surprised that Dorothea could pass the time quietly. He'd never known such a self-possessed woman.

"Are you hungry?" he asked.

"I wouldn't mind a bit of lunch," she replied, as

starchy as she'd ever been. Jack smiled to himself, enjoying every prim-and-proper inch of her, though her indignant responses to his teasing were even better.

He drove the carriage off the lane and into a small copse to the left. "I had Mrs. Atwater pack something for us," he said, amused by the expression of surprise in Dorrie's eyes. Jumping down, he circled the carriage and helped her out. They walked to the back and Jack reached in and retrieved the basket of food and a rug, then hobbled the horse.

He took Dorrie's hand and led her away from the carriage, walking on a narrow footpath through the trees. Her hand felt small and soft, and Jack was immediately struck by the memory of how smooth her bottom had felt against his hand, how soft. It was dangerous thinking, and he stopped it the minute he realized what he was doing.

He had only been looking for a place among the trees that would shade Dorrie's fair skin from the sun, but they soon came to a small, picturesque pond. Jack set the basket on the ground near it and turned to face her. "Nice spot."

He spread out the rug and knelt to open the basket, which contained bread and cold meat, cheese, a couple of bottles of water and some fruit. "Have a seat," he said to Dorrie.

Taking his hand, she lowered herself gracefully to the ground and pulled the items from the basket, laying the food out between them. They ate quietly while Dorrie watched the ducks on the pond and the ants on the rug. And avoided his eyes.

Jack didn't mind. He enjoyed looking at her, remembering her taste and the way she'd responded to his touch. She had disguised the passionate woman under her veil of propriety, but Jack knew what was underneath it.

When she was finished eating, she went over to the pond and scooped up some water to rinse her hands. It was clear that she was anxious to ignore what had happened between them that morning.

The trouble was that Jack couldn't stop thinking about her. He'd never experienced anything as arousing as her responses to him, and he wanted to test them again. He wanted to press his lips to her mouth, her neck, her breasts. He wanted to slip his hands across her buttocks and his fingers into her cleft.

"You're staring," Dorrie said. Her voice was soft, breathless.

Jack blinked to clear his vision. She was so beautiful, standing in the bright sunshine, with her hair and skin dappled by the light as it filtered through the trees. He took a step toward her, even as she took a step back.

But Jack wasn't going to let her retreat far. Watching as her chest rose and fell rapidly, he knew she felt the same pull of attraction that he did. Once he touched his mouth to hers, all her resistance would dissolve. When he pulled her against his all-too aroused body, she would melt in his arms.

"Dorrie."

"I—I think we should b-be on our way," she said, rubbing her hands together to dry them. "It's still a long way t-to York."

She was nervous, but there was no fear in her eyes. And she was right. They still had a long way to go until they reached the little inn he remembered from years past. Jack shoved his hands in his pockets and walked back to the rug. Tamping down the heated urges she roused in him, he knelt and began packing up what was left of their meal.

"You go on ahead and I'll meet you at the carriage," she said. "I, er…just…"

He took the hint. She wasn't the only one who needed a moment's privacy. He gave a quick nod and followed the path out of the woods to the place where they'd left the carriage. Placing the basket where it had been stored before, he walked around to the front of the carriage and waited for Dorrie to return.

An unexpected sound to Jack's right caught his attention. It was a man, coming out of the woods.

The fellow was big and burly.

He said nothing as he approached Jack, but Jack had the feeling the man was up to no good. His face was a road map of scars and his nose had been broken more than once. One ear was mashed out of proportion, but for all his faults, he moved with grace and ease.

A prizefighter.

His appearance was unkempt. Jack was no stickler for clean clothes, but the fighter's shirt and trousers had seen much better days. He approached Jack from the side, bringing his fists up in a fighting position when he got close enough to throw a punch.

Jack ducked, then threw his own punch.

"What's wrong with you!" he demanded.

The fighter did not reply, but swung his fist again. Jack dodged the blow and landed one of his own in the man's midsection. It felt like iron.

Jack asked no more questions but went about defending himself as best he could. Blows were delivered by both men, but for all the fighter's ferocity, Jack was younger and stronger.

And he had a lot at stake. If this bastard knocked him unconscious, what would happen to Dorrie?

Jack fought vigorously and was wearing his opponent down when he heard a shrill scream.

Dorrie!

He coldcocked his assailant and took off at a dead run toward the pond.

Chapter Eleven

When Dorothea heard someone coming out of the woods, she'd assumed it was Jack. Instead, it was two men—very disreputable-looking men. They closed in on her fast, before she had a chance to scream for help.

One of them covered her mouth with his hand, while the other grabbed at her body, looking for money, she supposed. She kicked and struggled with all her strength, but when they knocked her to the ground, she lost her wind and was unable to do anything against them.

When she felt the cold blade of a knife pressing against her flesh and slipping through her clothes, she renewed her efforts against them. Somehow, she managed to get out a scream.

The man with the knife laughed. ''Won't be no help for you now,'' he said. ''We got Byron to take care of your man.''

Dorothea's panic increased. What had they done to Jack? She tried to shove away from the men, but their hands seemed to be everywhere, and they were too heavy, too strong. She should have felt mortified to have her corset sliced open, leaving her bare, but she was too busy fighting, trying to catch her breath. And she was terrified—for herself, for Jack.

Refusing to make herself an easy victim, she kicked and clawed while they held her down. In the midst of her flailing, her hand closed around a large rock. Just as the weight of the man on top shifted, she brought the rock down hard against his skull. He yelped and fell away, holding his head.

Fighting now against only one assailant, Dorothea tried to scrabble away. But he held her in place, pinning her to the ground with one hand while he grabbed at her with the other. Dorothea tried kicking again, but could only manage to bring her knee up.

Whatever she did seemed to be effective. The man grunted and swore loudly as he started to fall back, but then he was pulled off her.

"Jack!" she cried.

The second man stood and faced Jack, though he had a large gash on his forehead from the blow Dorothea had delivered with the rock. A fight ensued while the first man lay on his side with his knees drawn up.

Dorothea picked the knife up from the ground, then got to her feet, holding her ruined blouse closed over her breasts. Her skirt was torn and filthy, but she was oblivious to it. Her heart pounded erratically, and she had trouble catching her breath, but she hardly noticed.

She winced every time Jack was hit, but she could see that he was more powerful than either of the two men. She had every confidence in him. Still, she screamed when the second attacker roused himself and stood, joining in the fight.

The air seemed to shimmer around Jack and the two men, and Dorothea stumbled, unable to take her eyes off them. She had to do something to help.

"Dorrie!" Jack called. "Move back!"

She spotted the rock she'd used before and reached down to pick it up. If only she could get close enough without ending up with a fist in her face, she might be able to knock one of those men off Jack.

Circling around them, she aimed at a likely target, but their movements were jerky and unpredictable. She could not hit the man without the risk of hurting Jack. Suddenly, one of the assailants jumped on Jack's back and attempted to hold his arms while the other one punched at will. Just as Dorothea went to crack the man's skull, Jack pivoted, then bent at the waist, throwing the man forward. He landed on the attacker in front, and they both fell.

"Jack!" she cried again.

"Are you all right?" he asked, turning to look at her. "God almighty, Dorrie," he said when he saw the condition of her clothes. "We've got to get out of here before these miserable devils decide to have another go at us," he said. "Come on."

He took her hand and led her quickly through the woods toward the carriage. They made it only about halfway there when one of the assailants grabbed Jack from behind. Dorothea screamed as the man swung once. Jack moved in time and landed his own punch, knocking the man unconscious.

"Let's go," he said, grabbing Dorothea's hand and moving her quickly along the path.

He led her to the far side of the carriage—opposite to where the prizefighter lay in the grass—and helped her up. Removing the hobble from the horse, he jumped into the carriage and drove off.

Jack wanted to put a few miles between them and the three who'd attacked them. At first, he'd suspected that Alastair had sent them to steal the map, but now he wasn't so sure. Alastair might be a crook, but he didn't think the man would sacrifice his daughter to those filthy clods.

The three men must have seen them lunching by the pond and decided to rob them and take advantage of Dorrie.

Jack did not think he'd ever felt so enraged as when he'd seen her in the grass, under attack. She had fought valiantly, but was no match for the two men who had her pinned to the ground and were tearing her clothes.

He'd never seen anyone so vulnerable before, and his instinct to protect her was entirely unfamiliar. He told himself it was only because he'd never been in such a dangerous situation with a woman before. He'd have reacted the same if it had been his mother or one of his sisters on the ground near the pond.

She'd been magnificent, though. Who would have thought she'd have the gumption to brain the first fellow, then kick the other one in his most vulnerable parts? And even then, she hadn't been finished. For all of her diminutive height, she had wielded that rock like a veritable Amazon.

To defend *him.*

He felt humbled and touched, all at once.

He looked over at her and saw that she was flushed. And her shoulders were shaking. No wonder, either. That had been as close a call as he'd had since Tanganyika. She had every right to break down and…

She glanced over at him and burst into laughter.

Jack was astonished. Her mirth was not the polite,

well-modulated merriment he would have expected from a lady as demure as Dorrie, but an all-out gale.

He felt himself smiling as their carriage rapidly covered ground. Dorrie had lost her hat, so her hair was loose and blowing in the wind. She held her bodice together with one hand and hung on to the carriage seat with the other while she laughed until tears streamed down her face.

When they were far enough away from their fateful encounter, he slowed the carriage, pulled off the road and stopped.

"Oh, Jack!" she cried, but could say no more because of her continued laughter. Somehow managing to keep the edges of her blouse together, she held her sides and laughed until her hilarity diminished to a few hiccups.

She wiped her eyes with the back of her hand and looked up at him with moist, green eyes. Her lashes were dark spikes that glistened in the sun. "That was the silliest... Oh, Jack, I don't know when I've ever been so ridiculous."

She was delightful, and Jack was speechless.

"Those men...they were just suddenly *there*," she said. "They grabbed me and—"

"They must have seen us by the pond and waited for us to split up."

She nodded. "I don't think I've ever been so frightened."

"You sure didn't show it," he said, using one hand to snag a lock of her hair. It was so silky, he wanted to bury his face in it.

"I don't know what got into me," she said. "I just... It all seemed so absurd."

"What are you going to do with the knife?" he

asked, gesturing toward the weapon she'd brought along.

She reached down to the floor and picked it up. "Keep it," she replied. "Maybe in my boot like your little gun."

Jack shook his head and laughed, then jumped down from the carriage and assisted Dorrie to do the same. "You'll need some other clothes," he said, reaching in for her bag. "I'll wait over there while you change."

He needed some space.

Leaning against a tree twenty feet from where Dorrie was removing her clothes, he allowed himself a moment to savor her reaction to their little misadventure. He realized he'd never seen her laugh, and she'd looked entirely unfamiliar with the experience.

He guessed she hadn't had much cause for gaiety in her life, judging by her usual starchiness, though he'd had more than a few clues that she possessed a fire beneath her cool and controlled surface.

He knew she liked to sing. He'd heard her humming several times, always quietly, always when she thought no one was near. And though her clothes could not have been more proper, Jack had seen what she wore underneath. Tantalizingly delicate cotton and silk caressed her skin all day and all through the night.

And when he kissed her, Jack did not think there was a volcano in the world as potent as her response to him.

He reached down and picked a flower—a weed, he guessed, though it was pretty. He got another and another, and soon he had a whole handful of them. Catching a glimpse of Dorrie, he saw that she was mostly finished dressing. She had only one more button or two to go when Jack started walking toward her.

Without thinking, he handed the flowers to her.

"Bluebells," she said. She took them and held them to her breast, tipping her nose to them. "They're... they're wonderful, Jack."

Jack wondered why, if they were so wonderful, she had tears in her eyes. Backing away from her before he did something even more foolish than gathering flowers, he said, "We'd better get going."

She bit her lip. "Not until I clean that cut on your cheek," she countered.

Dorothea could see that Jack wanted to argue, but she was having none of it. He had a gash on his cheekbone, just under his eye, and she had a ruined cotton chemise that she could use to wash it.

She poured water from one of the bottles they'd brought from the Boar's Head Inn and soaked the cloth. "Lean toward me," she instructed.

He eyed her warily, then rested one hand against the side of the carriage, backing her into it.

"I don't think it will hurt," she said, ignoring the close quarters.

"That's not much of a guarantee," he protested.

"Well, I wouldn't know," she said flippantly, "since I've never been scraped like this."

Jack grumbled and winced when she touched the cloth to the spot and began to rub.

"Ow."

"You're going to have a bruise here."

"Yeah, well, you should have seen the other guy."

Dorothea shook her head and continued cleaning his injury. She'd been this close to him before. Closer, even. She could feel his eyes on her, feel his breath on her cheek, see the muscle clench in his jaw.

Her knees suddenly felt weak and she had an odd feeling in the pit of her stomach. Jack had probably saved her life this afternoon. He'd taken on two—no *three*—men single-handedly in order to keep her safe.

She stopped swabbing the cut and met his eyes. A fly buzzed past, and a wren cheeped nearby. Bees worked over the field, and a light breeze hushed through the trees. Dorothea swallowed loudly. "Thank you," she said, "for being there today."

"Come here," he said, his voice husky and low. Dorothea went into his arms.

He whispered something she could not hear and touched his lips lightly to her forehead. Dorrie felt comforted by his embrace. She slipped her arms around him and stood still while he rubbed one hand across her back.

"Dorrie," he said. "You're all right now."

"I know," she replied quietly. "I guess it just now struck me how serious—"

"Don't think about it now. You're safe. I won't let anything happen to you."

She knew it was true. In all their travels, he'd seen to it that she was safe and comfortable, even if he did interfere with her privacy.

Somehow, though, he was always there when she needed him.

He handed her up into the carriage and Dorothea was glad there was no vase to put her bluebells in, because she wanted to hold them to her breast and savor this moment as long as possible.

She had never received flowers before.

They rode in silence again, though it seemed uncomfortable this time. Dorothea didn't know what had gotten into her, laughing like a madwoman when she'd just been accosted and might even have lost her life. Jack must think she was out of her mind.

Perhaps that was why he'd given her the flowers. It was nothing more than a gift meant to soothe her ragged nerves.

That thought deflated her, though why she should care was beyond her comprehension. They were still rivals, and she had every intention of finding the Mandylion without him and turning it over to her father.

Besides, once the Mandylion was discovered and she dealt with it, Jack Temple would be on his way to his next adventure. He probably had no roots other than a few loose ones in America, where his parents and siblings lived.

Dorothea wondered how it would be to live like Jack, like her father, traveling from place to place, on expeditions like this one…or even more exotic. How she would love to travel to Greece, to Rome, to Arabia! She felt her pulse rise at the thought of such adventures, though she knew she would never be able to go.

She had been warned about the weak condition of her heart too many times to indulge in such silly fancies as these. Travel would be too difficult. Extremes of temperature would be damaging. Foreign foods would upset her system and too much exercise would further weaken her damaged heart.

Some part of her objected to these arguments. She'd been traveling with Jack for several days and had suffered only the slightest discomforts related to her bad heart. Surely she could convince her father to take her on his next expedition. If she was careful, she would be all right.

Besides, she did not think she could stand to return to her solitary, sedentary life.

"There's York up ahead," Jack said. "We'll just circumvent the city and keep going south."

"Why not go through the city?" Dorothea asked. "Wouldn't that be the more direct route?"

Jack hesitated for a second before replying. "I'd rather not go through the city."

"Actually, I need to stop and replace my— Replace the items that were ruined this afternoon," Dorothea said. She had not brought many clothes with her, and when her assailant slashed through her chemise, corset and blouse, her wardrobe had been seriously diminished. Surely Jack would not begrudge her the opportunity to replenish what she'd lost.

"Dorrie, can't you—"

"We're right here, Jack," she countered. "It will only take a few minutes and then we can be on our way."

Dorothea could tell that Jack was not happy with the decision, but he agreed to take her to a shop in York.

"I'll need money," she said.

When he turned and cocked his head to look impatiently at her, she said, "Well, you *did* drag me from London against my will."

"You came along willingly enough," he said. "In fact, it was *your* idea to come along. Why didn't you bring any money?"

"Don't be petty, Jack," she said, glad of the argument. Not once had Jack been stingy with her, but this discussion helped Dorothea to put her relationship with Jack back into some reasonable perspective. "Besides, I'll see that you are reimbursed."

In a short while, they were driving through the city gates. Jack stopped once to ask for directions to the merchant's district and soon had her out of the carriage and into a ladies' apparel shop.

"Make it fast, will you, Dorrie?" he said as the shop girl approached. "I'd like to be on our way."

Dorothea did not understand his hurry. There was still a good bit of time before dusk. They would be out of the city and into their country inn well before dark.

"May I assist you, madam?" the clerk asked.

Embarrassed for Jack to overhear their discussion of her unmentionables, Dorothea stepped away and told the clerk what was needed.

"We have a good selection of ready-made lingerie, if you'll step this way."

Dorothea glanced back at Jack, who sat scowling in a pink brocade boudoir chair at the center of the shop. Smiling at his discomfiture, she followed the woman to the front of the store and looked over the fine linens and cottons displayed there.

In the midst of choosing her merchandise, she felt an odd prickle at the back of her neck. Placing her hand on the spot, she turned around.

In the window was a huge man with cocoa-brown skin and a completely bald head. His odd light-colored eyes lit upon Jack and stayed there. Dorothea didn't think Jack would have been oblivious to the man's scrutiny, but the difficult day had finally caught up to him.

He had fallen asleep on the chair.

Chapter Twelve

Jack let himself be convinced that a night at the Ainwick Arms wouldn't hurt. It was late afternoon, and he was tired. In reality, he was exhausted, having slept only fitfully the night before, then doing battle with those three villains near the pond. He'd gotten more battered and bruised than he wanted to admit, but he'd driven on, ignoring the ache that had settled in his ribs and the crick in his shoulder.

It was so unlikely that Alastair Bright would find them here in the city, Jack figured it had to be safe to stay here one night before moving south to the next site on the map.

He wasn't so worried about Dorrie sending a wire to her father anymore, but if they returned to the Ainwick, they would have to share a room again, if only because the hotel knew them as husband and wife. What *did* worry him was that he was starting to become accustomed to thinking of them as a pair. A partnership. A couple.

Jack had known her less than a week, but he could not imagine the day when they would part ways. And that was a thought that had him jabbing his fingers through his hair. He didn't need to be entertaining ideas about Alastair Bright's daughter.

What he *did* need was a good night's sleep.

"Mr. Adams!" cried the hotel clerk when they entered the lobby of the hotel. "What happened?"

"We met with a mishap on the road," Jack replied. "Have you got a room?"

"Why, yes sir," the clerk replied. They quickly took care of business and registered. For once, Dorrie did not complain about the arrangements. When they reached the staircase that led to the guest rooms, she stopped abruptly, then returned to the desk.

"We'll have a meal sent to our room, if that's possible," she told the clerk, then proceeded to order the dishes she wanted.

"Yes, madam," the clerk said, writing on a pad.

"And I'd like you to send up some clean cloths so that I can tend Mr. Te— Mr. Adams's injuries."

"Right away, madam," he replied.

A few moments later, they were in the same room they'd shared before. The bags were placed on the floor near the bed and a pitcher and a bowl of clean water were brought in.

Jack couldn't believe his eyes. Gone was the prim little kitten he'd brought from London. In her place was a tigress.

"Take off your coat, Jack," she said, once they were alone, "and sit here on the bed."

Amused, he did as he was told. He didn't have the energy to argue with her anyway.

"You're hurt," she said, unbuttoning his shirt. "I saw you wince every time you moved."

"It's not bad, Dorrie," he said, enjoying the sensation of her fingers trailing down his chest to his belly.

"I should not be doing this," she muttered. "I should have asked to have a physician sent—"

"No," Jack countered. "No doctor."

"Of course," Dorrie said, removing his hand from where he'd grabbed her wrist. She finished unbuttoning his shirt and pulled it out of his pants. "I knew that would be your reaction, so I didn't even suggest it."

Jack dropped his suspenders and pulled the shirt off.

"Oh heavens!" she cried.

"I don't think you're supposed to let the victim know how dire his condition is," he said dryly.

"I'm sorry, Jack," she said contritely. "It's just that it's so purple. And scraped."

"I don't think any of the ribs are broken," he said, looking down at his side. "Just bruised."

"I *am* going to call for a physician."

"Don't bother," he said. "He'll only bind my ribs and give me some laudanum…which I won't take, by the way."

"Why not?" she asked. She took a clean cloth and dipped it in the water, then touched it tentatively to his side.

"It makes me sick," he replied. "I took it once when I broke my arm."

She washed away the blood that had smeared across his abdomen. "How did you break your arm?"

"Hmm?" Jack did not want to talk. He closed his eyes and savored her touch. When she was finished cleaning the dried blood from his belly, she made him turn so that she could look at his back.

"Sore?"

"My right shoulder," he replied as she began to rub it. "I landed on it in the first round."

"First round?"

"Boxing."

"I don't understand."

"Prizefighting," he said. He stretched out on the bed and Dorrie kept rubbing his back. "Men fighting...for a purse."

"I've never heard of anything so ridiculous," she said. "Are you teasing, Jack? Because if you are..."

Jack couldn't remember the last time he'd felt so good.

But as he drifted off, he knew perfectly well that he'd felt even better, just that morning, when he'd kissed and caressed Dorrie Bright.

Jack was asleep when the tray arrived.

Dorothea considered waking him, but he was so peaceful, she decided against it. She was certain he would take a short nap and awaken refreshed and hungry. The tray could wait.

She picked up his coat and searched for one of the precious documents he always kept there. It was the key. Laying it flat on the table near the window, she went over to the bed and looked down at Jack. He was sleeping soundly. She should be able to slip the folded map out of his back pocket without waking him.

Carefully, she used both hands to unbutton the pocket, then slid one hand in. With two fingers, she drew out the map. Opening it up, she lay it next to the key and sat down to study them both.

What did they mean?

Obviously, the writer wanted to confound any but the most educated reader. Why else would the key have been written in three obscure languages?

Herein lies the precious cloth.

Did he mean that the cloth lies there at the abbey? The document was addressed to the abbot, so why not?

Herein lies the precious cloth.

Jack's interpretation made sense, too. This document might only be a letter or key for the abbot, indicating some clue that only the cleric would understand when he saw the map. Dorothea wondered if the mapmaker and the abbot had been friends. If she and Jack could figure out who the abbot was, they could determine who his friends were and then they might be able to make some sense of the clues.

She held the key up to the light and scrutinized it carefully, looking for a date inscribed somewhere. That would help them to determine who the abbot was at the time the map was created. But there was nothing hidden within the ornate borders of the page.

The map itself was plain. There were no flowery borders, no cherubs drawn anywhere. Nor was there a date. Only the child's rhyme and a circle of mangled geography.

Even Dorothea, who hadn't been anywhere in her life, knew that this map was horribly inaccurate.

Jack wanted to travel south of the city tomorrow. She traced one finger along the route from the city walls to the cross that was drawn just southeast of the city. One of the faces—a Templar head or not—was drawn nearby. It seemed a likely enough place to explore, though Dorothea could not understand how Jack thought he would find anything of value. The map was imprecise, and he couldn't just start digging somewhere with the mere hope that he would discover the cloth.

A small crenellated wall was drawn near the coast, directly east of York. At least, it was drawn that way. And another one of the Templar heads was nearby. Dorothea wondered at the significance of these faces. Did they truly signify something sacred to the Templar Knights, or did the faces represent something else? Jack could be entirely wrong in his assumptions.

Still, if this map was somehow related to the Mandylion, and the Mandylion had been in Templar possession, then Jack's reasoning made sense. The mapmaker could very well have had some connection with the Templars.

Dorothea ate from the tray and pored over the words on the map and key. She looked at them from every angle, checking the translations repeatedly, in case there was some nuance, some word that they had misinterpreted.

There wasn't.

She read the nursery rhyme again, looking for clues in the words. Was there a location indicated here? Certainly, there was no mention of a specific place, but two of the lines made her think of the sea. Perhaps the writer lived by the sea. Or was fond of the sea. Or had buried the map by the sea.

Frowning, she studied the map. The third Templar head was closer to the sea than the others. And it was drawn near the crenellated wall. They had assumed the wall represented a castle, but if the castle...

Wait, Dorothea thought. *A castle was usually a family seat. It would have been a nanny or a mother who recited this rhyme, perhaps at the castle drawn on the Mandylion map.*

This was the first glimmer of insight Dorothea had had since she'd started translating. And she didn't think Jack had any idea.

He seemed to believe the cloth would be hidden at a monastery or an abbey. Which made sense, of course. It was a religious relic. Why would he assume that it would stay in the possession of an individual family?

Unless he was investigating the least likely hiding places first. Maybe Jack had already come to Dorothea's conclusions. He'd been at this sort of thing a lot longer than she had and probably had a much better system of sifting through clues.

Dorothea stood and stepped away from the table. She knew she was right. The nursery rhyme was the only clue here.

Jack shifted in his sleep. Dorothea guessed he hadn't gotten much sleep these past few days, but he had only himself to blame. If circumstances had been different, and he had not brought her along....

She ran her hands up her arms. If Jack had not brought her to York, she would still be in London, trying to sort out some kind of life for herself in that dusty, dreary, neglected house of her father's. She'd have been sweeping, dusting, scrubbing every corner of the place in order to make it into a home. Trying to turn Creighton into a trustworthy employee.

Was that what she wished for herself?

For the first time in her life, she was free to choose, free to make her own decisions. She doubted they'd all been the correct ones, but she had survived. And become stronger for it.

Dorothea was beginning to realize that she and her mother were of very different temperaments. She did not know if she could ever be content again, sitting at her desk, in a dry and barren atmosphere, translating ancient Prakrit texts into modern English.

It was the adventure of life that made it worthwhile—the possibilities and uncertainties that intrigued her. She wanted to travel to the boundaries of York and beyond. She wanted to see the ancient statues and buried village sites that she'd only read about.

Her heart sank. Once Jack was gone, her adventure would be over.

Perhaps she could convince her father to take her on his next expedition. If she managed to find the Mandylion before Jack, it would be a strong argument in her favor.

Dorothea knew she would have to do something to impress on him her value. She was not going to stay in that dreary old house in London.

Jack could not believe he slept the whole night through. He was ravenous when he awoke, but Dorrie was not in the room and that was worrisome. He groaned with the discomfort in his ribs when he pushed himself out of the bed to take stock of things.

His bag lay on the floor at the foot of the bed. His spare trousers, jacket and shirt had been removed and were hung up so they wouldn't be too crumpled when he put them on. Dorrie had to have done it. One side of Jack's mouth quirked in a smile. It was just like Dorrie to think about his clothes.

Her bag stood next to the door, packed and ready to go. There were no other signs of her presence in the room. Jack even had to wonder if she'd spent the night there with him.

One glance back at the bed told him that she had. There was a depression on the pillow that answered that question. But where was she now?

In a flash, his hands were searching his pockets to see if the map and key were still in place.

They were.

Why hadn't she taken them and left? She wanted to find the Mandylion for her father, and last night would have been the perfect time to take the map and key and return to London. Jack smacked the heel of his hand on his forehead. He could not believe he'd allowed himself to be lulled to sleep by the soothing touch of her hands on his back. Not when so much was at stake.

Within minutes, he was in the lobby, the map in his back pocket and the key in his jacket.

"Did my...wife leave any message for me?" he asked the clerk at the desk.

The man nodded toward the dining room doors. "She said she would meet you at breakfast. Are you feeling better, sir?"

"Er, yes. Thank you." Before joining Dorrie, he checked them out of the hotel and gave instructions for their carriage to be brought around to the front entrance.

Jack went through the door to the dining room and

found Dorrie sitting near one of the windows, drinking tea and reading a newspaper. Her new hat was perched atop her burnished mahogany curls. She wore the blouse she'd purchased the day before under her jacket, hiding all the lush curves he knew she possessed.

He closed his eyes and took a deep breath. He'd been an idiot to give her so much leeway when she was the enemy's daughter. In all his travels, from India to darkest Africa, there had been nothing, there'd been *no one* who'd posed a greater danger to him.

God almighty. He enjoyed being with her.

And if that wasn't unsettling enough, he wanted her, too.

Everything had changed since yesterday, after lunch, when he'd heard her scream. He hadn't gotten into the brawl for the fun of it or to prove anything, as might once have been the case. His only care had been for Dorrie. Making sure she was safe. Taking care of her. Thrashing the ruffians who had put fear in her eyes.

He looked at her now, sitting so prim and proper in her traveling clothes. He didn't need the complications a woman would bring. He liked his life the way it was, with the freedom to do as he chose, whenever he chose to do it. He could drop everything on short notice and go on an expedition whenever he pleased, with the best group of fellows a man could want.

He wasn't going to let Dorothea Bright interfere with it, either. Once the Mandylion was safely in the hands of the curator he knew at the British Museum, Jack would return to New York. A visit with his family was long overdue, and he would have time to research an intriguing Egyptian legend before autumn and the return of all his academic responsibilities at the university.

He had no room in his life for a woman like Dorrie, but as he watched, her cheeks took on a captivating pink tinge. He thought of her smooth skin and the ripe curves she hid under her corset and bustle. She took a sudden deep breath and placed her hand gently in the center of her chest. Her eyes drifted closed.

Jack felt an answering throb in his own chest, a thud that didn't stop with one beat. And it annoyed him to think that his heart might beat in time with hers.

Chapter Thirteen

Dorothea didn't see why Jack had to be so surly this morning. It was another beautiful day, and they had all the time in the world to search for the Mandylion.

She poured tea into the cup at his place.

He scowled and waved the waiter to their table.

"Coffee," he said to the man. "Black."

"I'm sorry, Jack," she said. "I'd have ordered—"

"Are you ready to travel?" he growled.

"Yes, I—"

"As soon as I drink this, we'll go."

She did not reply to his bad-tempered speech, but finished her tea, folded the newspaper and placed it on the table beside her plate. Her palpitations had passed, even if Jack's temper had not. She imagined he must be in pain for him to act this way.

"How is your bruise?" she asked.

"Which one?"

She moistened her lips and refused to take offense at his treatment of her. Most of those bruises were the direct result of his fight to defend her, and she would not complain about his ill humor this morning.

His cheek was swollen and bruised, and the gash at

its crest looked awful. She longed to reach over and caress him, but would not dare. Besides being in a public place where such a gesture would be entirely inappropriate, Jack would surely bite her hand off.

He left money on the table and stood, helping Dorothea to ease her chair back. In a short while, they were once again on the road.

Dorothea looked down at the modern map and frowned. "I think you should veer east," she said.

He did not reply.

That was all right. Dorothea enjoyed the ride in spite of him, taking in the scenery, smiling and greeting the few passersby. She had yet to determine how she was going to get away from him to find the Mandylion alone. If he had any idea that she had figured out the clues, he would never let her out of his sight.

She sighed. She didn't particularly *want* to be out of his sight.

Something must be wrong with her. He was no different from the brash American who had burst through the front door of her father's house in London less than a week before. Well, he was cleaner now, but he was still an irresponsible adventurer.

And in the short time since they'd met, she had experienced more of life than she had in her twenty-five years in Oxford.

"Jack, look!"

She took hold of his arm and pointed into the distance, where a grouping of dark clouds hovered over neatly tilled ground. Bracketing the clouds were two rainbows.

"I'll be damned," he said, slowing the carriage and coming to a stop.

"I've never seen two rainbows at once," Dorothea remarked.

"They're rare, all right." She heard awe in his voice and knew he was impressed, in spite of himself. Then he became cool again. "The rain's headed this way."

It suddenly became windy and Dorothea was reminded of the night when they'd been caught in the rain. They hadn't been far from this spot, and they'd found shelter in a barn. She wondered if Jack would look for it again.

"What will we do?"

He looked at her then and she knew he was also thinking of the first time he'd kissed her. It made her breathless when his glance grazed her lips and returned to her eyes.

He cleared his throat. "It'll be a while coming. Let's keep going."

It was just as well. He was going to despise her when she slipped away and claimed the Mandylion for her father. Jack might even feel as if she'd betrayed him, though they'd never had more than a tenuous partnership. She had made it clear from the start that her loyalty was to her father. He could not possibly think she would help *him* to take such a discovery away from Alastair.

Jack continued to drive south while Dorothea kept an eye on the coming storm.

"There's a church near here. I visited it once with MacElroy, years ago," Jack said. "It might even be the site marked by the cross on the map."

Dorothea agreed that it might very well be one and the same, but she also knew that he would not find the Mandylion there.

They drove another mile, but the wind picked up and it was obvious that the storm was nearly upon them. Jack drove into a farmyard where a few plump chickens pecked at the dusty ground. A pretty young woman came out of the house, wiping her hands on her apron.

She smiled broadly at Jack and glanced at the sky. "Ye come just in time, I'd say. Drive yer carriage into the barn if ye like and wait it out in the house."

"Thank you," Jack said. "We will."

When they returned to the house, the woman was waiting at the door.

"It's going to be a downpour," Jack said.

"American, are ye?"

Jack nodded.

"Come in, then," the woman said. By her expression, she was glad to have company on this dreary day. "I've got tea and a few biscuits to offer."

Dorothea felt Jack's hand at the small of her back as she followed the woman into the cottage. She liked the way it felt, even as she admonished herself not to get too accustomed to it. If she ever saw him again after finding the Mandylion, she was certain it would not be on good terms.

"Is your husband at home?" Jack asked when they stepped into the kitchen.

"My—? Oh, I'm not married," the woman said. "I keep house for my father. He's out in the field, looking for a place to wait out the storm, I'm sure. What's yer name, then?"

"I'm Jack Temple and this is—"

"Pleased to know you, Mr. Temple," she said before Jack had a chance to introduce Dorothea. "I'm Alice Trevain."

To Dorothea's supreme annoyance, Miss Trevain smiled sweetly at Jack and batted her lashes at him.

"This is Miss Bright," Jack said, finishing the introductions.

"Miss Bright," Alice said, speculatively, dismissing her. The farmer's daughter barely gave her another thought while she focused all her attention on Jack.

Jack seemed oblivious to her blatant flirting, but leaned casually against the table with his arms crossed over his chest. He obviously enjoyed looking at the woman, and Dorothea could not blame him. Alice Trevain was quite beautiful. In an old-fashioned, country sort of way.

A loud rumble of thunder sounded in the distance, and a sudden gust of wind blew dust and light debris at the window.

"Miss Trevain, do you know of a church nearby? A old stone place with a—"

"Sure," she said, lifting the kettle from the stove.

"Let me help you with that," Jack said, taking the heavy kettle from her. She beamed at him and pressed her bosom against his arm. Intentionally.

Dorothea gritted her teeth and said nothing. They were warm and dry and would be staying only until the storm was over.

"It's Saint John the Baptist Church, about two miles east of here. But it's not used anymore. They've got a nice church down in Selby and most go there."

"No, I'm thinking of John the Baptist," Jack said, returning her smile warmly while Dorothea stewed. How could Jack's mood change so drastically in such a short time? He was as friendly to Alice now as he'd been hostile to Dorothea only moments ago.

Alice took off her apron and reached into a cupboard for a tin of biscuits, showing her assets to great advantage. She put the biscuits on a plate, then gathered three cups and set them on the table, brushing Jack's arm or shoulder every time she came near.

"I visited there a few years ago," Jack said. To Dorothea's dismay, he didn't seem to mind the close contact. "Are there any interesting stories about the church?"

Dorothea put her nose into her teacup. She sipped the hot brew and tried to ignore Jack's easy banter with this stranger. He could barely be civil to *her,* yet he hung on Alice Trevain's every word, soaked up every flutter of the woman's long eyelashes.

The rain came suddenly and in a downpour. It rattled the rooftop and ran down the windows in sheets. As annoying as Alice Trevain was, Dorothea was glad she'd opened her door to them.

"—abbess and the priest at Saint John's, ye mean?"

Dorothea looked up and paid attention to the woman's words. It was obvious to her that Jack didn't know what she was talking about, and he urged her to continue.

"They're just stories," Alice said with a shrug. "Who knows what happened five hundred years ago. And who cares? I'm much more interested in... Americans."

She laughed, and Jack smiled indulgently at her. Dorothea leaned back in her chair and studied the woodwork. She forced herself not to concern herself with the mutual flirtation going on in the room as if she weren't there. As if Jack were not *her* escort, *her* companion, *her*... As if he were not the man who'd kissed her breath away as recently as yesterday.

Jack told Wild West stories to pass the time. As far

as she knew, Jack was from New York. She did not think that had anything to do with the American West, but admittedly, she knew little of him. Only that he was an explorer like her father. That he dealt in antiquities.

"Tell me about the abbess and the priest," he finally said, at which point Dorothea decided to listen.

"There's nothing much," Alice replied. "Surely nothing as interesting as Jesse and Frank—"

"Where, exactly, is the abbey?"

"Holywake?" she asked. "Why, it's about a quarter mile from the church, I suppose. The ruins, anyway. Everyone knows it burned some time after the wars, during Henry VII's reign."

"There must not be much left of it or else it would show up on the map," Jack said.

"Ye're right," Alice replied. "Nary a wall standing. Only the foundation still in the ground."

"Any other stories, besides the one about the abbess and Saint John's priest?"

"Now, that's a wicked story," she said.

Dorothea put her elbow on the table and her chin in her hand, and absently drummed the fingers of her other hand on the tabletop. Alice's cloying was more than a little irritating, and Dorothea doubted she had anything of value to impart.

"The abbey provided fare for the priest's table," she said. "And, of course, he got to know the abbess...*intimately,*" Alice added suggestively.

"Were there any stories about a hidden, er, artifact? Something from the Holy Land?"

"You mean from the Crusades?"

"Exactly," Jack said. Dorothea thought he sounded awfully self-satisfied.

"Well, there's a tale of a lay brother who passed through," Alice said.

"Go on," Jack urged.

"They say he came to York from Jerusalem," Alice said. "Stayed a fortnight at the abbey and went on to claim his rightful estate somewhere in Yorkshire."

"Who was he?"

"Awk, it's probably not true, but just a children's tale," she said with a shrug, "told on cold nights to amuse and pass the time."

"But that's all there is to it?"

"Dull, don't you agree?" Alice asked. "Nothing as bold and daring as you dashing gunslingers from the West." She lowered her voice and batted her lashes— for the last time, Dorothea decided.

Just as Alice laid her hand on Jack's chest, Dorothea stood up. "The rain seems to have stopped," she blurted. She slipped her arm through the crook of Jack's elbow and pulled him away. "Shouldn't we be on our way, *darling?*"

He was so startled, Dorothea almost laughed. Instead, she pressed her body against Jack's in a gesture of pure female possession. "Thank you so much for tea, Miss Trevain," she said, making her voice sickeningly sweet. "And for giving us such a warm and hospitable shelter from the storm."

She continued to lead Jack to the door, actually pulling him through it once it was open. There were deep, muddy puddles everywhere, but Dorothea managed to step around them as she headed toward the barn.

"There was no need to rush, Dorrie," he said. "I was just finding out—"

"There was nothing more to learn from Miss Trevain," Dorothea said, and then muttered, "except how she tastes."

Luckily, Jack did not hear her last words. They got into the carriage and drove toward the front of the house, where Miss Trevain waited. Her hungry eyes practically devoured Jack as they approached, and Dorothea reacted without thinking. She took Jack's face in her hands. Meeting his startled gaze, she kissed him.

She had meant to give him a quick peck that would demonstrate to Alice Trevain that Jack was not available, in case she had any ideas about following them to Saint John's Church. But the heat of his mouth seduced her. The carriage came to a halt and Jack slipped a hand around her waist, never breaking contact with her mouth. He took control of the kiss and Dorothea's eyes drifted closed, while her bones melted.

He released her suddenly and flicked the reins, starting the carriage once again.

"You have quite an aptitude for theatrics," he said once they were back in the lane. It was slow going now that there were muddy ruts to avoid.

"Don't I?" she said, unwilling to admit just how seriously she'd been affected by that kiss.

Jack gave all his attention to steering around the pitfalls in the lane. He did not know what to think of that kiss, and it was best that he forget it for the time being. Otherwise, he might be compelled to drive the carriage into an isolated field and do what he'd been wanting to do from the moment he'd met her.

He had to get some breathing space.

Besides, there was a new location to consider. He'd

thought the cross on the map was indicative of the church—Saint John the Baptist—but now he wasn't so sure. The cross north of York indicated Rievaulx. The one to the south probably meant the abbey.

Holywake.

It must have been an insignificant little place in the twelfth or thirteenth century. Probably made of a combination of stone and timber, which is why fire had destroyed all but the foundation.

The story of the lay monk was interesting, too. Jack knew that many of the monasteries hosted lay brothers—men who had not taken the sacred vows of the brotherhood. If one of these men had actually arrived from Jerusalem, he might have carried the Mandylion with him. He may have had Templar connections in the Holy Land and could have brought the cloth to England for safekeeping.

Jack would bet it was hidden on the Holywake grounds.

He grinned and turned to look at Dorrie.

"What's wrong?"

"Have you ever been to the American desert?" she asked.

He nodded. "I've been a lot of places. Why?"

"It just occurs to me that I don't know much about you, Jack," she said. "I know you have two sisters—"

"And three brothers," he said.

She nodded. "And you travel."

"All over," he agreed. "Wherever there's something of interest to see."

He didn't know what she was getting at. But if he knew Dorrie at all, he knew he'd never be able to predict her thoughts or actions.

He grinned. It sure made things interesting.

Chapter Fourteen

There was nothing at the Holywake site. Nothing but a few signs of a stone foundation, mostly overgrown by grass and weeds. Jack was disappointed, to say the least. Disgusted that he'd wasted his time.

"It's, well, it's old," Dorrie said.

"There's nothing here," Jack remarked. "Not one single place to start looking."

Dorrie walked quietly alongside him without offering empty sympathy or any other comfort. He appreciated that more than she could know.

"Look," she said, pointing into the distance. A man was walking away from the hedgerow, carrying a walking stick. Jack glanced up, then returned his attention to the site.

They meandered all around, looking for something, although Jack knew it was useless. He would need a large team of men and plenty of equipment to excavate this kind of site. The same was true of Rievaulx.

He kicked a rock in the path. This search for the Mandylion was proving to be anything but simple.

"Maybe the cross on the map *does* mean the church, as you first thought, Jack," Dorrie said.

"I suppose it's possible," he replied. "We can go tomorrow. When there's good light. It's getting late now."

"Hullo," the man with the walking stick said as he approached. His hair seemed nicely trimmed under his cap, and he wore his gray beard closely cropped.

Jack put out his hand and the other man took it.

"Interesting place here," he said to Jack.

"Are you familiar with it?" Jack asked. "Know anything about it?"

"Well, it's what's left of Holywake Abbey," the man replied. "Built in the year 1232 and burned to the ground in 1493."

"Do you know if any records were kept?"

"Not a one," he said. "They rotted and were discarded years ago. You're American, aren't you?"

"Yes," Jack said, frustrated.

"I wouldn't mind a ride back to the village," the fellow said. "Tell you what I know about the old abbey and where to find more. You planning to stay the night?"

"Yes."

"Elmswood Arms," he said, climbing into the back of the carriage. "I'll show you."

The room was shabby. And Dorothea was going to have it all to herself.

For some reason, that thought wasn't particularly comforting, even though she'd fussed every time Jack had insisted they share. She had gotten accustomed to having him near, even last night, when he'd been dead to the world and had not stirred in the least when she'd come to his bed.

Dorothea did not know what was wrong with her

today. Early in the morning, she'd had ample opportunity to take the Mandylion map and the key and
leave Jack. Instead, she'd left the documents where
she found them and gone to the dining room to await
Jack.

He'd been as unpleasant as a man could be, but she
had ridden beside him, enjoying the day until they'd
reached the Trevain farm. Dorothea did not know what
had come over her then. Alice Trevain's overt flirtation had embarrassed her. And the way Jack had
played into the woman's hands had annoyed her.

Dorothea had to amend that. It did more than annoy
her. It brought out feelings that were entirely unfamiliar to her. She had been angry and hurt all at once.
She had felt belittled.

She guessed that was why she'd kissed Jack. The
gesture had not been born of affection or lust. She'd
wanted both of them to know that she was not a timid
mouse who could be ignored.

She presumed Jack understood that now.

His disappointment in the Holywake site had been
palpable, and Dorothea found herself sympathizing
with him, even though they were rivals in the search.

Dorothea opened her bag and took out the items she
would need for the night. Then she hung up the clothes
she intended to wear in the morning, while she waited
for Jack to collect her for supper. It would be difficult
to face him now, after his disappointment, knowing
that she had the clue to the Mandylion and would soon
claim it for her father.

It only remained to be seen exactly how she was
going to do it.

Should she leave him and strike out on her own
toward the castle indicated on the map? Or remain

with him and go through the motions of exploring
Saint John the Baptist Church and the records of Holywake.

Dorothea felt very torn. Guilt was not something
with which she felt very comfortable. In fact, she
could not remember another time in her life when
she'd felt so culpable. She had always been an obe-
dient daughter and an honest scholar. Yet here she
was, playing along with Jack Temple—actually helping him—as if she would meekly allow him to discover the location of the Mandylion and take it from
her father.

Even though she was ashamed of herself, Dorothea
knew there was no other way. She could not let Jack
win. And, beyond that, she had to prove to him that
her father was not the charlatan he believed. Alastair
Bright might have been an unsuitable husband, but
Dorothea's mother always assured her that he was a
reputable antiquarian. He had academic connections
all over the world, Honoria had said many a time, and
the respect of scholars on every continent.

Dorothea wondered if Jack Temple could say the
same.

She answered a light tap at her door. "Ready?"
Jack asked when she opened it.

Dorothea's heart thudded in her throat. He had
washed his face and combed his hair and, though she
knew it was ridiculous, he seemed more devastatingly
handsome than he'd ever been. She swallowed.

"Your room's not too bad," Jack said, glancing in
behind her. "I think they gave me a closet, though."

Dorothea did not want to discuss their rooming arrangements, or she might be tempted to offer to share.
And that was out of the question.

"I'm famished," she said. "Shall we go?"

She scooted around him and went to the stairs, leaving him to close the door. The less she talked to him, looked at him, the better it would be. She might be able to live with her guilt that way.

Jack took Dorrie's elbow and wondered what had come over her. He couldn't pinpoint exactly what it was, but something was different.

They went down to the main room which was no more than a smoke-filled tavern. It was no place for a lady, but Jack didn't see any alternative. The village was small and this seemed to be the only place a man could get a pint and a meal if he chose.

"Stay close," Jack said, tucking Dorrie's arm into the crook of his own.

Every man in the tavern turned and looked at them, eyeing them suspiciously. Jack had not expected anything less, but he knew it would make Dorrie uneasy. The smoke, the smells, the rough clothes—all were foreign to Dorrie Bright, in spite of the fact that she was Alastair's daughter.

They found an empty table in a back corner and sat.

"Jack, can't we have some food brought upstairs?"

"Not in a place like this," he replied. "In fact, we'll be lucky if anyone comes to the table for our order."

Jack didn't wait for the barkeep, but left Dorrie long enough to put in a request for food and get a pint for himself. The man behind the bar reluctantly agreed to brew some tea for Dorrie.

A few minutes later, a boy came with their food and a pot of tea. The mutton stew was nothing like the tasty meal they'd had at the Boar's Head Inn near

Rievaulx, but it was filling enough, taken with the coarse bread that was served.

"Hear you been looking at the old abbey," one of the men said to Jack. He pulled up a chair and straddled it while he sipped his beer.

He did not appear threatening, but Jack knew better than to relax. He'd been caught off guard the day before when the three men had sneaked up on them, and he didn't intend for anything like that to happen again.

"Interesting old place," Jack remarked noncommittally.

"Been there for centuries," the man said. "Burned down years ago."

"Yes, that's what we were told," Jack said. "I also heard some story about a monk sniffing around the nunnery centuries ago..."

"American, aren't you?"

Jack didn't understand why it was necessary for everyone to state the obvious when they met him, but he gave a nod. "From New York. Just doing a little sight-seeing."

"In our backward little part of the country?" the man asked sarcastically. "There's better abbeys. You ought to go on up to Rievaulx or over to Fountains."

"Thanks for the tip," Jack said, grateful that Dorrie had decided to keep quiet. "We'll do that."

"Now, our abbey," the man said, "Holywake, was a small place on the scale of things. Only housed about fifty nuns at most, late in the thirteenth century."

"Any truth to the story of the monk?"

"Well, now," the fellow said, "there may be. Nobody's ever proved nothing, but the stories have gone round the district for many a year."

Jack felt Dorrie take a breath, and he knew she

planned to speak. He found her hand under the table and squeezed it to get her attention. He did not want anyone to take more notice of her than was absolutely necessary.

"They say he seduced one of the nuns," Jack said, deliberately altering the story.

The man laughed. "Yeah, that's one of the versions."

"What's the version *you* believe?" Jack asked.

"I think the simplest one is the true story," he said. "That the monk was only passing through on his way home from the Holy Land. That he sought shelter from the weather and stayed a few days, then went on to his home."

"Which was where? Rievaulx?"

"No, as the story goes, he was a lay brother," the villager said, "and a fierce fighter."

"In Jerusalem?"

"Most likely. He may have had something to do with the Knights of the Temple—no one knows."

Dorrie grabbed Jack's thigh. If his breath caught, it was because of the reference to the Templar Knights and not from the heat of her hand.

"But he only stayed at Holywake until he could travel to his home?"

The man nodded, but added nothing more. Jack wanted to know where this monk's home was. That was the most important part of the story. If he'd had some connection with the Templars, then it was entirely possible he'd been given the cloth to carry safely to England. Once he returned to his home, he'd have found a secure place to hide it.

"Somewhere east of here," the man said. "Nobody in these parts knows where."

Jack took a drink of his beer. He did not want to appear too interested or ask pointed questions that would arouse the other man's curiosity.

"What about the connection with Saint John's Church?" he asked.

"Father Robson and the abbess?"

"You know his name, then?"

"We know plenty," he replied. "A scandal it was...once the lovers were discovered."

"What happened to them?"

The man tipped his mug and finished his drink, then stood. "Not fit for a lady's ears, if you take my meaning," he said. He turned and walked away.

Jack gave a knowing nod and tried to ignore the way Dorrie's hand had clamped around his thigh. He would be able to get a lot more information later, when she wasn't with him. He would deposit her in her room, then come back to the tavern and drink with the locals and find out everything he could. It wouldn't be difficult.

Getting Dorrie to cooperate with the plan would be the tough part.

"Go after him, Jack!" she said in an urgent whisper.

"Hush," he replied, spooning another bite of stew into his mouth. "Finish eating."

"I cannot believe you're just going to sit here and—"

"Dorrie, the man doesn't want to talk around you."

"But—"

"Look at this place," he said. "Do you see another woman in it?"

"Well, no," she answered.

He put his spoon down. If she'd done any traveling

with her father, as Jack suspected, she would be familiar with the concept of men wanting to socialize without women present. That's why there were pubs and taverns.

"I'll come back later and see what I can find out."

"Jack—"

"You're going to have to trust me on this one, Miss Bright," he said.

They finished their meal, and Jack escorted Dorrie to her room. He followed her inside and lit the oil lamp that sat on the table next to the bed.

"Ugh. My clothes smell like smoke," she said.

"Comes with the territory," Jack remarked offhandedly. "Listen. I want you to keep your door bolted, and don't let anyone in. My room is right next door, but I won't be back for a while. Still, you'll be safe enough here."

But leaving her made him uneasy. They hadn't been separated in days, and this little inn was far from ideal. She looked slightly forlorn.

"Will you knock on my door when you get back?"

"Sure," he said. He would do anything to make her stop looking so worried. Gently, he cupped her cheek in his hand. "You'll be all right."

She'd thought he was going to kiss her before leaving, and Dorothea was surprised by how much she'd wanted it. Their kiss at the Trevain farm had only fueled her need for more, even though she had no business wanting any more intimacies with Jack. Within a day or two she would leave him and go on her own search for the Mandylion.

She knew Jack had asked the villager about the priest and the abbess only to divert attention from his real interest, the lay brother who had passed through on his way home from the Holy Land. It was only a matter of time before Jack understood the clue of the nursery rhyme. He would head toward the last site on the map, and there was a very good chance he would find the home where the Mandylion had been hidden.

Dorothea had to get there first.

She undressed and slipped on her nightgown. It was late enough to go to bed, but Dorrie did not think she'd be able to fall asleep until Jack returned. Besides, the bed was lumpy.

After blowing out the lamp, Dorothea lay down and closed her eyes, but the voices from the tavern traveled upstairs. She tossed and turned awhile, but finally gave up and lit the lamp again.

Then she heard a sound coming from Jack's room.

A heavy scraping sound was accompanied by a thud against the wall. Instantly, she realized Jack had returned without stopping in her room first. She threw off the blanket and slid out of bed. Pulling a shawl from her bag, Dorothea wrapped it around her shoulders and went to the door. She dared to open it only a crack, to peer out into the hall.

No one was there.

As anxious as she was to find out what he'd learned, she crept out of her room and slipped down the hall to Jack's door. Glancing quickly in both directions, Dorothea tapped on the door.

It was yanked open by a brown giant, who grabbed her by the fabric gathered at her chest and pulled her into the room, clamping a hand over her mouth before she had a chance to cry out.

Her heart fluttered wildly in her chest as the man pinned her to the wall and spoke. ''Where the map be?'' he demanded with a kind of accent Dorothea had never heard before.

She tried to speak but could not. Then she attempted to move her head, but he held her fast. How did he expect her to answer him?

"You be Bright's daughter."

She was finally able to nod.

"I come from Bright," he said. "To get map. You tell me where."

She nodded again, and he loosened his grip.

"I don't h-have it," she said.

"Temple."

"No!" she cried, then said more calmly, "No. Temple put it away for safekeeping. He didn't want—"

"You be lying, woman!"

"No, I'm not!" she replied indignantly. How dare he assume she was being untruthful, even if she was. She was not about to turn the map and key over to this overgrown buffoon without verifying that he was truly her father's man. Besides, she doubted Alastair would hire such a ruffian. "Where is my father?"

"Not far," he said. "He will contact you."

A moment later, the man was out of the window and gone.

Chapter Fifteen

''That was all he said? That the lay brother was some kind of Yorkish gentry?'' Dorrie asked.

Jack handed her into the carriage and pulled himself up beside her. The hours he'd spent in the tavern had been essentially wasted. He knew only a fraction more than he'd known before, and what he'd learned was hardly useful information.

''What about the priest's story? Was there anything to that?''

The tale of Saint John's priest and the Holywake abbess was indelicate, to say the least, and he didn't want to impart it to her now. Or ever.

''Jack!''

He took the eastern road out of the village. The third Templar head on the map lay in that direction, so that was where he had to go. Jack figured there would be more than enough castle ruins for him to examine, once they got closer to the coast, and he had to determine how he was going to proceed with his search for the Mandylion.

''Jack!''

He wished Gauge O'Neill were here. The man had

a knack for unearthing useful information from unusual sources. That wasn't to say that Jack couldn't
get the same information, but it always took him a lot
longer. He wondered if he could excavate without
drawing attention— "Ouch!"

"You are ignoring me, Jack," Dorrie said sweetly
after pinching him.

"Yes, I am."

"Tell me what you heard last night," she said.
"You didn't tell me anything when you got back."

Because he could hardly speak when he'd seen her
standing there in her nightclothes, the same gown he'd
nearly removed from her delectable body when they'd
stayed near Rievaulx. His fingers had itched to touch
her, his blood had burned with his need to hold her,
to make her his own.

But instead of taking her in his arms, he'd forced
himself to turn and leave her. He spent the night without her, just as he had at the Boar's Head Inn. Wanting
her. Wishing she were anyone but Bright's daughter.

"There was nothing of use to us," he said.

"Well, can't you at least tell me what happened
with the priest and the abbess," Dorrie countered.

He supposed he could tell her the story without em-
bellishing it the way he'd heard it.

"The abbess had a child," he said. "The priest
died. That's it."

She turned in her seat and grabbed his arm. "What
do you mean, 'that's it'? It must have been terrible for
them. Can you imagine?"

"I'm sure it was terrible," Jack replied. "The child
was a girl, and she was raised in the convent. Became
a nun. Her mother, ah, was banished."

Dorrie frowned. She did not let go of Jack's arm

but shifted her body closer to him, sending a shock of heat through him. "That is so sad."

Jack swallowed.

"I wonder where she ended up," Dorrie said. "The abbess."

"They didn't say," Jack remarked. He was glad that Dorrie still had a grip on his upper arm, or he'd have been tempted to wrap it around her shoulders and pull her even closer. And that was something he had to avoid.

The truth of the matter was that he was going to take the Mandylion from her. He was going to see to it that her father was exposed as the criminal he was. And when all was said and done, Dorothea Bright would hate him.

He was not going to have her seduction on his conscience, too.

Jack would never have thought it possible, but he liked Dorrie Bright, in spite of the fact that she was Alastair's daughter.

Hell, he more than liked her. She had more spunk and spirit than any three women he knew, and he had yet to spend a dull moment with her. But their differences were vital. She was the daughter of a scoundrel, a man who thought nothing of desecrating ancient excavation sites, of stealing important timeless artifacts meant for posterity.

Jack's principles were too firmly ingrained for him to ignore all that.

If Dorothea had worried that Jack would discover why she was preoccupied this morning, it had been needless. It seemed he had his own worries.

She had attempted to keep him distracted with her

questions about the Holywake abbess, but he was not going to share any more than he had already. Instead, they rode in silence, while Dorrie pondered the meaning of her late visit by the brown giant.

Not that he had visited *her*. When she thought about it, she realized that the man had been searching Jack's room for the map and key. She supposed her room would have been searched next when the man didn't find what he was looking for.

Dorothea shuddered at the thought of that hulking man coming through her window as she undressed. Her encounter with him in Jack's room had been terrifying enough, and she had been adequately covered in her gown and shawl. She did not care to meet with him again, under any circumstances.

She took frequent furtive glances behind the carriage, wondering how her father had found her, and how he planned to meet with her. She was hardly ever apart from Jack. Surely Alastair did not intend to confront Jack. If he did, he'd have shown up himself at the tavern last night or on the road.

Dorothea clutched her fist to her chest, as if she could slow her beleaguered heart, and worried that that was exactly what her father had in mind. With the big chap to force the issue, Alastair could take the map from Jack and—

"Are you all right?" Jack asked.

"Yes, of course," Dorothea replied. "Why wouldn't I be?"

He turned his eyes back to the road.

Dorothea could not bear it if anything happened to Jack. He might be an American, and he definitely had some raw edges, but she had grown fond of him. He had taken care of her for days, seen to her needs, risked his life for her safety... He'd been more than kind, even if he was singularly responsible for every unpleasant situation from which he'd had to rescue her.

Still, she knew that in years to come, she would remember this adventure warmly. When she thought of Jack...

Dorothea could not place Jack in the past tense. She could not imagine a day without bantering with him, arguing with him, loving him.

Her breath caught in her throat. What a ridiculous notion. To fall in love with someone in a week's time? It was not possible. They'd spent a great deal of time together, that was all. And he'd been kind when it had not been strictly necessary. He'd given her bluebells.

When the memory of his kisses came to mind, Dorothea did not know what to think. Her mother had always admonished her to remain chaste. The touch of Albert's lips on the back of her hand had been acceptable but nothing more. Dorothea had not even been allowed to ride alone in a carriage with him.

Her mother would be appalled at her recent behavior. Bluebells would not have impressed her.

"You keep pressing your hand to your, uh, bosom that way," Jack said, "and I'm going to start thinking you intend to draw my attention to it."

"Why, of all the—"

"But that crease in your forehead tells me I'd better keep my eyes on the path and my thoughts on the Mandylion."

The Mandylion. The only reason they were together.

"When we find it—"

"We'll take it to the museum in London," he said. "Archibald Crowe is the curator of antiquities there, and he knows what he's doing. He'll see that the cloth is sent to the proper experts to be authenticated. Studied."

And Jack will not be paid for his trouble, Dorothea thought. The museum will not pay him for the cloth, though perhaps he might receive a stipend for his effort.

"You are going to a great deal of expense just to take your revenge on my father," she said, prying although she did not want to appear to be doing so.

He shrugged. "It's only half of what I'd like to do to him."

"You are certain it was my father who stole the fertility god from the tribe?"

"Without a doubt," he said almost carelessly. His sparkling blue eyes engaged her, and though he was in good humor, he seemed ready to argue about Alastair.

But Dorothea was distracted. She wished Jack would pay more attention to his surroundings. The man who'd climbed into his room at the inn could be lurking in the trees beside the path, on horseback perhaps, just waiting to overtake them and force Jack to give him the map.

And Dorothea knew Jack would not back down from a fight, even if their assailant was double his size.

"And when the tribe realized one of us had taken it, all hell broke loose."

"Um. So you said," Dorothea commented absently.

"Dorrie, it's obvious that you aren't ever going to believe me, and I guess there's no reason that you should. Alastair's got you convinced that he's a reputable dealer, and your loyalty to him is admirable," he said. "But misguided."

She did not believe that for a second. There *had* to have been some misunderstanding in Africa. Her mother would not have spoken so highly of Alastair had he been the sort of man Jack alleged. Her father was a reputable explorer—and a collector, she had to admit—but she'd seen no evidence that he was a fraud.

In fact, if anyone's methods were questionable, they were Jack's. He'd broken into her father's house and stolen the map and even come back later to search for the key. If anyone was a charlatan....

"What's got you so jumpy today?" Jack asked.

"That place," she said without hesitation. "The inn. It was as unsavory an establishment as it could be."

"But it was either that or a night under the stars," Jack replied. "And I didn't think you'd want to sleep in the carriage."

"You are entirely correct," she said.

"We'll find a better place tonight."

"One can only hope," Dorothea replied.

"As I recall, there are numerous little villages between here and the coast."

Dorothea shrugged. She was unfamiliar with this part of the country. She didn't know Oxfordshire well, either, due to the restrictions her mother had placed on her activities.

"Quite a few castle ruins, too."

Oh dear. Dorothea wondered if Jack intended to search every one of them. She was certain the Mandylion, if it actually existed, would be found somewhere near the sea. It was a waste of time to explore every ruin between here and the coast. "Do you have the map?" she asked. "The modern one?"

He gave it to her, and she opened it, hoping to get an idea of where the castle and head were drawn. If she was not mistaken, the castle they sought would be overlooking the sea, halfway between the Humber River and Flamborough Head. It could be near a town, or not...the medieval map was not very specific, and things had probably changed in five hundred years.

"Any idea where to start?" Jack asked.

Dorothea raised her eyebrows and shrugged. "It's all the same to me," she finally said.

A stone tower was all that was left of the first castle ruins. There was no town or village nearby—no one around whom they could question about the history of the place. Jack and Dorrie wandered around the site for a while, and Jack jotted a few notes and made some drawings in a tablet, even though he didn't believe this was the site where the Mandylion was hidden.

Since he had little else to go on, he had to rely upon his instincts. Nothing that was written on the map or in the key led him to believe the Mandylion would be hidden in one of these inland estates.

At the ruins of the fourth castle, Jack watched Dorothea sit down on a broken stone wall. Her arms were braced on the wall behind her, and she leaned back to hold her face toward the sun. Her hat lay on the wall beside her, so his view was unobstructed.

Purposely, he walked away from her. He enjoyed looking at her far too much for his peace of mind.

Many of the walls of this castle were intact, and Jack examined the stonework of the fireplace in what would have been the great hall. He walked the length of the hall and stepped outside, wondering who had lived here so long ago. Was it the man who had made the map?

He'd been so sure that the cloth had been hidden in a church or some other consecrated place. Why not Rievaulx or Holywake? Those seemed to be the most likely connections to the Mandylion, yet he didn't think it was hidden in either place.

He glanced at Dorrie, sitting so patiently, waiting for Jack to finish his examination of the site. She had not seemed anxious to walk these grounds. It was almost as if she, too, were certain the cloth was not hidden here and was just biding her time.

Gritting his teeth against a growing suspicion, Jack continued walking around the periphery. They had seen the same clues. There was nothing in the words—

Unless she'd fabricated the Arabic lines of the poem. Jack supposed that was possible, although he could pick out a few words himself. And the way she had translated was in line with what he saw.

What other clues were there? The markings on the map were geographically questionable. Rievaulx was shown in the correct *general* location, but it certainly was not exact. Nor was the face that seemed to indicate Holywake Abbey.

It suddenly seemed as if the simple, straightforward search for the Mandylion was becoming more complicated by the hour. With every castle site they explored, Jack's pessimism grew. He didn't know why he'd thought he could find the Mandylion without his men.

This was going to require a lot more investigation, inquiries and actual digging than he had been prepared to do. In fact, when he'd stormed into Bright's house the week before, he'd only planned on throttling the man. The idea of taking the Mandylion from him had been a direct result of Bright's absence.

If he couldn't do any physical damage to the man, he was going to go for the next most important thing: the cloth Alastair had bragged about while they were in Africa.

Jack jabbed his fingers through his hair. He was going to have to wire his men in London, and have them meet him here in York, with all their equipment. If O'Neill was better, he could probably put a proposal together and go to Crowe for financing. Obviously, the British Museum would love to have the Mandylion in its collection and would want to fund a legitimate expedition. Jack had the credentials needed for such a purpose and had worked with Crowe before.

He circled around the outer wall as he thought through his future course of action and came upon Dorrie, lying on her back in the sun. The sight of her hit him like a punch in his midsection.

She was on the same stone wall, her eyes were closed, and she appeared to be asleep. Her arms were outstretched beside her, hands on the ground, palm up. One leg was bent at the knee and the position would have been indecent but for the bright burst of petticoats around her legs.

Jack had the most compelling urge to sneak up to her and slide his hands up the length of her legs through that feminine froth of petticoats. She would be shocked, but he would turn her protests into acquiescence with his kiss. He wanted to taste her, more than he wanted to take his next breath.

Somehow, he'd managed to keep his lust at bay for the last two days, but seeing her now....

He balled his hands into fists and forced himself to

look away. There were so many other things that should occupy his mind—he had plans to make. A wire to send. Supplies to procure. He should not be thinking of all that smooth, white skin hidden under so many layers of clothes.

Dorrie's sigh reached his ears, and he turned to face her. Her smile was soft but radiant, as if she took pleasure in the quiet, peaceful surroundings.

She attempted to push herself up, but it was an awkward move. "Help me up, will you, Jack?"

Jack hesitated only a heartbeat, and then he was at her side, giving her a hand and helping her to her feet.

But he did not let go.

They stood facing each other, only inches apart. Her scent enticed him, and her clear green eyes, with their thick, dark lashes, drew him even closer.

Tipping his head, he touched his lips to hers as one arm slipped around her waist. It became a slow, deep melding of lips that raised his temperature, tripped up his heartbeat. He felt one of her hands at the back of his head, pulling him in. He hadn't thought it possible that every time he kissed her it would get better or more consuming, but when their tongues danced, he groaned, breaking the kiss.

Swiftly, he picked her up, carried her inside the great hall and lay her on the grassy ground before what was left of the hearth. Kneeling, Jack threw off his jacket and slid it under her.

Chapter Sixteen

There was no roof, so the sun shone in on them, illuminating every inch that was exposed as Jack unbuttoned Dorrie's blouse. He touched his lips to her throat, then moved down, slowly tasting, feasting on her soft flesh. One hand worked the laces of her new corset, and when he freed her breasts from their confines, she sighed deeply.

Jack cupped one breast in his hand and licked its delicate pink tip. It hardened in reaction, as did its twin. He looked up into Dorrie's eyes and saw astonishment, as well as the reflection of his own passion.

She placed both hands on the back of his head and held him to her breast, while her breath came in short gasps. Her eyes drifted closed, and she lay back, her head pillowed in a rich, lustrous mass of auburn curls. She was so beautiful that Jack couldn't take his eyes off her face.

And he wanted her more than he'd ever wanted anything.

He slipped a hand down the fine, feminine expanse of skin to her waist and was impeded from further exploration by the securely fastened waist of her skirt.

Caution was beyond him at the moment, and he slid his hand lower while he pulled at the fabric, drawing it up as his hand moved steadily down.

When he slipped under the edge of her skirt, he still did not meet with skin. He felt stockings, garters and thin cotton drawers. Dorrie made a whimper, then whispered his name when he finally found bare flesh.

"Open for me, honey," he said, impossibly swollen with his own need.

She shifted slightly, and he found her moist heat. Shuddering, he closed his eyes and pressed his fingers to her most sensitive part. Dorrie rocked against his hand and he heard her breath catch when he slipped one finger inside.

She raised her head and looked at him, arousal and bewilderment in her eyes.

No one had ever touched her so intimately before, and Jack felt the impact of that knowledge to the core of his being. He moved again, raising himself up to capture her lips. He kissed her deeply, using his tongue and teeth while he pleasured her with his fingers.

Breaking their kiss, she cried out softly and pressed her legs together. A deep shuddering breath followed, even as she pulled Jack closer.

He took her hand and kissed it, then carried it downward, pressing her palm against his arousal. "Feel how I want you," he said.

Her touch was exquisite torture. Jack tensed his jaw as Dorrie explored the length and breadth of him, her innocence evident in her tentative touch. Feverishly, his hand went to his belt, then to the buttons of his trousers. He could think of nothing besides burying himself in her, of possessing her completely.

"Jack?"

"I know, sweetheart," he said, taking her mouth once again. He positioned himself over her and looked into her eyes.

They were wide and fearful. His heart thudded in his chest while his blood pooled uncomfortably. One thrust of his hips and he would be in heaven. One word of reassurance and he could convince her that this was right.

The most primitive of urges impelled him to continue, but he braced himself to retreat. "Dorrie, I..."

"Are you, I mean, are we..."

He tipped his head and pressed his forehead against hers. "Finished? Yes," he said. "This was a mistake."

He pushed himself to his feet. As he walked away, he ignored the disturbing thought that he had been searching for Dorrie Bright his whole life.

Dorothea pressed her hand to her heart and willed it to slow while she blinked back the tears she refused to shed.

She'd had no idea.

Her mother had never warned her of the intense pleasure that would accompany a man's intimate touch. In fact, Honoria had told her that it was something to be avoided at all costs until the marriage bed, when her husband's touch would have to be tolerated.

As if it were an awful thing.

Dorothea could not help but wonder in what other ways her mother had misled her. She did not know if Jack had been kind to her just now, or if she should be horribly offended by his abandonment.

She put her clothes to rights, then got up and straightened her skirts, brushing off bits of grass and dirt. Casting a sidelong glance in his direction, she saw that his back was to her, and he was standing stiffly, facing a row of dark clouds in the distance.

It was going to rain.

Dorothea did not know what to do. To her knowledge, the rules of etiquette did not cover such a situation, and Jack was quite obviously vexed.

She decided to ignore him. Their attempt at lovemaking had been a dismal failure, and though she'd never experienced anything as wonderful at his intimate touch, it was clear that Jack had no intention of repeating it. At least, not with her.

She reached down and picked up his jacket. She brushed it off and then went over to him, holding the coat at arm's length. "We should, um, be on our way," she said.

Too embarrassed to look at him, she was surprised when he dropped the jacket to the ground and reached for her.

"I apologize," he said, pulling her into his arms. "I had no right to take advantage."

Her heart jumped.

"But you—"

"Should never have touched you."

Dorothea felt the solid muscle of his chest against her cheek, the strength of his arms around her. She closed her eyes and reveled in his raw masculinity, and wished she would never have to let him go.

He regretted their intimacy, and she did not know how to change his mind.

He set her away from him and looked into her eyes. His gaze traveled to her forehead and her cheeks, and her lips tingled with want.

But he did not kiss her again. He began to unbutton her blouse.

"You, uh…"

She glanced down and saw that she'd skipped a button, putting the entire blouse askew, and Jack was correcting her mistake. His big fingers were awkward, but Dorothea was touched by his gentle manner.

She felt a lump in her throat, but swallowed it before she spoke. "I'm not upset that you…that we…"

"Dorrie," he said. He hesitated and she saw a muscle flex in his jaw. "This…attraction…that we feel. Nothing like this has ever happened to you before, has it?"

She shook her head.

"It's not going to work," he continued. "We…" He hesitated and Dorothea frowned.

"I don't understand."

Jack let go of her and stepped away. "Come on," he said. "We've got to go."

They did not reach the coast by dusk, as Jack had intended. There had been so many ruins to catalog, Jack had gotten bogged down writing the details of their structures and settings and the likelihood of whether or not the Mandylion was hidden at any of them.

He scrubbed one hand across his face and admitted that the cataloging had been secondary. He hadn't been able to keep his mind on his work. It was so full of Dorrie, he could hardly think.

She was bewildered, as she had every right to be. He had seduced her, then backed away, then offered a partial explanation that made no sense. Hell, it made no sense to him, either. He wanted her in a way he'd never wanted any woman. On the surface, she was as prim and starchy as could be, but underneath, Jack knew Dorrie was the most sensual, passionate woman he'd ever known.

But she was Alastair Bright's daughter. The blood of a charlatan ran through her veins, and Dorrie was loyal to him. Jack knew she would use any method at her disposal to discover the Mandylion herself and present it to her father. He still didn't know whether he could trust her translation of the key or if she'd withheld information crucial to figuring out the cloth's location.

And he could not help but wonder if she would take any satisfaction from cheating him out of the Mandylion.

Jack supposed he might have been able to seduce Dorrie out of her staunch loyalty to her father, but that would have been unscrupulous. He was a better man than Alastair Bright. He was no fraud.

He would not make love to Dorothea Bright until they'd settled the Mandylion with the proper authorities in the British Museum. After that, Jack had plans for her.

He was going to take her to his hotel suite in London. After champagne and a light meal for two in his rooms, he would undress her slowly. Her hair would come down, pin by pin. When she was naked, he was going to taste every inch of her and make her writhe in ecstasy. And when she was ready, Jack was going to possess Dorrie Bright in the most intimate, intense way that a man can possess a woman.

He shifted uncomfortably and threw her a sidelong glance. Christ, he was thinking in terms of a future with her, after all this was settled. He must be out of his mind.

Dorrie studiously avoided looking at him while her hands twisted and tortured the edge of her jacket. There was no telling what she was thinking, though he knew she was confused about what had happened between them. He took great satisfaction in knowing he was the only man who had brought her such pleasure, and he looked forward to sharing it the next time.

"Is that a village?" she asked, pointing into the distance.

It was, and Jack headed for it, hoping there'd be a small hotel or inn where they could stay. In two rooms.

Jack felt a prickle at the back of his neck and glanced toward the trees at his left, the only place where a man could stand watch—or follow—without being seen. Then he turned toward Dorrie and wondered if she'd experienced the same odd sensation of being watched. He narrowed his eyes, but did not ask her.

He would just have to be more diligent as they traveled. His bruises were too fresh to risk being accosted again.

The village was small, but there was a public house with rooms to let on the second floor. They registered, and while Dorrie got herself settled in her room, Jack went back outside to scour the surrounding area with his eyes and satisfy himself that no one had followed them. If highwaymen had followed them, looking for easy prey, the scoundrels were out of luck.

If it was Bright, and he'd somehow caught their trail, he, too, was out of luck. Jack wasn't planning on sleeping tonight.

* * *

Dorothea was certain they'd been followed. Even after she was standing safely in the tiny room Jack had gotten for her, she felt as if she was being watched. She pulled her curtain aside slightly and looked out at the street, but no one was about, besides Jack.

She wondered what he was doing.

She flopped back on her bed and stared at the ceiling. She wondered what he *had done* to her.

Nothing so astonishing had ever happened in her life. Jack's touch had made her feel as if she were the most important, most beautiful woman in the world. Somehow, he'd made her crave even more kisses, more caresses than before, but he'd withdrawn from her just before... Dorothea did not know what would have happened if he had not left her so suddenly. Certainly there would have been something more if Jack had not changed his mind.

Images from her father's collection came to her then, and Dorothea began to grasp the primitive need that drove her to him.

She heard voices outside her room and then footsteps. Finally, a knock at her door brought her to her feet.

"Got supper for ye, ma'am," said a young woman in an apron. "Yer cousin said I should fetch ye."

"I'll be right down," she said. She returned to her room and rearranged her hair. She straightened her clothes and wished she had something a bit more... elegant...to wear to dinner with Jack. She looked at her face in the glass. She was pale, and her eyes looked enormous. All out of proportion. She pinched her cheeks to get more color in them and bit her lips.

Perhaps if she were more attractive....

What foolishness, she thought as she turned away from her reflection and left her room. She and Jack were rivals. They both wanted the Mandylion for different reasons, and when Dorothea was the one who discovered it, she was going to have absolutely no regrets. She had told Jack from the start that she intended to beat him to it.

It was fortunate that he'd kept that promise in mind this afternoon.

They ate a quiet meal together. Jack concentrated on his food while Dorothea concentrated on Jack.

His jaw was shadowed by dark whiskers and his hair was overlong and uncombed, though it looked as if he'd raked his fingers through it to gain some order. He wore no coat, and no collar with his white shirt, which was rolled up to the elbows, revealing corded forearms liberally sprinkled with dark hair. His tan trousers were held up by dark brown suspenders, and he looked as dangerous as he had the day he'd barged into her father's house in London.

Only she felt differently about him now.

Her heart fluttered in her chest, and she had to take a moment to catch her breath.

"Go down the wrong pipe?" Jack asked, noticing her distress.

He patted her back, glanced at the lack of progress she was making with her meal, then returned his attention to his own food.

"Where will we go tomorrow?" she asked, thinking of his naked chest and the broad, muscular back she'd rubbed the night he was injured.

"Toward Hornsea, I think," he replied, opening the map lying on the table. "The third face is drawn right about here,'' he indicated a point just west of the seaport, ''so we might get lucky.''

Dorothea did not take notice of the location, her attention fully focused on the strong hand spread out over the map. She pressed her legs together to stifle the wave of heat spreading out from her center, but the sensation was only made worse. She swallowed and looked away, so unsure of herself, of him, that she had to leave.

''Are you feeling all right?'' Jack asked.

''N-no,'' she replied. ''I think I'll say good-night. I'm…just tired.'' She stood, with Jack quickly following suit, pulling her chair away for her.

''You've hardly eaten anything.''

She nodded. Everything was suddenly too confusing. The Mandylion, the days of travel, Jack's kiss, his touch.

She did not want to care about him, but she did. She did not want to crave his caress but it seemed that she was powerless to stop it. Worst of all, she did not want to take the Mandylion from him.

Turning quickly away, she headed for the stairs, only to discover that Jack was right behind her. But Dorothea's mind was muddled with too much confusion to face him now. There was a dangerous chance that she would plead with him to join her in her room and continue what they'd started in the grass earlier in the day.

She pressed her hand to her chest and composed herself. ''I'm fine, Jack,'' she said, though she sounded too breathless, even to herself. ''I just need to sleep.''

''Dorrie.''

''Really,'' she said, putting on as genuine a smile

as she could muster. "Go back and finish your supper."

She must have been convincing, because he retreated as soon as she unlocked her door. Though her heart lurched at his departure, she knew it was for the best. She knew she would do something foolish if he stayed.

Once inside her room, she lit a lamp, then started to undress. Something near the bed caught her eye, and she saw that it was a sheet of paper, folded. A note.

Dorothea picked it up. It said:

My dear daughter,
Your travels are of great interest to me. If you would be so good as to meet me tonight—I will be waiting for you after Temple retires. Come to the village church.

With greatest affection,
Alastair Bright

Chapter Seventeen

It was ridiculously easy to slip away into the night. Nothing impeded Dorothea but her own conscience. She and Jack had had a partnership of sorts.

Now that was about to change.

She walked silently, keeping to the shadows. She had no choice. Alastair was her father, and she owed her loyalty to him. She could not ignore his request for a meeting, any more than she could disregard the request he was sure to make.

Her heart thudded heavily, and Dorothea pressed her hand against her chest in a vain attempt to settle it down. She kept going until she reached her destination. Pausing in the lane across from the church, she took a deep breath and crossed over.

"This way," came a deep voice out of the darkness.

Dorothea circled around to the side where a door was ajar. She hesitated and a man came out.

"Dorothea," he said.

"Father?"

In the shadows, she was able to make out a man's form. He tipped his head slightly, then took her hand. "Follow me."

A few minutes later, she found herself standing at the bottom of a set of stone steps, where one candle illuminated a small landing. Two other men were present, the tall brown one and another fellow of a more normal size. "We'll talk here," Alastair said. "You didn't tell Temple you were coming?"

"N-no. Of course not."

He was much shorter than Dorothea remembered, his height only slightly greater than her own. And he was thin and wiry. His hair seemed to be the same color as hers, though there was silver at the temples and in the muttonchops he wore. His eyes sparkled with bright intelligence, and he had a vibrant energy about him.

"Have you figured out where it is? The Mandylion?"

"I—"

"You have to be careful with Temple," Alastair said. "He's a canny bastard and if he gets any inkling that you know where it is, he'll figure some way to wheedle it out of you."

"But he—"

"Now, where does he plan to go tomorrow?"

"Hornsea," she said, overwhelmed.

"Why? Because of the location of the faces on the map?"

She nodded.

"What does he make of them?"

"He thinks they have some connection to the Templar Knights—the faces they—"

"I concur," Alastair said. "The Mandylion is all tied up with the Templars. No doubt about it." The big brown fellow unrolled a document that appeared to be a map and held it up to the light. Alastair turned his attention to it.

"And what of the key?" he asked as he perused the map. "Anything useful there?"

"N-not really," she said. "It seems to be just a letter to the abbot of—"

"Rievaulx. I know."

Dorothea was astonished by Alastair. He was as quick as the crack of a whip with his questions, yet he hadn't asked a single personal thing about her. They had not laid eyes upon each other in twenty years, but all he wanted to hear was what she knew of the Mandylion.

She pressed a hand to her chest and tried to rub away the ache.

The action caught Alastair's attention. "Heart troubles, eh?" he said, confusing her once again. "Your mother wrote to tell me all about it."

"She did?" Dorothea asked, dumbfounded. She had been unaware of any communication between her parents.

"I was amazed you've been able to keep up with Temple," Alastair said absently. "He's not one to slow down for anyone."

"My heart doesn't—"

"And that bit about bearing children," her father said. "Any truth to that?"

"What do you—"

"No need to be bashful," he said, turning to look at her. "Honoria said there'd be problems, and I just wondered if any of that's changed."

Shock took Dorothea's breath away. Her mother had never said anything about—

"How about the swelling?" he asked, pushing aside

her skirts in order to see her ankles. "Not noticeable. Maybe your mother was wrong about the other."

The tall brown man interrupted, rolling up the map. "We best start tonight," he said. "Get to Hornsea first."

"Let's not be hasty, Paco," Alastair said. He gave Dorothea a pat on the cheek. "All in good time."

"What will you do with the Mandylion when you…find it?" Dorothea asked.

"Ahh, now there's a question," Alastair remarked.

"We've got to douse this light and get out of here, Al," the third man said.

"In a moment, Neville," her father said. "My daughter wants to know what we will do with the cloth once we find it…and we *will* find it, won't we, my dear?"

Dorothea gave a nod and gained a smile from her father.

"It will be presented…to the queen, of course," he said. "Victoria will decide where it goes, and she will grant it to the most worthy of recipients."

The breath Dorothea held in her lungs escaped her now. This was perfectly acceptable. Though Alastair was an abrupt—well, rude—fellow, his intentions were honorable. He would do the right thing with the Mandylion.

After all, it was a much grander gesture to hand the precious cloth to Queen Victoria, allowing her to bestow it upon a likely beneficiary, rather than giving it to some curator in the bowels of the British Museum.

"Well, come now," Alastair said. "You must return to your room before—"

"Quiet!" Neville called out in a harsh whisper. The

candle was suddenly extinguished and Dorothea felt
lost in the dark. She also felt like a thief in the night.

"Father."

"Hush, girl," he whispered, taking hold of both her
arms. "We don't want Temple to know we're on his
heels. If anyone were to discover us here, then Temple
would find out, and all would be lost, wouldn't it?"

Dorothea supposed he was right. Alastair must have
been in any number of difficult situations and known
how to extricate himself. This was no different.

They waited for a few long moments, then Alastair
helped her up the steps in the dark. They stood by the
door at the side of the church until he decided it was
safe, then opened it a few inches and gave her a nudge.

"I won't contact you unless something urgent
comes up," he said. "If you want to reach me—" he
thought for a moment "—just leave a note in the back
of your carriage. Neville or Paco will find it."

"But I—"

"It's all clear now," Alastair said, poking his head
outside. "Scoot back to your room, love. And do it
carefully."

Dorothea was quiet and distracted again, and Jack
wondered if she was coming down with something.
She didn't appear to be ill, but she sure was acting
differently this morning.

When he went out to hitch the horse to the carriage,
several of the village men were milling about, curious
but wary of the strangers. They asked a number of
questions about America, but Jack was eventually able
to turn the conversation to the cloth.

"Are there any stories about a Templar Knight
coming through here in ancient times?"

"Templar Knight?"

They knew nothing of the Templars or their role in protecting Christian pilgrims in the Holy Land. The sect had been disbanded five hundred years before, and it had been primarily a French order, though the Templars owned a number of properties in England.

"I've heard of such a thing," said one old fellow who was missing most of his teeth. "Well," he said, drawing out his words, "I don't think they called him that…Templar…but maybe."

"What did you hear?" Jack asked, anxious for any information at all. He hoped the old fellow wouldn't fabricate something just to impress a stranger.

"It was in the reign of Edward," the man said. "The first."

"Oh, aye," said another. "I remember, too. A monk it was, not a knight, though."

That was all right with Jack. The Templars were monks as well as knights, honest defenders of the pilgrims before greed and secrecy destroyed them.

"He was heir to a grand estate east of here," said the first man.

"How could that be, if he was a monk?" asked another.

"The story goes that he was wed, too."

"Then he *couldn't* have been a monk."

"Maybe he had a woman, but she wasn't his wife."

As they argued among themselves, Jack doubted he would learn anything useful here. At least he knew there'd been a mysterious character in the correct time frame, who'd wandered through here on his way to an estate farther east. That was where Jack and Dorrie were going, and the discussion here only confirmed that they were heading in the right direction.

"Thank you, gents," he said, leading the horse to the front entrance of the public house. He only had to collect Dorrie, and they would be on their way.

She came out of the building with the landlord's wife, smiling and talking cordially with the woman. Jack was unaccountably relieved that her mood did not seem to change when she laid eyes on him. In fact, he saw a spark of something that she quickly quelled.

Jack felt an odd wave of something he couldn't define when he looked at her, too.

They traveled all morning. By mutual agreement, they bypassed every castle ruin on the way to the coast. It was threatening to rain, and they agreed it would be best to get to Hornsea before the sky opened up. Jack was still somewhat worried about Dorrie, though she assured him she felt fine.

He felt certain that something was bothering her, but it was clear she wasn't inclined to discuss it with him.

After an hour's ride, Jack could smell the ocean and hear its waves, though it was a short while before they even arrived in town.

"There's a hotel," Dorrie said, pointing out the first place she saw.

But this was a resort town. Jack knew there would be lodgings closer to the water, and he wanted to stay somewhere picturesque. Something compelled him to find a unique place, unlike anything Dorrie had ever seen before.

He turned to look at her and felt a surge of arousal. She was leaning forward in her seat, taking in all the sights, her eyes gone round with delight.

"You act as though you've never been to the shore

before,'' he said in an attempt to subdue his unwelcome reaction to her.

"It's wonderful,'' she said. "Might we go down to the beach later?"

"Of course,'' he said. "Do you swim?"

"In the ocean?'' she asked.

"Lots of people do,'' he replied, even more puzzled about her than before. "Want to try it if the weather warms up?"

"I don't know how to swim,'' she replied. "My mother wouldn't allow... I just never had an opportunity."

Jack fully intended to pursue the conversation once they'd checked into a hotel. He drove all the way to the beach and saw exactly the kind of accommodation he'd hoped for. He turned and drove down the lane on which stood an elegant inn overlooking the sea.

There was a wide porch facing the water, and bits of color in the planters at the windows.

It was just the type of place Jack would bring a new wife—

He frowned at that ridiculous thought, then glanced at Dorrie: his adversary, his partner. She was the only woman who'd ever put such thoughts into his head, and he was going to make it stop. For all her starch and decorum, she was intensely attractive, beautiful, desirable. And she puzzled him, but that was all.

In all the time they'd spent together, he'd learned very little about her travels with her father and heard only vague references to her mother, whose recent death weighed upon her. She seemed to know practically nothing about her father's collection of ancient erotica, yet she had a facility with the antiquated languages that would be very useful to Alastair in his work.

"Oh, how lovely!" she said. "Jack, may we stay here?"

"I'll see what I can do," he replied. They turned their carriage over to a groom and entered the lobby of the Marine Hotel.

Dorothea tried to appear sophisticated, but the beautiful room, with its polished floors and beautiful rugs, the glossy desk and softly glowing lamps were beyond anything she'd ever seen before. Plush sofas and an ornate fireplace graced the far end of the lobby, where the members of a young family gathered their belongings for a trip onto the sand. The handsome young husband held a small child in one arm while he circled his wife's expanded waist with his other. A child of about four or five years dashed toward Dorrie.

"We're going to the beach!" she cried.

"Yes, I see," Dorothea replied, observing the small metal pail and shovel in the little girl's hands.

"And Daddy is going to make a sand castle," she continued. "While Mum gets a nap."

"How wonderful," Dorothea replied.

"Sorry," the young mother said as she took the child by the hand and cradled her ballooning belly with the other. "Our Sara is a mite outgoing, while Davy," she said, gesturing to the boy in his father's arms, "is rather too shy."

Dorothea smiled. "They're no bother," she said. "Lovely children."

With a quick thanks, the young couple took their children and headed toward the door. Dorothea pressed her hand against her abdomen and thought again of her father's words. Had it only been a few days ago that she'd imagined herself bearing Jack's child? Now she knew she would have difficulty with childbirth. Her dream—no matter how remote it had been—was shattered.

Honoria had never said anything to her about it, and Dorothea wondered if this condition had something to do with her weak heart. She'd never had any problems besides her restricted activities, and always believed she'd have a husband and children. She was planning on it with Albert Bloomsby, though the prospect of Albert as her husband had become less attractive with every day that she passed in Jack's company.

When a tear slipped from one eye, Dorothea quickly turned away and brushed it from her cheek, before Jack or anyone else nearby had an opportunity to notice.

Everything had changed since last night. Her father was not at all the proper academic her mother had led her to believe, and Dorothea learned that Honoria had kept a very important piece of information from her.

She could not have children.

"Adjoining rooms, if that's all right with you," Jack said, interrupting her thoughts. He picked up her hand and dropped a key into it while Dorothea schooled the expression on her face to betray none of the emotions flying through her.

"Perfect," she said, keeping her voice steady.

A man in livery carried their bags ahead of them. Dorothea's heart thudded heavily in her chest as she climbed the stairs to the second floor and followed the man into the first room.

Jack went to the far wall and pulled back the curtains, then opened the long windows that overlooked the sea. Dorothea was spellbound by the view. She had never seen anything to compare to the majesty of the ocean.

It seemed impossibly quiet to her, even though the sound of the surf was loud in her ears. Gulls flew overhead, then landed on the water or the sand, squawking at each other and the people who walked the beach.

"I'll be in my room next door," Jack said. "Why don't you get settled, and then we'll go find some lunch. I'm starving."

She nodded absently, then turned and watched him leave through the adjoining door. He closed it behind him.

The wind suddenly kicked up, making the curtains billow around her. Keeping the window open so that she could still see and smell the ocean, Dorothea stepped away from the window and sat down.

She could not think about her father's words now. When she saw him next, she would question what he knew of her condition, and if there was nothing more, Dorothea would write to Doctor Bates—the physician in Oxford who'd looked after her since childhood.

She had to know the truth of it, but the matter of the Mandylion had to be resolved, too. Her theory on where to look for the cloth was a good one. She knew it would be found in a castle somewhere near here— overlooking the sea or at least nearby. The search was not going to be easy, and Dorothea's conscience told her that it was time to part ways with Jack.

She could not pore over the map or key or search another castle ruin with him. Though he'd known from the start that she intended to work toward finding the cloth for her father, it felt altogether too unethical now, to stay with him. When she next met with her father, she would stay with him. That was where her loyalty had to stay, not with Jack.

"Ready?" Jack's voice accompanied a knock at the adjoining door, startling Dorothea out of her thoughts.

He had washed his face and combed his hair. He did not give her his usual easy smile but wore a slight frown when he came in.

Dorothea knew she'd been unusually quiet all morning. She had been so preoccupied by her thoughts and worries after her meeting with her father that she had hardly spoken to Jack at all. And now he was suspicious of her.

That would never do. She had to behave as if nothing had changed, at least until she was in contact with Alastair again and had somewhere else to go.

Yet the thought of leaving Jack brought no peace, either.

"The dining room is not serving," he said. "But the clerk offered to find us something to tide us over until tea."

"That sounds fine," she said. She started to walk past him, but he caught her arm.

"Dorrie."

He turned her to face him. "You have no idea what it takes for me to keep my hands off you," he said gruffly. "I want to lay you on that bed and kiss you until your mouth is swollen. I want to fill my hands with your breasts and bury myself so deep inside you that you'll know that you belong to me."

Dorothea felt her eyes fill and her face burn. If not for Alastair and the Mandylion, she would want these things, too. She would want Jack to love her and care for her and give her the children she'd always wanted.

But it could never be. And they both knew it.

"Once the Mandylion is safely locked up at the museum," he said, his voice tightly restrained, "there will be nothing to keep me from you."

Unable to speak, Dorothea swallowed and blinked back her tears. She bit her lip and nodded, certain that Jack meant everything he'd said.

However, she doubted he would still want her after she betrayed him.

Chapter Eighteen

A gentle rain fell while they lunched, but as soon as it cleared, Jack was determined to visit the ruins of an ancient castle that lay just north of Hornsea, near the water. It would be a distraction, at least.

Dorothea remained quiet, and any fool could see that she was upset, as much as she tried to hide it. Was it because of his promise to make love to her as soon as they resolved the Mandylion issue? She had been a willing participant yesterday, but she had to be having second thoughts now. Jack wondered if it wasn't frustration and confusion that was making her incommunicative.

It was clear that she'd never experienced anything like what had happened—or *nearly* happened, if Jack hadn't come to his senses in time. Even now, it took all his willpower to keep from taking her upstairs to his room and taking possession of her in the most primal way possible.

A man in hotel livery approached them, just as they were finishing the meal. "Mr. Adams?" he asked.

Jack nodded.

"One of the wheels of your carriage is cracked,"

the man said. "I thought I'd see if you'd like me to have it repaired for you."

Jack leaned forward. "Can you fix it here?" he asked. The man looked like a groom, not a mechanic.

"No, I'll send it over to Alf Tindall, in town," the fellow said. "He'll have it ready by tonight if you'll be needing the carriage."

"That will be fine, but I'll need a couple of horses this afternoon, if you have any for hire."

"Jack, I don't ride," Dorothca said.

"Just one, then," he said to the groom. That suited his purpose even better.

"I'm not staying here alone," Dorothea said after the man left.

"I didn't intend for you to stay behind."

"Well, then, how—"

"You'll ride with me," Jack interjected. "You've done it before." And he remembered every minute of that ride.

Dorrie started to protest but apparently thought better of it. She finished her tea and when Jack stood, she followed suit.

Though he was no closer to understanding what was bothering her, she carried herself proudly, as if to deny there was anything amiss. And he admired that.

Nothing was going to defeat Dorrie Bright.

"You have time to change into your plain skirt," he said when they reached the door of the lobby. "It'll be easier for riding."

She agreed and left him for a short while. When she returned, she seemed calm, composed and ready to go. They went outside and found one of the young men holding a sturdy roan mare, saddled and ready to ride.

"Here you are, Mr. Temple," the fellow said.

"She's used to the sand and the surf if you've a mind to ride the beach."

"Thanks," Jack said. He mounted, then turned to give Dorrie a hand up. With a mounting block and the groom's help, it was accomplished with greater delicacy than the last time he'd thrown her onto a horse's back.

She sat sidesaddle in front of him, and Jack slipped his arms around her, pulling her close. They rode to the path that led to the beach, and then headed north across the sand, wet from the storm.

"I thought all English country ladies learned to ride," he said.

"My mother would not allow it," she replied. He felt her body relax somewhat, as she became accustomed to the rocking movements.

"What about Alastair?" Jack asked. "Didn't he have anything to say about it?"

"I don't know what he would have said," she replied. "He wasn't there."

Jack urged the mare into a canter, and Dorrie wrapped her arms around his waist. She tucked her head under his chin, and when he pressed his lips to her hair, he was instantly aroused. He wanted her badly, though he was determined not to act on his insatiable hunger. At least, not now.

She turned her face to the wind, and he felt her breath catch. "This is wonderful!" she cried. "I feel as if I were flying!"

When he poked the mare into a full gallop, Dorrie twisted her body and pressed her back against his chest. She spread her arms like a gull on the wind and giggled with pure joy. It was not the reaction Jack had expected from her, but if he'd learned anything about

Dorrie Bright, it was that she never acted predictably. He hugged her to him and breathed in her scent.

At least the doldrums that had possessed her all morning were gone. Now, if only they could find something of value at Clyfton Castle, something besides crumbling rock and overgrown weeds, Jack would be satisfied.

"Look, Jack!" She pointed into the distance, where the rotting tower of Clyfton Castle was silhouetted against the gray sky. "Is that it?"

"Must be," he said, glad to have something to think of, besides Dorrie's soft bottom pressed against him.

He slowed the mare's gait and visually surveyed the area. This was his last chance to locate the Mandylion without additional help. If he saw anything that spurred a memory of something on the map or in the key, if there was any indication of a secret place, he would bring a shovel and do some digging on his own later.

If there was nothing, he would start asking questions in town and see if there were any stories about a lay brother, a Templar Knight or a sacred cloth hidden somewhere in the vicinity.

Jack dismounted after they'd ridden inside what had once been the castle's outer curtain. Dorothea leaned down and placed her hands on Jack's shoulders. He eased her down, but did not let go of her when her feet touched the ground. He closed his eyes and tipped his head so that his forehead touched hers.

His thumbs moved at her waist, and her breasts grew sensitive in anticipation of his touch. She cupped his face, taking his strong jaw into her hands. Her fingers moved over the rough whiskers, his lips.

He took one finger into his mouth.

Dorothea made a sound that was unfamiliar to her own ears and leaned into Jack. When she would have thrown her arms around him, he took hold of her hands and kept her from embracing him.

He started to speak, but changed his mind. Instead, he kept hold of one of her hands, then gathered the horse's reins and started walking. They went through what was once the great hall of the keep. The stone walls were relatively intact, and, although the floors were missing above them, various fireplaces were visible on the upper level.

A circular stone staircase led to the high tower.

Jack kept Dorothea's hand in his as they walked through the grass and weeds to the far end. "Abgar was king of Edessa in the first century," he said as Dorothea forced herself to quiet her shaky nerves. "It's said that he suffered from leprosy and that someone brought him a cloth bearing an imprint of the face of Christ."

She moistened her lips. "Was he cured?"

Jack nodded. "So the story goes. And in gratitude, a likeness of the face on the cloth was painted and displayed at the city gates."

"What happened to it?"

"Those were turbulent times," Jack said. "A pagan king followed Abgar. Then there were the Romans. The cloth was hidden away by whatever members were left of the Christian sect."

"How did it turn up again?"

"There are several different versions," Jack said. He poked his head into the stairwell that led to the tower but went no farther. "The most likely one is that it resurfaced in the sixth century during a flood or some other natural disaster.''

Still holding Dorothea's hand, Jack began to walk the inside perimeter of the keep, just as he had in all the other castles they'd visited.

''But it was taken to Constantinople several hundred years later.''

Jack nodded. ''There is documentation of its existence in the city, but when the Crusaders invaded, it disappeared again.''

''Only to resurface as the Shroud of Turin in France in the fourteenth century,'' she said. ''Except that you believe the Shroud is a different cloth.''

Jack kicked at a mound of dirt next to one corner of the hall. Then he let Dorothea's hand go and stepped back to study that part of the wall, from the ground to the uppermost edge of the second story. He shook his head.

''What?''

''Nothing here that I can see,'' he said. ''At least, nothing obvious. Which is why I'll have to go over all my notes and try to make an educated guess as to the most likely location.''

''Then what will you do?'' she asked. She was just as puzzled as Jack. She'd assumed that once she stepped inside the ruins of Clyfton Castle, she would know it was the Mandylion's hiding place. That she would somehow sense it. She'd been wrong.

Unless it wasn't here.

She thought again of the clues and knew with certainty that it was the rhyme written on the map that somehow pointed to the cloth's location. Nothing else was consequential, at least not in any way that she could see.

"I have a team of men—still in London," he said, "who will bring whatever equipment is necessary for an excavation."

"So you think the Mandylion is underground?"

"Not necessarily," Jack replied. "Look at these walls. They're stone, and they're thick. In Edessa, the Mandylion was hidden for centuries in one of the walls of the city. Why not here?"

"It would be poetic," Dorothea agreed.

"My men know how to search a site, without destroying it or covering up important evidence."

Dorothea wondered if the two men with her father also knew how to excavate a site. She assumed they had accompanied Alastair for that purpose, although they were no closer to discovering the Mandylion's hiding place than she was.

It looked as if she was going to have to tell her father that she had no useful information for him. However, she would not just leave him a note in the back of their carriage. She wanted to meet with him again and ask the questions she hadn't had the wherewithal to ask before.

"Come on," Jack said.

They walked back to the horse, and Jack lifted her up then mounted behind her. He wrapped his hands around her waist and turned the mare, returning to the beach. "Shall we ride some more?" he asked, his breath warming her ear.

"Yes!" she exclaimed, glad of the diversion.

Jack spurred the horse into a gallop, and they rode across the long expanse of sand. It was just as wonderful as before, and Dorothea delighted in the speed, the sense of freedom and the closeness to Jack. She placed her hands over his and turned her head slightly—just enough to meet his lips with her own.

The gait of the horse prevented a deeper contact, but Dorothea was warmed by that slight touch. They were not going to find the Mandylion.

There was nothing to give her father—no new clues, no information regarding the most likely castle ruin, no ancient cloth to turn over to him. Her adversarial relationship with Jack was finished.

Dorothea wondered if Jack realized that.

She leaned into his chest and closed her eyes. There was no reason they could not pursue this…attraction… between them. With so little experience with court-ship, all of it overseen by her mother, Dorothea did not really know what to expect.

She was not going to worry about it now. This moment was so perfect, she wanted to relish every bit of it.

They galloped across the sand as if they had all the time in the world. Dorothea knew nothing of Jack's plans or the responsibilities that awaited him, but she had nothing pressing to return to in London. As they rode into the wind, Dorothea wished she could remain this way forever, locked in Jack's arms, without a care in the world.

Eventually, Jack turned away from the beach. He made his way up past the hotel and into the center of town, where a large cross stood.

''Where are we going?''

''To church,'' he said.

They rode on until they reached a long, low building of ashlar and cobble. A crenellated tower rose from one end of the church, and a variety of headstones marked the ground in the adjoining yard.

Dorothea read the plaque. "Saint Nicholas Church."

"We might find something of use here," Jack said. He dropped to the ground and helped Dorothea down.

"Do you suppose the vicar will be here?"

"Let's go inside and see," Jack replied.

The interior of the church was dimly lit and apparently empty. They walked up the center aisle, and didn't see the old woman until they'd almost reached the sacristy. She was mopping the floor.

"Awk! You startled me!" she cried, dropping her mop. "Took a few years off my life," she added, tapping her chest.

"We're so sorry," Dorothea said. "We never meant to frighten you. It didn't look as if anyone was here."

"And what do you want at St. Nicholas's?" she asked. "Services have been long done."

"We're looking for the vicar," Jack said, bending to pick up the mop handle. "Is he here?"

"No, went home hours ago," she replied.

"Is the vicarage nearby?" Jack asked.

"Of course," she said and gave them directions.

It wasn't far, so Jack and Dorothea walked to the house. Clouds still hovered overhead, and a strong wind was blowing off the sea, but they'd had no more storm than the light rain that had come during lunch.

"The vicar might know something about our mysterious lay brother, or there may be old records stored somewhere in the church or the vicarage," Jack said. "It's the last thing I need to investigate before I decide what to do."

Dorothea hadn't thought about searching records.

"Were there any records for Holywake?" she asked.

"No," he answered. "I tried to get information at both Rievaulx and Holywake, but there was nothing left."

"Why do you think there's something here at St. Nicholas?"

He laughed. "I don't. Not really. But to be thorough, I'll go through the motions and see if there's a hint of anything useful."

The vicarage was a large, gracious home with a wide drive leading up to it. Jack tethered the horse, and he stepped up on the porch with Dorothea and knocked.

A few minutes later, a pretty woman answered the door. She was well dressed and carrying an infant. "May I help you?" she asked.

"Ma'am, I'm Jack Temple, and this is Dorothea Bright. We've come to see the reverend if he's available."

"Reverend Browning is in the garden, if you'll come this way," she said, allowing Jack and Dorothea into the house. "I'm Mrs. Browning," she said, turning to lead them through to the back. "My husband likes to spend his Sunday afternoons in the garden, reading or playing with the children."

"Very restful, I'm sure."

"Mr. Temple," she said, shifting the infant, "you're American?"

"Yes, ma'am. From New York."

They went out a door at the back of the house and found Mr. Browning sitting in a chair on the lawn, reading to a young boy in his lap. Two other children played with toy soldiers on the ground nearby.

"Dear," Mrs. Browning said, "Miss Bright and Mr. Temple have come for a...visit."

The men shook hands, and Dorothea listened as Jack told the vicar what he sought.

"Your children are beautiful, Mrs. Browning," Dorothea said wistfully. For a short while, she'd been able to forget her father's dire warning about child-bearing.

"Thank you," the woman replied. "They're a bit of a handful. Boys, you know. I'm just glad this one's a girl."

"Yes, she's very pretty."

As if she heard them talking about her, the infant became fussy and started to wail. Mrs. Browning shrugged, then begged Dorothea's pardon and left the garden, retreating to the house so as not to disturb her husband and his guests.

"At the vicarage?" Jack asked. He had sat down on one of the chairs near Reverend Browning, and the two were conversing as if they were old friends, recently reunited.

"Yes, boxes and boxes of old records," Mr. Browning was saying. "I've never gone through them, though. Couldn't see any point."

"No, I don't suppose there would be any reason for it," Dorothea remarked.

"Would you mind if Miss Bright and I had a look?"

"Now?"

"Whenever it's convenient," Jack replied easily. "We're in no rush."

"Well, I'd hoped you'd stay for tea. Marjorie!" he called toward the house.

"We wouldn't want to trouble you, Reverand Browning," Dorothea said. Her mother would have disowned her for arriving unannounced at teatime.

"Nonsense," he said. "We always have plenty. Marjorie!"

"Shall I see if she's in the kitchen?" Dorothea asked. "I hear the baby."

"Good idea, Miss Bright," he said. "I'm sure she's not far."

Dorrie approached the house and heard the baby's sporadic cries. Mrs. Browning's voice was audible as well, singing a bright tune as she soothed the child.

"Rumble, roar and crash away," she sang as Dorothea raised her hand to knock.

The next part of the song was inaudible as the baby screeched, but Dorothea clearly heard the woman sing the words, *"Though wee and tiny you may be, God's Angels will guard over thee."*

Her heart leapt into her throat. Was it possible that the nursery rhyme written on the map was a song?

"Rumble, roar and crash away, Wind and waves and autumn's haze. Mama will always stay with thee, 'Til flowers come with summer bees."

Dorothea swallowed her excitement and knocked.

Chapter Nineteen

"You'll be staying for tea, won't you?" Mrs. Browning asked pleasantly, rubbing her daughter's back. The baby's cries had turned into occasional whimpers, so it was possible to talk.

"Reverend Browning invited us, but I really—"

"No, now don't feel you must decline," Mrs. Browning said. "We will have plenty. We always do on Sundays." She murmured quietly to the baby and walked to the front of the house where there was a cradle. Gently laying the baby in it, Mrs. Browning let out a happy sigh.

"Their nurse has Sundays off," she said, joining Dorothea once again.

"All the more reason Mr. Temple and I should leave you in peace."

"I wouldn't hear of it," the vicar's wife said. "Truth be told, I've never met an American before, and I love his accent."

Dorothea smiled. She did, too.

"I heard your song just now," she said. "I don't believe I've ever heard it before."

"No, I don't suppose you would," Marjorie said,

taking plates from a cupboard. She placed three of them on a table in the kitchen, then took four more to the dining room. "It's an old song that originated with one of my ancestors. Whether she composed it or not, I'll never know, but it was handed down through the ages."

Dorothea felt she might faint. This was impossibly good fortune. Containing her excitement, she asked, "Was your family from Hornsea, then?"

"They were the lords of Clyfton," she replied. "My father was earl, but when my brother died in India, our male line ended."

"I'm so sorry," Dorothea said.

"More than six hundred years the Bretons were the earls of Clyfton," Marjorie answered wistfully. She brushed her hands on her apron. "Well, the title and estates wouldn't have passed to me or my children anyway."

"I'm fascinated by the song, though," Dorothea said. "Do you know how many generations have sung it?"

Marjorie laughed as she began setting food on the table. "Untold numbers, I'm sure. According to family lore, it was Lucy Breton who originated the song in the thirteenth century. Since she had at least eight children, I'm sure she would have made good use of the song while she raised them all at the manor."

"The manor?"

Marjorie paused dramatically and covered her heart with her hands. "A very romantic story. Lucy's husband was Alex Breton, brother of the Clyfton lord. Alex was returning home from the Crusades when he rescued Lucy from brigands on the highway. They fell in love, and he carried her off to his manor near Clyfton.''

''Does the house still stand?'' Dorothea asked, almost breathlessly.

''Oh, certainly,'' Marjorie replied. She leaned one hip against the table and looked into the distance. ''I hardly ever think of that old place. It's just north of the castle, right on the beach now, though I suspect it was a bit farther inland when it was built. Still, it's in ruins—the walls remain only because they're stone.''

Dorothea took the milk bottle from Marjorie and poured milk into the three cups at the table.

''The boys will have their tea in here,'' the vicar's wife said, ''and leave us to have a little peace.''

''You lived in Oxford with your mother?'' Jack asked as they rode back to the hotel. She had never mentioned it before, and he had been surprised to learn that she was not part of her father's household in London.

Dorrie nodded. ''My father was gone, and my grandfather let us use his house in Oxford.''

''But your mother died recently.''

''It's a long story, Jack,'' she said. ''Very dull.''

He doubted it, but she clearly did not want to speak of it. She burrowed into Jack's chest to share his heat. It had become quite cool while they were at the vicarage, and she had nothing more than her thin jacket to keep her warm.

Jack closed his arms around her and realized that his preconceptions about her had been wrong. Dorrie had not traveled the world with her father but had lived a sheltered existence in Oxford with her mother. He wanted to know why she'd left Oxford, and what she'd been doing at her father's house, why she felt such loyalty to a man who had to have been gone more than he was home.

He would get her to talk about it sometime, but he knew it wouldn't happen tonight.

"Reverend Browning's tale of the lay brother who came to Clyfton Castle from the Holy Land narrows things down nicely," he finally said. "I'll wire my men tomorrow and have them meet us here at Clyfton Castle. Since Mrs. Browning gave her consent to the excavation, we can begin work right away."

Jack understood that Dorrie wasn't enthusiastic about his discovery. It meant that he had the upper hand and was likely to take the Mandylion out from under her nose. There was nothing more that she could do.

And Jack wondered if she would stay to see him unearth it.

He ignored the sinking feeling in his chest when he considered finishing alone. She had been with him from the start, puzzling over the documents, picking away at stone and earth at countless ruins all across Yorkshire.

"I know you're upset, Dorrie," he said, "but it's for the best. Archibald Crowe…"

He blew out a breath of frustration. He didn't want to talk about the Mandylion now. He didn't want to hear her defend her double-dealing father or the great things Alastair would have done with the Mandylion had she gotten it first. He just wanted to hold her.

Jack had never experienced a more hollow victory. He would have the Mandylion, and his revenge against Alastair, but he could feel himself losing Dorrie. The closer they came to the hotel, the more distant she became.

He rode to the stable and dismounted, while one of the grooms jumped up from his bench and took the reins. "Mr. Adams, sir," he said. "Your carriage is repaired and ready for you."

"Thanks," Jack replied, assisting Dorrie down. "Appreciate it."

Jack took her hand and placed it in the crook of his arm, and they headed for the hotel. They climbed the stairs to the second floor, and Jack unlocked Dorrie's door. He had every intention of following her inside, but she turned, holding the door cleverly enough to stop his progress.

"Thank you, Jack," she said, "for taking me riding today. It was...I've never..." She stopped, and he watched the muscles in her throat work as she swallowed heavily. She seemed to be on the verge of tears, and Jack could not have felt worse if he'd been punched in the gut.

"Honey, it had to go one way or the other," he said, trying to be conciliatory. "I won't tell you that I'm sorry I'm going to take the Mandylion from Alastair, but I *am* sorry that you got caught in the middle."

He wanted to pick her up and carry her into the room and cover her face, her mouth with kisses. But when she bit her lip and looked away, Jack knew she wouldn't welcome his kiss. He couldn't blame her. For him, it would be a kiss of victory. For her, one of defeat. "I know, Jack," she said. "And I wish you the best. I..."

"Dorrie?"

"I think I'll turn in early," she said. "It'll be a long day tomorrow."

* * *

Dorothea dried her tears of frustration. It wasn't fair that she should be put in this position. Either she betrayed Jack or she betrayed her father. How was she to choose?

Pacing the length of her room, she tried to sort out her options, but no matter how she looked at it, she owed her loyalty to her father. It did not matter that she'd fallen in love with Jack.

Sitting down at the writing desk, she opened the drawer and took out pen, paper and ink.

"Father, I know where to look for the Mandylion," she wrote. *"It's—"*

Should she be so specific?

No. Someone other than Alastair might come across it. Anyway, she wanted to talk to her father again, ask him what else her mother had kept from her. She folded the paper and dropped it in the small wicker basket next to the desk and gave serious consideration to the wording of the note. *"I think I know where it is,"* she finally wrote. She considered adding more, but decided this was enough.

After waiting for the ink to dry, Dorothea folded the paper and slipped it into an envelope. It would be some time before it was late enough to venture out to the stable where she'd seen their carriage. Somehow, she would have to get past the grooms to slip the note into the back. Her father would have to do the same.

Resuming her pacing, she thought about her visit at the vicarage. She and Jack had stayed much too long, but the reverend and his wife had seemed to honestly enjoy their company. Charles questioned Jack at length about America and his travels. Marjorie wanted to know about life in Oxford.

And the old song that had been handed down through Marjorie's family had not been mentioned again.

Dorothea was torn between guilt and elation, and she wrung her hands as she paced. How could she betray Jack this way? In spite of everything, they'd developed an easy partnership, sharing clues and ideas, searching the old ruins together.

And he'd given her bluebells.

Tears trailed down Dorothea's cheeks as she opened her bag and reached to the bottom where she'd placed the carefully wrapped bouquet of flowers that Jack had given her. Whatever happened, she would keep these forever, for she doubted there would ever be another who would fill her heart the way Jack did.

She set them on her pillow and when she lay down next to them, she thought about the consequences her actions would reap.

A noise woke her.

Dorothea could not tell if it had been someone in the hall or if it was Jack in his room next door. She got up quickly and looked outside.

It was very late.

She went to the door between her room and Jack's and pressed her ear to it. There was no sound. Deciding that it would have to be now, Dorothea put her jacket on, placed the note in a pocket and opened her door.

It suddenly occurred to her that she would need some reason for going to their carriage in the middle of the night. She considered the problem for a moment, then went back and took her comb from the dressing table and placed it inside her jacket along with the note. Then she slipped silently out of her room.

Staying as far from Jack's door as possible, she headed toward the far end of the hall and went down a back staircase until she reached the main floor and a side door leading out of the hotel. She stepped outside and took a moment to get her bearings.

There were several paths, and Dorothea found the one that led to the far side, where the stable was located. Gas lights lit the entrance, and a single liveried groomsman was in attendance.

Seated on the bench with his arms crossed over his chest, he appeared to be asleep. Dorothea realized she would not need the ruse of searching for her comb in the middle of the night, after all. Stepping quietly, she moved past the man and went into the stable.

The horses were housed on one side, the carriages separately. She wandered through the shadows, taking care to stay quiet. All she had to do was find her carriage, drop the note in and sneak away. It should not be too difficult.

Another moment and she saw it. She deposited the note on the seat and scurried away. Ten minutes later, Dorothea was back in her room, and no one had even known she'd been gone.

Jack knew he should have stayed in bed. He couldn't remember the last time he'd been hungover, but he vowed never again to drink as much as he had last night.

His head pounded, and his stomach felt as if he'd swallowed an old shoe. The bright light of morning hurt his eyes and every sound went off like a cannon in his ears.

And he still hadn't been able to forget Dorrie's sad eyes when he'd left her in her room.

He was a bastard for beating her to the Mandylion, but there was nothing he could do about it now. He'd gotten the information he'd needed from Charles Browning, and there was nothing more to say about it. His men would come, and they would excavate until they found it.

Or decided that the cloth did not exist.

He washed and shaved and tapped on Dorrie's door. Since there was no answer, he went down to the dining room and found her finishing breakfast.

He ordered coffee.

"You're up nice and early," he said. "Did you— No, I guess you didn't sleep all that well."

Her skin was so pale that the circles under her eyes made her look like a raccoon. Certain that she wouldn't care to hear herself compared to a rodent, Jack said, "You're pale this morning."

She gave a quick nod. "I know," she said, and he was glad she didn't remark on the green tinge to his own complexion. "I...I had trouble sleeping."

"Yeah. So did I," he said. He reached across the table and took her hand. "Dorrie, let's call a truce. I want peace between us."

Her eyes held such a poignant sadness that Jack almost gave in to the urge to turn the Mandylion over to her. But he wouldn't. Not when Alastair Bright owed him so much, owed his men so much.

"Jack...I've made plans to return to London," she said. She took her hand from Jack's and kept her eyes on the plate in front of her.

It was not what he wanted to hear.

"You don't need me to translate anything else," she

continued, "and your men will be arriving soon, so you'll have all the help you need. I, uh, I'll only be in the way."

Ignoring the headache and the screeching in his ears, Jack stood abruptly, bringing Dorrie up with him. Gently, he pulled her out of the dining room and through the lobby until they reached the stairs. Then they continued on until they were inside Jack's room.

Without giving her a moment to think, Jack took her in his arms and kissed her because his life depended on it. He didn't want to lose her. He wanted Dorothea Bright in his life forever, even if she was Alastair's daughter.

"Jack!" she cried, pulling away to draw air into her lungs.

"Tell me you don't want me to hold you," he rasped, tasting the soft skin below her ear and tracing kisses down her neck. He eased her back against the wall and put his hands on either side of her head. He gave her enough space that she could move away if she wanted to do so. He didn't think she would. "Say you don't want my touch, my kiss."

She tipped her head to the side to give him better access, then slid her hands up his shoulders. Jack shuddered with the pleasure of her touch and the anticipation of a more intimate caress.

Her hands slid through his hair and she made a low sound of acquiescence.

"I want you, Dorrie," he said. "Forget about the cloth. This is about us and nothing else."

She dropped her hands and pushed him away. Tears welled in her eyes and she covered her mouth with one hand. "I can't forget, Jack," she whispered. "I only wish I could."

A second later, she ducked under his arm and went to the door without turning back.

When she walked through it, Jack wondered if it was too early to order a pint.

Chapter Twenty

Dorothea went directly to the beach. She had to pay a toll to walk along the north promenade, but she didn't care. She had to get away from Jack.

He was going to hate her. And she was too cowardly to stay here in Hornsea and face him after he learned that she'd given her father the real clue to the Mandylion. As soon as she met with Alastair again, she would ask for enough money to see her back to the house in London.

She wiped her eyes again with her handkerchief and continued along, half running, oblivious to everything...the scenery, the fashionably dressed people. None of it mattered.

"Been keepin' an eye out fer you, miss," said a masculine voice, coming to her from behind. She started to turn, but he said, "Keep lookin' straight ahead. It's me, Neville. I'm here to take y'to yer father. We got yer note."

Dorothea's breakfast threatened to rise in her throat. This was it. The betrayal. She'd put it in motion during the night when she'd left the note for Alastair to find, and now she would complete it. Soon she would be on her way to London and would never see Jack again.

"We've got a ways to go yet," Neville said. "Just keep movin'."

There were fewer people once they left the promenade, and as they moved farther north, there was no foot traffic at all. Neville kept pressing her to a faster pace, which made Dorothea short of breath.

By the time they left the promenade, her heart pounded heavily in her chest. She felt palpitations and knew that her heart was not keeping up with her activity.

"I don't understand why we must rush!" she said in frustration.

"Just keep on," the man behind her said.

She began to feel nauseous, light-headed and uneasy with Neville. He might be her father's man, but his eyes were cold. Untrustworthy. The sooner she got to her father, the better. She would have a word with Alastair about the kind of men he employed, both here and in London. They were disrespectful and slack in their duties.

They continued north, hurrying in the direction of Clyfton Castle, where she and Jack had ridden the day before.

How she wished they'd kept on riding and had never heard of the Brownings.

Neville came up beside her and took her arm to keep her moving. Dorothea noticed that he repeatedly glanced back in the direction of the hotel, though it was no longer in sight. His movements were furtive and suspicious, and Dorothea became increasingly uncomfortable. "I need to rest a moment," she said.

"Al's got a wagon up ahead," Neville said. "Keep goin'."

His tone was harsh, and Dorothea felt as if she were on some sort of forced march. She was unaccustomed to moving at this pace and knew that if she continued, she would collapse. She now had proof that her heart was as weak as her mother had always told her.

"Come on, get movin'," he said, shoving her. "We ain't got all day."

She saw it then. A rough wooden wagon partially hidden in a stand of brush, a good distance up from the beach. Her father and the man he called Paco were sitting in it, waiting.

She stopped and placed one hand over her pounding heart. Her breath was coming in short wheezy spurts, and she didn't know if she could make it as far as her father's wagon. "Wait!" she gasped. "I...can't..."

"Come on, girl," Neville said. He took Dorrie's arm again and gave a tug, but she lost her balance and fell into the sand.

"Stand back, mon."

Alastair's large companion had come over to assist her. Dorothea had been frightened of him once, but he redeemed himself by bending down and picking her up. Then he carried her all the way to the wagon. Dorothea still had trouble catching her breath. She couldn't remember ever feeling so helpless or so weak.

Of course, she'd never stormed off in such a frame of mind before, unaware of her surroundings or her frantic pace. Her mother had been right about limiting her activities. Dorothea could barely tolerate a brisk walk.

"There you are," Alastair said as Paco set her in the back of the wagon beside an assortment of tools.

"You've got the heart of an old woman, love, just as your mother said."

Dorothea would have gasped at her father's cruel words if she'd been able to catch her breath.

"I just...need to rest..." she finally managed to say, slumping down in the wagon.

"Your note said you know where it is," her father said. "I presume you meant the Mandylion."

"Yes," she wheezed. She did not have enough breath to go into detail about her reasoning. If only she could rest, she was sure she would feel better. "There is a house... It's north of...Clyfton Castle." Her heart still fluttered heavily in her chest. If only it would slow down, beat more normally....

"Go on," Alastair said.

"The man who...owned the house...came from... the Holy Land," she said. "Hundreds of years... There is a song...written on the map...."

"The French rhyme?" her father asked.

Dorothea nodded. "His wife's song."

"And you believe that's the clue?" Alastair asked.

Dorothea nodded. "Nothing else...I translated it all... There was nothing."

Alastair looked skeptical. Dorothea could see him mentally weighing his options as he gazed out at the sea.

"And what about Temple?" he asked.

"He believes...it's here...Clyfton Castle," Dorothea said, still struggling for air. Once she told her father what she'd discovered, perhaps she could persuade him to take her to a physician. "Jack...doesn't know...song was from the house...not the castle."

"Let's go," Alastair finally said.

"But, Father..."

There was an overgrown track that led past the castle ruins she had visited the day before with Jack. Alastair ignored her plea and drove the wagon several more miles until they reached a much smaller pile of stone walls. Dorothea continued to struggle for breath, and now that she was resting, she improved marginally. Perhaps she did not need a physician after all.

"Is this it?"

Dorothea shrugged. "I think it must be," she said.

Alastair jumped down and walked around the broken-down walls. He spoke quietly to Neville and Paco, who both followed. From her place in the wagon, Dorothea could hear him analyzing the site aloud.

Her mother had been right about him. Alastair really was a learned man. He talked about the stone and mortar and the style of house it had been, based on the configuration of the walls. He walked the length of the building, testing the soil beneath his feet, looking for remaining traces of the structure.

After a word about support beams, he pointed toward the spot that would have been the center of the house. The wind shifted suddenly, carrying his voice away, so Dorothea could no longer hear what he said to the men. She closed her eyes and lay back against the side of the wagon and willed her heart to slow.

She wished she did not feel like such a traitor to Jack. This *had* to be the right thing to do. Jack would move on to his next expedition and Dorothea had to live with her father. Or, at least, in her father's house.

She'd been right to leave Jack. Even if there had been no Mandylion, no betrayal, Dorothea had no doubt that Jack would begin to resent her when she proved incapable of the most basic physical exertion.

She would never be able to hike into the ruins of anything more challenging than the few castles they'd visited in York.

Maybe not even that, she thought, remembering how she'd felt after walking all over Rievaulx and then climbing the hill that overlooked it. Sadly, she admitted she would never be able to keep up with Jack. She was doomed to a dull and sedentary life in that dismal house of her father's.

When she looked up again, there were short posts in the ground, and the men had strung twine between them, forming a grid. They were digging now, all three of them, in separate squares. Dorothea did not know how Alastair had decided where to dig or if he thought he would actually find the Mandylion this way. She had to assume, however, that her father had the knowledge and experience to follow the right course.

And then it occurred to her that he did not have permission to dig on Mrs. Browning's property.

Dorothea frowned. Jack had made quite an issue of the Brownings' permission, to the point of having them sign a document stating their consent. Shouldn't Alastair do the same?

She tried to call out to him, but her voice was weak and he did not hear her. Or he chose not to hear.

Since she could do nothing about it now, Dorothea leaned back and closed her eyes again. She was breathing more easily now, and her racing heart seemed to have settled down. With luck, she would feel fine after resting awhile.

Rain woke her. Judging by the amount of digging that had occurred, Dorothea estimated that she must have slept for hours. The afternoon had turned cool, and there was a brisk wind coming off the ocean.

She shivered and watched as dirt continued to fly out of deep holes. Wouldn't the men climb out and look for shelter from the rain?

Dorothea looked up at the sky. The last time she had been caught in the rain, she'd been with Jack. And he had found them a warm and dry place to stay.

Deciding that perhaps her father hadn't noticed the rain, Dorothea managed to climb out of the wagon. She walked to the place where the old house once stood and stepped over some broken rock. Mindful of her footing, she went to the first mound of dirt and looked in.

Paco stood in a hole that was just slightly deeper than his height. He was intent upon his digging, so Dorothea moved on to the next mound.

She discovered Neville, tapping at what appeared to be a solid stone wall beneath ground level. Curious, she remained standing in the light rain, shivering, looking down at him as he worked.

The wall seemed to be solid. Dorothea readily admitted that she knew nothing about it, but wondered if perhaps it was so well preserved because it had been under the ground. Was it a section of one of the main rooms or part of a cellar?

She moved on and found her father digging just opposite Neville. Facing the other man's site, Alastair had cleared the other side of the wall, and was prodding at it with a small pick.

"Father?" she called.

Alastair did not respond.

Dorothea called louder and got him to look up at her.

''What is it?'' he asked, giving her only a moment's attention. He turned quickly back to his work.

''You probably haven't noticed, but it's raining.''

He kept on tapping.

''Father?'' she said again. ''I'm getting soaked.''

She thought she heard grumbling, but he eventually looked up at her. ''There's a tarpaulin in the back of the wagon. Get back in there, pull it over you and you'll stay dry enough.''

Dorothea stood there for a moment longer, wondering if she'd heard him correctly. Perhaps her earlier exertion had made her more light-headed than she thought. She could not imagine that her father wanted her to stay out in the cold and rain, with a filthy old canvas tarpaulin pulled over her.

''Father?'' she called down to him again.

He squinted up at her and spoke sharply. ''Look, girl. I haven't the time for your troubles. Go on and leave me to my work.''

Stunned by his words and the rudeness with which they were delivered, Dorothea retreated. She backed away from the deep holes dug by the three men and tripped over a tool, sprawling on her bottom in the mud.

Somehow, she managed to get back on her feet. She held her hands out in the rain to rinse them, then hobbled back to the wagon in her ruined clothes and her mud-caked shoes. This was not at all what she had envisioned when she placed her note in the carriage the night before.

Thoughts of Jack crossed her mind, but Dorothea forced her attention to the situation at hand. She could not afford to think of him now. She had to get out of the rain, or she would suffer a chill, and there would be no Jack Temple to warm her in a cozy bed.

The tarpaulin was neatly folded and rested on the wagon floor, under a heavy wooden box. Luckily, it was mostly dry. Dorothea climbed into the soggy wagon bed and pushed the box off it. The canvas was heavy and unwieldy, but she managed to open it and tent it over herself while she waited for her father and the men to finish for the day.

Surely they would not continue much longer in this rain. Besides, it would be dark soon, and they would not be able to see what they were doing.

By midafternoon, Jack was worried.

Dorrie had not come back to her room, unless she was purposely not answering. He picked the lock on the door that adjoined their rooms and glanced in to assure himself that she truly was not there.

At least she hadn't left for London. He knew she had only a few coins with her. Her bag remained in its place on the stand in the corner, and her spare dress was hanging in the small closet.

But where had she gone?

There were plenty of places she might be, and Jack decided he would check them all. He went down to the beach and visited all the little shops nearby, then headed back into town to see if she had taken herself off on a long walk.

When it started to rain and Dorrie was still missing, Jack figured she must have gone to visit the Brownings. They were the only people in town that she knew, and it was obvious she would stay there until the rain stopped.

He quit worrying for a while and went down to the

hotel desk to see if a wire had arrived from O'Neill or any of his other men.

The message had been succinct. They would arrive on Wednesday or Thursday. There was no word about O'Neill's condition or whether he would be joining the group, but at least Jack knew they would come ready to excavate.

The rain continued and Jack remained in the lobby, waiting for it to pass. He managed to refrain from pacing but kept an eye on the main entrance of the hotel. He also watched the ocean through the front windows and refused to entertain any thoughts about Dorrie and the sea.

Hadn't she told him she did not swim? If he remembered correctly, Dorrie had not been allowed to swim, and the thought gave him some measure of calm. She was sensible enough to stay away from the water.

One hour passed, then another. The rain did not let up, and Dorrie did not appear. Jack could wait no longer.

He made his way to the stable and hired a horse. Impatiently waiting for the groom to saddle the same mare he'd ridden with Dorrie the day before, he finally mounted and was off, riding through the streets of Hornsea until he reached St. Nicholas's Church.

He encountered Reverend Browning, staying reasonably dry under a large black umbrella.

"Why, Mr. Temple!" Browning called out. "What are you doing out in this?"

"I was on my way to the vicarage," Jack replied.

"Come with me to the church," the minister said. "Dry off a bit. Maybe I can scare up a cup of tea for you."

Jack dismounted and walked alongside the man. "Sorry, Reverend, I've only come to ask if Miss Bright is at the vicarage."

"Why, no," Browning replied. "Nasty day to be out and about, don't you think?"

Jack nodded, though he barely noticed the rain. His thoughts were too intent upon finding Dorrie. "I thought she might have gotten out of the rain at your place."

"Not today," the reverend said. "Perhaps in one of the cabanas alongside the hotel?"

"I'll check," Jack said. "Thanks, Reverend."

"Let me know if there's anything—"

"No, I'm sure she'll turn up soon, nice and dry in some corner of the hotel where I haven't looked."

He'd spoken with a lot more confidence than he felt. She'd been upset with him when she'd gone off, and she was clearly not anxious to be found. He'd tried to force her affections, and he wasn't proud of that. Still, he hadn't believed he'd need too much force.

Turned out he was wrong.

A short while later, Jack returned to the stable soaked and in a foul temper. He hadn't been able to find Dorrie anywhere.

"Do you have a private parlor in the hotel?" he asked the clerk. If Dorrie had been sitting in a nice cozy spot while he scoured the town....

"Yes, sir," the man replied. "On the third floor, opposite ends of the hall. Both rooms have lovely seaside views."

Jack bounded up the stairs and heard the sound of a piano playing in the distance. He bypassed the young couple with the pregnant wife and their two children and headed for the third floor, toward the music. Moving quickly down the hall, he went all the way to the end and entered the room.

A young lady was playing the piano, while several hotel guests passed the time playing cards and listening to the music. Dorothea was not among them.

A quick visit to the other parlor and Jack was certain she was not in the hotel. Puzzled, he returned to his room and wondered for the hundredth time where she would have gone.

He let himself into her room again and stood by the window with his hands on his hips, looking out. He had to assume that Dorrie had not checked out and returned to London, unless she'd left without her belongings. Crossing to the other side of the room, Jack opened her bag and lifted out the few items inside.

Her nightgown, drawers and stockings…something enclosed in paper at the bottom. Carefully pulling it out, he set it on the bed and peeled the paper away.

The package contained the flowers he'd given her.

Jack sat down on the edge of the bed. He knew he hadn't been wrong about her feelings for him. He had sisters. He knew there was only one reason that a beautiful woman made a keepsake out of a bunch of lousy weeds.

She was in love with him.

He stood abruptly and started pacing. *Then where the hell was she!*

The rain gave no sign of slowing, and Jack knew it was time to involve the local magistrate. For some reason, Dorrie was not able to get back to him. He doubted there was reason to suspect that anything was wrong, other than that she was stranded somewhere and could not get back, but he would not risk her safety.

He gathered up the flowers and put them back in the paper, then set them carefully in Dorrie's bag. Then he brushed the few torn leaves into his hand and dropped them into the wicker basket next to the desk.

One sheet of paper was in the basket, and Jack had no qualms about picking it up. Perhaps she'd started a note to him but changed her mind.

His stomach burned when he unfolded it and read the message to her father.

Chapter Twenty-One

It had been hours since Dorothea had huddled herself under the heavy canvas. She was wet and covered with mud. She was so cold she could not feel her feet and shivering so badly she could hardly catch her breath.

She hovered between a drowsy wakefulness and unconsciousness, continuously struggling with every breath to draw air into her lungs. At times, she thought she heard Jack's voice, and she tried to call out to him, to tell him she was there, in the wagon.

If he ever heard her, he didn't come and get her out from under the tarpaulin.

Dorothea should have felt better after the rain stopped, but it got no warmer, and she could feel the wind as it blew over the canvas. There were times when she thought she would suffocate under there.

When she heard voices again, they were accompanied by the clang of tools being thrown in the back of the wagon. Something hit her leg, and she cried out. There were quiet mutterings, and Dorothea cringed when she heard a curse or two. Someone pulled at the tarpaulin, and she was suddenly fully exposed to the cold night air.

The three men looked like coal miners in the light of their lanterns. They were covered in black mud, but Alastair and Neville were grinning in spite of it. The man called Paco wore no expression at all, as usual.

"You were right, missy," Alastair said, raising a long metal tube into the air. In Dorothea's dazed state, he looked like a victorious warrior, holding the spoils of battle. "You figured out the puzzle, and now we have it!"

"You...?"

"What did I tell you, eh?" he jabbed Neville with an elbow. "Didn't I say she'd be useful?"

"The Mandylion?" she asked, feeling faint, confused. She thought the Mandylion was a cloth—not an ornately etched shaft of silver. "May I..."

"Why not?" Alastair asked rhetorically. "You were the one who told us where to look—you may do the honors."

Alastair handed it to her.

The silver sheath felt strangely warm in her hands. Reverently, she ran her fingers across the scrollwork and energy pulsed through her.

Alastair scowled and grabbed the end of the silver rod. He worked at it, twisting and pulling, but was unable to do whatever it was that he intended.

"Paco," he said impatiently, "do what you can."

Dorothea did not let go while Paco worked on the end. She held it steady for him, every bit of her strength centered on her hands. When finally a cap of some sort came off with a harsh squeak, she jerked back and landed on the wagon bed with the silver scroll in her hands.

"It's inside," Alastair said, paying no heed to his daughter's fall.

With two fingers, she reached into the tube and felt heat. Warmth spread through her fingers and into her hand, then down her arm. The chill suddenly left her bones, and she stopped shivering.

Pulling at the cloth rolled within, Dorothea slipped it out of the beautiful tube. She closed her eyes and pressed it to her breast before opening it. There were voices—angry, impatient voices—clamoring at her to unroll the cloth, but Dorothea barely heard them. She was filled with a peace and sense of well-being that she had not had since she was a child. Since before the illness that had damaged her heart.

After several moments, she knelt and took a deep breath. She held the cloth by the edge and gently unrolled it, keeping it close to her body.

"That's it, by God!" Neville asserted. "Look at that face! Just like y'said, Al."

Alastair did not comment but trained his gaze on the cloth that draped his daughter from bosom to knee. It was made of heavy linen and was yellow with age, frayed at the edges. A hazy brown imprint covered the center of the cloth, giving the impression of a man's face.

Dorothea knew it was the true Mandylion. Jack had been right.

Paco grabbed the cloth from Dorothea's hands and rolled it up. Quickly, he shoved it into the silver rod. "You not put eyes on dat. Very powerful. Very dangerous."

Neville's eyes widened as Paco thrust the tube with the cloth under the tarp beside Dorothea.

"We go now. Turk comes in morning," Paco said. "We trade cloth for pounds."

Dorothea was not sure she understood the man. His

English was heavily accented, and he spoke rapidly, making it difficult to decipher his speech. But she was sure he said they would receive pounds for the cloth. Pounds of what? And who was Turk? One of Queen Victoria's men?

She was breathing much easier now, and when Neville finished hitching the horse to the wagon and they all jumped on, she realized she felt comfortably warm, too. She was still wet and covered with mud, but it didn't seem so bothersome now. Glancing at the sky, Dorothea realized the storm must have passed. That was surely the reason she felt so much better.

"Where exactly will Zengui be?" Neville asked. "And will he have the money wi—"

"Stow it," Alastair hissed. "We'll talk later. I don't want..." He gestured with his head and shoulders, and Dorothea could not tell if he meant it as a shrug or if he was indicating that he didn't want her to hear what Neville was going to say.

She had a suspicion that it was the latter.

Dorothea settled into a corner of the wagon bed and drew her legs under her, thinking that perhaps, if they didn't notice her, they would forget she was there and speak freely again. But they rode on for quite a distance in silence.

When the wagon stopped, Neville jumped down and told her to get out. Paco got out of the wagon and pointed to a steep hill. "We go there," he said.

Dorothea groaned inwardly. She knew she could not make it, especially after the night she'd had. Her heart had beat erratically and, just as her mother had predicted, she had suffered the ill effects of too much exertion. She *did* feel better at the moment, but she knew that the terrifying hunger for air could easily return.

Alastair did not seem to have much patience for her weakness and did not even glance her way as he drove the wagon up the steep path.

"Come on, girl," Neville said harshly. "Ain't got all night."

The moon was a bare sliver in the sky, and its light was frequently obscured by clouds. Somehow, though, Dorothea managed to follow the men up the hill without falling and rolling all the way back down. The others were well ahead of her by the time she reached the top. At that point, she was able to follow the light that emanated from the broken windows in a battered old house.

She approached it warily, carefully pushing the door open. The house had obviously been abandoned for many a generation and was little more than a hovel on a hill. Dorothea tried not to judge her father by these surroundings, but she was beginning to think that Jack might not have been entirely mistaken about Alastair.

He kept company with two ruffians, and he dug up the ancient manor house in the dead of night and without permission.

It didn't seem right, but perhaps it was difficult to find men who would leave their homes and travel all over the world so that Alastair could pursue his quest for ancient treasures. Perhaps her father was no happier about the men who worked for him but had had to settle on these two out of necessity.

"You'll want to bed down in the back," Alastair said. "There's still a blanket in there, isn't there, Nev?"

The other man nodded, and Alastair tipped his head toward the room, gesturing her into it.

"Father," she said. "I'd hoped to ask you... You spoke of things my mother told you—"

"Go on, girl," Alastair said brusquely. "Out of here while I make some plans."

Chagrined at being brushed off so easily, Dorothea retreated into the other room. She found a blanket on the rotted floor and wrapped it around her shoulders, though she wasn't cold. She supposed she did it out of habit more than anything, and then it occurred to her to wonder why she did not feel cold. Nor was she short of breath.

She placed her hand on her heart. It was beating normally, without palpitations, as she would have expected after such exertion.

It was strange. Dorothea should have felt awful, but she did not. She felt strong and healthy, as if there was no obstacle she could not overcome.

She glanced around the dark room and saw no furniture. There was a dankness to the place that made Dorothea's skin crawl, but she knew she could do nothing until her father finished with his men. Then she would ask him what she needed to know.

They kept their voices low in the other room, and their furtive tones made the hairs on the back of Dorothea's neck rise. She crept closer to them in order to hear what was being said and considered herself fortunate that the floor was mostly dirt and did not creak.

"—too sickly to bother with us," she heard her father say. "She won't be a problem."

"Then we get the cloth to Salim Zengui tomorrow, and he pays us right away," Neville said. "We don't wait for any middleman, agreed?"

"Nine thousand pounds," said Paco, his voice deep and curt. "In three parts, Bright."

"Three *equal* parts," added Neville.

"All right, all right," her father said in a harsh whisper. "You'll get your money. And we won't hand over the cloth until the Turk pays up. Satisfied? We take the cloth down to the cove—wave a torch. Zengui will send a boat."

"He better have the cash on his little boat, or he won't be seein' no cloth."

"I promise you, he will," Alastair said. "I've dealt with him before."

Dorothea could not believe her ears. Jack had been right all along. Her father was exactly the rascal Jack described.

"Dis cloth have power," Paco said. "Zengui... He will burn it."

"He can hang it in his privy for all I care," Neville said. "I just want my money. It ain't been no garden party, chasin' after Temple all week and then diggin' half the night in the rain."

"You're lucky we didn't have to dig for a week," Alastair said. "*I'm* the one who knew where the wall would be. *I'm* the one who pointed us in the right direction."

"Not until yer brat figured out the clues."

Thoroughly disgusted, Dorothea considered confronting them all at once, but realized that was a foolhardy notion. These men intended to make a great deal of money with the sale of the Mandylion and would not take Dorothea's interference lightly.

She wished Jack were here to help her figure out what to do. Somehow, she had to get the cloth back and into Jack's hands. Perhaps then he would forgive her for being such a blind, trusting idiot. She felt sick about the way she had defended her father while she doubted Jack's story. All her life, she had trusted everything her mother had told her, including the stories about Alastair.

Obviously, Honoria had known Alastair well, but had kept the truth to herself. It wasn't just his wanderlust that had made them incompatible. Her mother must have been aware of Alastair's chicanery and refused to live with it.

Unfortunately, she had been less than candid with Dorothea, who wondered what other things Honoria had kept from her.

Retreating into the back room, Dorothea sat on the floor. She raised her knees and laid her head on them, pretending to doze. If her father happened to come in, she wanted him to believe she'd been asleep all through their discussion. She did not fear any reprisal from Alastair, but she was not so certain about the other two men. To Dorothea, they did not seem like fine, upstanding Englishmen.

Unfortunately, neither did her father.

A couple of very long, uncomfortable hours passed and Dorothea finally heard the sound of snores coming from the other room. She stood up, dropped the blanket and stretched to get the blood flowing in her arms and legs.

She crept toward the front of the house and listened for any sounds besides those that would be made by sleeping men. When she dared, she peeked around the corner.

In the faint light coming in through the window, she saw that all three were lying on the floor. Her father snored loudly, while Neville's snores were much quieter. Paco made no sound, and Dorothea stood watching him for several long minutes to assure herself that he was asleep before she ventured into the room.

She was going to run away, but not until she found the Mandylion to take with her.

It was next to Alastair. He lay flat on his back, with one arm folded over his chest, the other at his side. The silver rod lay beside him, within easy reach of his hand, and Dorothea knew that he must have fallen asleep holding it.

Silently, she moved toward him, afraid to breathe.

She closed her hand around the ornate silver shaft and felt the same heat as before. Confidence welled in her heart, and she slipped away as quietly as she'd come in. Without a sound, Dorothea returned to her place in the back room. She did not attempt to leave through the main door, because she remembered it had stuck when they'd first come in and was likely to be stuck now. One push and everyone would awaken.

There had to be some other way out.

She closed her eyes and took a few deep breaths, forcing herself to stay calm. She was not trapped here. There was a way out. Perhaps she could crawl through a broken window or a rotted door somewhere.

Dorothea only knew that she had to get back to Jack, and she wanted to take the Mandylion with her.

Somehow, she was going to have to search the house for an exit. All the windows in the back room were broken, with edges of jagged glass protruding from the window frames. Dorothea attempted to raise the sash, but the wood would not budge.

Carrying the Mandylion, Dorothea took a few steps toward the room in front. A short passage led to another room on the opposite side, and she decided to explore it.

Moonlight shone in, better than in the other rooms, and Dorothea examined each of the windows. Only one was passable, but not without some danger of being cut. Dorothea returned to the other room and picked up the blanket she'd thrown around her shoulders. She wrapped one hand with the thick wool and took hold of the longest piece of glass. Closing her eyes, she held on tight.

It seemed as if her heart stopped when the snap of the glass reached her ears. She did not know if the sound woke anyone but wasted no time in climbing out through the window. She landed heavily on the wet ground outside and did not stop. She gathered her skirts in one hand, the Mandylion in the other and ran.

It occurred to Dorothea that she had the strength of a healthy woman as she ran. Her heart pumped, her lungs took in air. Nothing was amiss as she exerted herself far beyond anything she'd ever done.

Yet just a few short hours ago, she had lain in the wagon bed under a filthy canvas tarpaulin in desperate distress. Her heart would not slow, and she had felt as if she were drowning. Now she felt renewed. Whole.

She pressed the Mandylion to her breast and kept running. The steep hill she'd climbed earlier was difficult to descend, but with care, she made it to the bottom. She could hear the ocean next to her and knew she was on the right path. Following the sound of the surf, she continued running in a southerly direction and knew that she could keep on running as long as it took, to get back to Jack.

If necessary, she would kneel and beg his forgiveness. She had been stupid to offer her loyalty so blindly to Alastair, especially when she knew how honorable and ethical Jack Temple was. He had taken special care of her, even though she'd insulted him and insinuated that he was no more than a scoundrel who wanted to cheat her father out of his rightful prize.

Never again would she question his character, his honor. He had proven a hundred times over that he was a virtuous, reputable man, and Dorothea loved him. And if he would allow it, she would be honored to join Jack on his future expeditions.

A loud crack behind Dorothea made her turn to see what had made the sound. It was Paco, and he was not far behind. The turn threw her off balance, and she fell to her knees.

Quickly scrambling up, she started to run again, but he grabbed her. "You don' take what's Paco's," he said.

He raised his hand to her and then everything went black.

Chapter Twenty-Two

Jack stood looking at the ruins of Clyfton Castle and wondered why Dorothea and her father weren't here. With Jack in direct competition for the rights to excavate the site, he could not understand why Alastair was not here already, staking his claim.

Gazing out at the sea in the distance, he had to admit that he had never given Dorrie any reason to believe he was a better man than her father. For all she knew, Jack was an adventurer just like Alastair, a man with no roots, no loyalties beyond his next acquisition and the money it would bring him. He should have told her the truth. His university credentials would have proved that he was a reputable man.

Jack mounted his horse and rode back toward the hotel, then changed his mind and took the path that went into town. Dorrie knew that he had received exclusive permission from Marjorie Browning to excavate the castle site. Either Alastair planned to wait until Jack and his men unearthed the Mandylion so that he could steal it from him, or there was another site that Jack did not know about.

It was much too early to visit the vicarage, but Jack

didn't see that he had any choice. He'd been up all night, worried about Dorrie. By her own admission, she did not know Alastair.

But Jack did. And he didn't trust the old scoundrel to take care of her.

The front door of the vicarage opened and a matron, wearing a dark blue gown and a crisp white apron appeared. "Yes, sir?" she asked politely.

"I know it's early, but…would Reverend Browning or Mrs. Browning be available?"

"Why, the Reverend has already left for church, sir," the housekeeper said. "Mrs. Browning is taking her breakfast with the children."

The cumbersome etiquette required was frustrating, and Jack wanted to ignore it all and storm past the woman to find Marjorie. Instead, he said, "Would you ask if she will see me? I'm Jack Temple. It's urgent."

"Please wait here," the woman said, ushering Jack into the foyer of the house.

A few minutes later, Jack was shown to the kitchen, where Marjorie sat with the three boys and their nurse, while the baby lay in her cradle nearby.

"Why, Mr. Temple!" Marjorie said. "It's so pleasant to see you. Mrs. Delwood said there was something urgent?"

Jack remained standing, even though a chair was offered. "Mrs. Browning—Marjorie," he said. "During our visit the other night, we discussed your property—"

"To which do you refer, Mr. Temple," she asked. "The manor house or Clyfton Castle?"

Jack knew nothing of a manor house, but it was the most promising lead he had yet.

"The manor house."

"Oh, well," she said. "Can you not stop for a cup of tea, Mr. Temple? There's—"

"No, no thanks," Jack said, placing all of his effort into being civil. "What about the manor house?"

"Well, Miss Bright was fascinated by the story of my ancestors who settled there."

"She didn't mention it to me."

"That's strange," Marjorie said. "She was quite taken by the song, and the story of the lay brother who returned from the Holy Land—"

"What song?"

"Just an old children's song that's been in my family for centuries. A few of us—cousins and such—still sing it to our children."

"How does it go?"

Jack saw Marjorie's cheeks color. "I'm not much of a singer, Mr. Temple. Freddie, sing the Rumble song for Mr. Temple."

Two of the boys began. *"Rumble, roar and crash away...."*

Jack listened to the rest and made the same connection Dorrie must have done. The castle was not the place at all. It was the manor house.

"Marjorie, where is the manor where this song originated?"

"Oh, it's just up the beach, a few miles north of the castle. It's in ruins now...only a few walls standing. Mr. Temple, what's this all about?"

"The other night, we spoke of a valuable artifact that might be buried at the castle site," he said. "I'm afraid a rather unscrupulous man will try to steal it if he finds it. If he gets to the manor first...."

Marjorie frowned. "I would rather he didn't," she said. "Is there anything you can do—"

"I don't know, ma'am," he said, "but I'll try."

* * *

They hadn't bothered to hide their tracks. Jack looked at what was left of the old manor house and saw mounds of dirt and sand that had been shoveled away from underground walls. He saw the long, narrow niche where the Mandylion must have been hidden.

The bastard had it!

And Jack had only himself to blame. If he hadn't spent the week letting Dorrie go on believing he was nothing but a mercenary, out for revenge against her father, against her only living relative....

He had to find her. Once she realized what Alastair had in mind for the Mandylion, she would be indignant. And she wouldn't keep quiet about it.

Jack doubted that Bright would actually harm his daughter. But he didn't know about Fleming, and he'd never trusted the old man's other cohort, Neville Stockton, either. He had to find Dorrie and get her away from them before anything happened.

With a quick glance around the perimeter of the site, Jack discovered the tracks of wagon wheels in the mud. A minute later, he was following the trail Alastair had left.

The path led north and inland. Jack was certain the wagon had traveled this way, because clumps of mud that had fallen from the wheels were noticeable along the trail for the first hundred feet or so.

He followed the path, but at the base of a large, steep hill, Jack was stymied. The trail disappeared. Since the only way to go was up, and he didn't know what he would find when he got there, he tied his horse and started to ascend.

He wondered if Dorrie had managed to climb this hill. She'd had difficulty handling minor exertions, and Jack didn't think she was capable of getting to the top of this steep incline by herself. Paco Fleming might have carried her, but the thought of Fleming's hands on her made Jack's blood boil.

Fleming was too ruthless a brute to handle a woman as delicate as Dorrie.

Driven by his need to find Dorrie and get her away from her father, Jack quickly made it to the top and saw that there was an abandoned house nearby. He took cover behind what trees and shrubs there were and inched his way to the building.

The windows and doors were all broken, and the place was uninhabitable. Still, he went inside.

Most of the floor had rotted away, so he walked across the dirt, looking in each of the decaying rooms. It was clear that someone had been inside recently. The remains of a few meals and other refuse were here, as well as a blanket on the floor near one of the back windows.

And a woman's shoe.

Jack bent and picked it up. It was Dorrie's.

"Two thousand pounds," Bright said to the dark-skinned man in the turban.

Jack forced himself to remain in place, silently watching from his well-hidden niche behind a fishing boat. He'd followed horse tracks to the cove and discovered Alastair and his cohorts at the far end of the quay. Fishermen's boats as well as several pleasure boats were moored here, and a formidable steamship was anchored some distance out. A good many sailboats plied the coastal waters, too.

Jack felt a muscle spasm in his jaw as the Turk stepped around Dorothea's unconscious body, then knelt beside her. He wanted to break the man in two when he lifted her eyelids, then slid his hands around her waist, up her torso, and back down to her hips.

The Turk looked up at Bright and spoke. "She is damaged. One thousand."

"Bloody hell, she's worth ten times as much. She's a virgin and as fair as you are dark. That bruise will be gone in a few days. Two thousand."

"Fifteen hundred."

"Seventeen and we'll have a deal."

When their business was concluded, the man in the turban had one of his men haul Dorothea off the sand and load her into the dinghy. Jack almost came out of hiding to toss the fellow into the sea, but he waited. He would not be able to take on the two Turks with their scimitars, as well as Alastair and his men.

Jack saw Neville shove a thick leather purse into his shirt. He unwrapped his horse's reins and mounted. "I'm off then," Neville said. "See you in London."

Bright moved to do the same, but Paco stepped in front of him, preventing him from going to his horse. "My cut."

"You got your cut."

Paco crossed his arms over his massive chest and shook his head. "I think to sell girl. My cut." He held out one beefy hand. "Now."

"Forget it, Fleming," Bright said. "She was mine to sell. There's no commission."

The best thing to do was to take one of these boats and go after Dorrie while her father and Fleming were arguing. With any luck, he thought, the two would come to blows and beat each other senseless.

Taking his derringer from its usual place in his boot, Jack put it in his pocket. It had only two shots, so if Jack needed to shoot, he would have to make it count.

Fleming and Bright continued to argue, and Jack looked over the boats that were moored on the wharf. Most were fishing boats, too large for one man to handle. A couple of skiffs, a dinghy and several small sailboats were tied there.

Though it had been years since he'd sailed, Jack decided a sailboat would serve his purposes best. It was likely to move faster than he could row, and it would not seem out of place in these waters. The men who had Dorrie would not think twice when they saw a pleasure sailboat in their vicinity.

Dorothea came to consciousness slowly. She felt ill, though her heart seemed to be beating normally, and she did not feel short of breath. Her head ached abominably, and nausea assailed her. Something was wrong with her hands—she could not feel them.

When Dorothea finally gathered enough courage to crack one eyelid open, she could not get her bearings. She had no idea where she was.

Squinting against the flickering lights in the room, her surroundings came into focus. A wooden floor with a thick rug woven in an intricate pattern of colors. A massive desk with papers. A chair.

A powerful wave of dizziness hit her, and she closed her eyes again. Nothing was familiar. Not the sights, not the smells.

Dorothea tried to sit up, and realized that her hands were bound behind her. She was a prisoner! Had her father tied her up and locked her away in this room?

She did not doubt that the scoundrel would do such a thing to his own daughter. But where was she?

She struggled to swing her legs around and push herself to a sitting position without using her hands. A large, heavily curtained window was behind her, and when she managed to turn and look out, she discovered she was on the water. She was in some kind of boat.

Fighting dizziness, Dorothea stood up and realized she wore only one shoe. Puzzled by its loss, she knew there was nothing to be done about it now. She had to get free. Hoping there would be something sharp with which to cut her bonds, she made her way to the desk and turned her back to it, twisting her neck so she could see what she was doing.

She shifted the papers, then pulled out drawers in her search. But the most likely drawer—the center one—was locked. No matter how hard she tried, she could not get it to open. Remembering the last time she'd come across a locked drawer, she wished for Jack's small gun.

Then she let out a laugh that sounded more like a sob. If she had Jack's gun, she wouldn't need a knife, would she?

Turning her attention back to the drawer, Dorothea looked for something she could use to pry it open. She was sure there had to be something, if not on the desk, then somewhere in the room.

Voices from somewhere outside caught Dorothea's attention, and she froze in place. They did not sound like her father or the two men who worked for him.

Some instinct made her move quickly to the soft mattress she'd been lying on when she'd awakened. She had not been harmed while unconscious, so she could only think that whoever held her captive would leave her alone until she awakened. She lay down, closed her eyes and feigned insensibility while she wondered if she could make herself violently ill if the situation demanded it.

The door opened, and Dorothea discerned the voices of two men. Their language was not English.

As frightened as she was, she forced herself to remain limp and try to figure out what they were saying. For the next few moments, they were silent, then one of them touched her.

The man's hands were all over her, and Dorothea forced herself not to react in any way, even though it was the most awful, demeaning thing that had ever happened to her. As much as she wanted to let her mind go blank, she had to remain aware, in order to determine who they were and what they were going to do with her.

When they spoke, she was able to translate most of what was said, but it made no sense to her. The context of their conversation was strange—a lot of talk about money and percentages. Then, as one of the men spoke of her hair color, the other pulled up her eyelids and gasped sharply.

"Very unusual!" he exclaimed.

"What did I tell you," the first one said. "With all this soft, fair skin and those eyes, she will bring a fine price."

"Bright said she was a virgin. Have you tried her?"

"Of course not, lord," the man said, his voice sounding aghast. "She is yours. My gift...."

Dorothea was shocked and appalled but did not react visibly to their conversation, though she quaked with panic inside. As soon as they left, she would find a way to get her hands loose, then get out of there. There *had* to be a way.

A few minutes later, the two men stepped away from her. They argued about whether or not the one would keep her or if it would be better to regain the money they'd paid her father, by selling her when they returned to Istanbul.

Horrified, Dorothea swallowed repeatedly to keep from being sick. She had to keep her wits intact if she was going to have a chance at escape. The first challenge would be to get her hands freed. Then she would see about getting out the door, and after that… Maybe she would be able to find someone on this boat who would help—

The door crashed open and the two men ducked back into the room, followed by Jack Temple. He was barefoot and soaking wet, and Dorothea had never seen him look so fierce.

He struck at once, using his fist on one of the two men, knocking him to the floor. The second man drew his sword, but Jack ducked away from the jab and picked up the desk chair. He swung the chair, knocking the sword out of the man's hand, but the one on the ground suddenly stood and attacked Jack from behind.

Dorothea got herself to a sitting position and watched, terrified for Jack. But he grabbed the man behind him and threw him forward as if he weighed no more than a sack of feathers. The man crashed into the first attacker and landed heavily upon him.

Jack kicked the sword aside and pulled his little gun out of his pocket.

"Don't move," he ordered. "Dorrie, are you all

right?'' he asked without taking his eyes from the men.

"Jack!"

"I guess that means yes," he said as he knelt and began searching the two men. "Stay where you are. I'll get you out of those ropes in a minute."

When Jack was satisfied that he'd disarmed the men, he kept the gun trained on them and took a quick glance around the room. Reaching down, he picked up the sword and went to the window. In one quick slice, he'd cut the cords that held the heavy curtains open.

Before long, he had both men tied and gagged. Seeing that they were no longer a threat, he shoved the gun back into his pocket and turned to Dorrie.

"Hold out your arms, honey," he said. In an instant, she was free, but her hands burned with the tingling pain of her returning circulation. He pulled her into his arms, and Dorothea knew there was no place she'd rather be.

"Jack, I'm so sor—"

He kissed her, cutting off her apology. His hands cupped her chin, her cheeks, then slipped into her hair. "God, Dorrie, you had me worried."

She swallowed and pressed her forehead against his chin, so happy to be in his arms, yet afraid they would never escape. "How will we get out of here?" she asked. "How did *you* get here? How did you know how to fi—"

"Sweetheart, listen. We're going to have to steal a boat," he said. "This isn't going to be easy, but we can do it. Take the gun."

"Jack, I don't know how to shoot."

"That's all right, because it's full of seawater anyway. It won't shoot."

"Then what—"

"We might need to use it again, like I did with these two. Just as a threat." He pulled away from her and knelt at her feet. Taking hold of her one remaining shoe, he pulled it off. "You'll be cold but better off barefoot. Quieter."

He stood and took her hand, pulling her up to face him. "I was unfair to you, Dorrie," he said. "I could have told you any number of things that would have verified what I told you about your father, but I was stubborn. I wanted you to take my word for it."

"Jack, I know what he's like now."

He nodded. "But I never gave you credit for your loyalty to him. You put your faith in him and never heeded my accusations. I admire that, and I want you to trust *me* now, just as you did Alastair."

"I do, Jack," Dorothea said, then she added in a whisper, "I love you."

"Dorrie," he said, and an instant later, his lips came down on hers. She felt as if he were taking possession of her, body and soul. And when he tipped his head slightly to deepen the kiss, her bones melted.

He pulled away abruptly and shoved his fingers through his hair. "We've got to get out of here. Now," he said. "Follow me."

"Jack," she said, stopping him. "What about the Mandylion?" she asked. "Is it here on the ship?"

"I suppose, but there's no time to search for it," he said. "I've got what I came for, anyway."

He opened the door just a crack and looked outside. When he decided it was safe, he took Dorothea by the hand and led her from the room. They padded quietly down a short corridor that was dark but for a couple of oil lamps hanging from hooks in the walls. Dorothea jumped at every shadow and hoped they would meet no one.

They had almost reached the stairs when a man came out of nowhere, running at them, shouting for them to stop. Jack pushed Dorothea out of the way and met the attack, fighting fiercely until another crewman joined in. Dorothea fingered the small pistol and wondered if she could threaten these men with it.

She decided against it. What if she were forced to pull the trigger and nothing happened?

One of the men punched Jack's face and Dorothea saw blood streaming from a cut in his lip. Jack got in the next punch, but the second man reached for a length of something made of wood or possibly metal. He would have struck Jack with it, but Dorothea went down to the floor and, with both hands, yanked one of his legs out from under him. The man yelped as he fell heavily, and Dorothea scooted quickly away.

With one powerful punch, Jack slammed the other man into the wall, knocking one of the lanterns down. The wooden floor caught fire immediately as the oil spilled out and began to spread down the corridor. Both crewman shouted and started working to put out the flames, while Jack grabbed Dorothea's hand and ran up the stairs. Once on deck they kept running, and Dorothea knew Jack wanted to lead them away from where the crew would soon be concentrated. The fire was serving as an effective diversion.

When they got to a railing, Jack quickly looked around for any free crewmen, then pointed out toward shore. "There's no time to steal a lifeboat," he said. "See that little sailboat out there?"

Frowning, Dorothea shaded her eyes and looked into the distance. "Yes."

"That's our transportation," he said.

Panic welled in Dorothea's throat. "But Jack, I—"

"Do you trust me, honey?"

"Of course I do, but Jack...."

He sat on the edge of the rail, then picked her up and climbed over the side. And then he jumped.

Chapter Twenty-Three

It wasn't until they surfaced that Dorrie stopped fighting him. He knew she trusted him, but instinct made her flail her arms and legs in an effort to rise to the surface.

Holding on to her, he spoke while he swam, reassuring her that they were going to be fine.

He wasn't sure that was true, though. The fire on the Turk's ship had spread and black smoke billowed over the water. It was dangerous to be so close to such a fire, and he hurried to get to the small boat he'd anchored a discreet distance away.

It was a struggle to get on board once they reached it, but Jack managed to climb aboard, then pull Dorrie in after him. Once inside, she lay panting on the floor of the sailboat.

"Are you all right?" he asked.

Apparently unable to speak, she nodded and turned over. She threw her arms around Jack's neck and pulled him down, holding him close. "I don't know how you did it, but you saved my life, Jack," she cried. "Thank you."

"No thanks necessary," he said. "I did it for myself."

"What?"

"I plan on spending the rest of my life with you, honey," he said. "I *had* to come for you."

He kissed her mouth, her eyes, her neck, and then they started laughing.

"We'd better get out of here," he said, pulling up the anchor. The first explosion sounded just as Jack unfurled the sail and took hold of the tiller.

There was a steady wind, so he was able to put a good deal of distance between them and the burning ship. A few minutes later, there was another explosion and the steamship began to sink. Men were dropping lifeboats and jumping ship as Jack and Dorrie watched. They sailed away to a safe distance and watched as the Turkish ship sank, the Mandylion with her.

"It's tragic," Dorrie said. "The Mandylion was real. I saw it. I held it, and it healed what ailed me."

Jack didn't understand. "What do you mean?"

"My heart," she said. "It's been weak for most of my life."

Jack frowned, remembering all the times Dorrie had seemed too taxed by some minor physical exertion.

"I could never do the things other girls did," she said. "No swimming or riding, nothing vigorous... Whenever I got a chill, I couldn't warm up again."

Jack remembered that.

"My mother kept me close to her," she went on, "and made sure I did nothing to overexert myself, or I would end up in bed with fluid in my lungs and swelling in my ankles. The doctor said my heart was failing."

The thought of losing her made Jack's blood run cold. In a short time she had become everything to him. He wanted to show her all the exotic places in the world, and he wanted to take her to New York.

"Come home with me, Dorrie," Jack said, pulling her into his arms. "We'll find a doctor in New York who specializes in heart ailments, someone—"

"Jack," she said, taking his face in her hands. "My heart is, well, it's all right now. Last night, when my father and his men were digging at the manor house, I was sick. So sick that I could feel my heart beating out of control, my lungs filling with fluid, and...I thought I was dying."

"Christ, Dorrie—"

"No, listen. When they unearthed the Mandylion, I held it in my hands, and I felt something change. I wasn't weak and sick anymore. My heart beat strong and true. In a short while, my lungs were clear."

Jack looked down at her in puzzlement.

"Then, all night long, I overextended myself," she said. "I stayed up all night at Alastair's hideaway and stole the Mandylion when they went to sleep. I ran for miles, trying to get to you—"

"I would have found you."

"Paco found me first."

It had been a close call. Had he waited another hour, had Marjorie Browning not mentioned the song and the manor house...Jack might have lost her.

"Come here," he said. She scooted closer and, while keeping one hand on the tiller, he put the other arm around her. He kissed her forehead.

"What about the Mandylion?" she asked.

He shrugged. "What about it?"

"Do you think it will ever be recovered?"

Jack looked back at the ship going down in the deep waters of the North Sea. "No, honey. I don't think it's meant to be."

Several officials awaited them when they returned to shore. They were given blankets and hot tea and taken to the magistrate's office to give their version of the morning's events.

Dorothea watched through one of the windows as her father and his cohorts were taken away in manacles. She felt nothing but emptiness, watching him go.

Once their official statements were signed, Jack and Dorothea returned to the Marine Hotel, where they both bathed and dressed in their spare clothes. Neither of them mentioned the words they'd spoken while they were in the midst of danger.

After dark, when it was time for supper, Jack knocked on the door that adjoined their rooms. Dorothea finished buttoning her dress and called to him to come in.

He gave her half a smile, and Dorothea didn't think she'd ever seen him more rugged. More dangerous. His cheek was bruised and his lower lip battered, but he had never been more handsome.

His hair was dark, and too long, but it was mostly combed back, all but one rebellious lock that fell over his forehead. He'd recently shaved, so his jaw was smooth, touchable. He wore shirtsleeves and carried his collar in his hand. His suspenders hung down and his khaki trousers rode low on his hips.

His expression was dark and dangerous, and Dorothea watched as a muscle in his jaw clenched. "Are you very hungry?"

She shook her head and devoured him with her eyes. "Not really."

He walked toward her and tossed the collar onto the desk. "Would you consider postponing supper?"

"I could be persuaded," she said, hiding her nervousness.

He came closer and touched a wisp of hair that curled in front of her ear. Bending down, Jack touched his tongue to the spot and Dorothea shivered with arousal. "What's the key?"

"To persuading me?" she asked breathlessly.

"Mmm, hmm," he said, pressing his lips to her forehead, her jaw, her neck.

He continued with his little kisses while Dorothea opened the first button on his shirt. Her fingers moved steadily down, inch by inch, revealing his strong, muscular chest. When she reached his trousers, she pulled the cotton shirt out and pushed it off his shoulders. Then she touched the brown, pebbled disks that were hidden under a mat of dark hair.

"This is the key," she said, flicking her tongue over his nipple.

Jack's breath caught, and he grabbed her upper arms while she licked and teased the sensitive spot. She knew it was sweet torture. She remembered it well.

"Did I tell you what a hero you are?" she asked.

"No," Jack rasped. "Dorrie—"

"Kiss me, Jack," she said and raised up on her toes to reach him.

He slid his arms around her and when he touched her lips with his own, a burst of fire shot through Dorothea. She ached for him, for his touch. This meeting of mouths and tongues was not enough and she pressed her body against his, desperate for more.

When Jack slipped his hands to the buttons at the front of her dress, Dorothea was certain he'd read her mind. He slid the gown off her shoulders, letting it fall to the floor. Next, he worked on her corset laces, quickly freeing her from its confines.

"Jack...."

"You are so beautiful," he said, removing her chemise. A moment later, she stood before him clad only in thin cotton drawers and stockings. He cupped her breasts in his hands and teased the tips with his thumbs, then with his lips and tongue. "I want you," he said.

He picked her up and, taking her mouth with his, carried her to the bed. Gently setting her down, he stretched out beside her and pulled her to face him.

He made love to her mouth again, while his hands slid across her body, seeking the places that would give her the most pleasure. Dorothea sighed and began her own exploration, until they were both fully naked and Jack was poised above her.

His blue eyes had darkened with intensity, the planes of his face fierce with his passionate arousal. Though she was nervous, she did not fear him, did not wish to stop.

"I love you, Dorrie," he said, pressing a kiss to her breastbone, then moving lower, caressing, tasting. "Marry me."

Her eyes drifted closed, and she felt as if she were floating. Blood pooled low and hot and when his tongue touched her most sensitive place, her hips rocked in a spasm of such exquisite pleasure, she thought her heart—whole as it was—would burst.

The euphoria was both physical and spiritual, and it continued, even as Jack entered her, making her part of him. Him part of her. He drove into her again and again, and she wrapped her legs around him to hold him inside her, forever.

Finally, keeping his eyes locked with hers, he made a low sound and shuddered violently, even as he gathered her into his arms. "Dorrie," he whispered in her ear.

She wrapped her arms around him and pulled him down to her, rolling with him to the side. Emotion clogged her throat, preventing her from saying what was in her heart. She felt fulfilled in a way she'd never imagined, completed by this man who had so recently been a stranger to her.

Of course she would marry him. She had been renewed and made whole again. And Jack was a part of her. She loved him and trusted him with her life.

He trailed one finger across her collarbone, then down to one sensitive breast after the other. He touched her face and wrapped a tendril of her hair around his finger.

"Give me your answer, Dorrie Bright," he said.

She nipped his earlobe lightly with her teeth. "Will you teach me everything there is to know about the sheela-na-gig?"

"Right after you learn a few lessons about the linga," he said, his voice husky and full of love.

"In that case, I'm all yours, Jack Temple. Forever."

*   *   *   *   *

Travel back in time to the British and Scottish Isles with Harlequin Historicals

On Sale July 2003

BEAUCHAMP BESIEGED by Elaine Knighton
(England, 1206-1210)

*A feisty Welshwoman and a fierce English knight
are used as political pawns—and discover
the passion of a lifetime!*

THE BETRAYAL by Ruth Langan
(Scotland, 1500s)

*When a highland laird fights his way into the
Mystical Kingdom to prevent a grave injustice,
will he become spellbound by an enchanting witch?*

On Sale August 2003

**A DANGEROUS SEDUCTION
by Patricia Frances Rowell**
(England, 1816)

*An earl hell-bent on revenge discovers the fine
line between hate and love when he falls for
the wife of his mortal enemy!*

A MOMENT'S MADNESS by Helen Kirkman
(England, 917 A.D.)

*With danger swirling around them, will a
courageous Danish woman and a fearless Saxon
warrior find their heart's desire in each other's arms?*

Visit us at www.eHarlequin.com

HARLEQUIN HISTORICALS®

HHMED31

HAVE A HANKERIN' FOR SOME DOWN-HOME WESTERNS? THEN PICK UP THESE SPICY ROMANCES FROM HARLEQUIN HISTORICALS®

On sale May 2003

WYOMING WIDOW by Elizabeth Lane
(Wyoming, 1865)

A pregnant widow in dire straits pretends to be the sweetheart of a missing bachelor. But will her best-laid plans fall by the wayside when she becomes irresistibly drawn to her "darlin's" dashing brother?

THE OTHER BRIDE by Lisa Bingham
(New York and Oregon, 1870)

You won't want to miss this first installment of an exciting two-book series about a titled Englishwoman and her maid who decide to switch places when they reach America!

On sale June 2003

BLISSFUL, TEXAS by Liz Ireland
(Texas, 1880)

When a prim and proper lady sets out to reform Blissful, Texas, she never expects to have such *im*proper thoughts about the town's roguish saloon owner!

WINNING JENNA'S HEART by Charlene Sands
(Oklahoma, 1869)

A spirited ranch owner tends to a handsome amnesiac she believes to be her long-distance fiancé. But will he be able to reclaim her heart once his true identity comes to light?

Visit us at www.eHarlequin.com

HARLEQUIN HISTORICALS®

HHWEST25

Three brothers, one
tuxedo…and one destiny!

Date With Destiny

A brand-new anthology from
USA TODAY bestselling author
KRISTINE ROLOFSON
MURIEL JENSEN
KRISTIN GABRIEL

The package said "R. Perez" and
inside was a tuxedo. But which
Perez brother—Rick, Rafe or
Rob—was it addressed to? This
tuxedo is on a mission…to lead
each of these men to the altar!

DATE WITH DESTINY
will introduce you to
the characters of
Forrester Square…
an exciting new continuity
starting in August 2003.

Forrester Square
LEGACIES . LIES . LOVE .

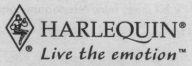

HARLEQUIN®
Live the emotion™

Visit us at www.eHarlequin.com

PHDWD

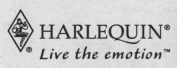

LOOKIN' FOR RIVETING TALES ABOUT RUGGED MEN AND THE FEISTY LADIES WHO TRY TO TAME THEM?

From Harlequin Historicals

July 2003

TEXAS GOLD by Carolyn Davidson

A fiercely independent farmer's past catches up with her when the husband she left behind turns up on her doorstep!

OF MEN AND ANGELS by Victoria Bylin

Can a hard-edged outlaw find redemption—and true love—in the arms of an angelic young woman?

On sale August 2003

BLACKSTONE'S BRIDE by Bronwyn Williams

Will a beleaguered gold miner's widow and a wounded half-breed ignite a searing passion when they form a united front?

HIGH PLAINS WIFE by Jillian Hart

A taciturn rancher proposes a marriage of convenience to a secretly smitten spinster who has designs on his heart!

Visit us at www.eHarlequin.com

HARLEQUIN HISTORICALS®

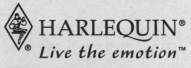

COMING NEXT MONTH FROM

HARLEQUIN HISTORICALS®

- **THE NOTORIOUS MARRIAGE**
  by **Nicola Cornick,** author of LADY ALLERTON'S WAGER
  Eleanor Trevithick's hasty marriage to Kit, Lord Mostyn, was
  enough to have the gossips in an uproar. But then it was heard that
  her new husband had disappeared a day after the wedding, not to
  return for five months…and their marriage became the most notorious in town!

  HH #659 ISBN# 29259-7 $5.25 U.S./$6.25 CAN.

- **SAVING SARAH**
  by **Gail Ranstrom,** author of A WILD JUSTICE
  Lady Sarah Hunter prowled London after dark to investigate the dis-
  appearance of her friend's children and unwittingly found herself
  engaging in a dangerous game of double identities with dishonored
  nobleman Ethan Travis. Now, would Ethan's love be enough to heal
  the wounds of Sarah's past?

  HH #660 ISBN# 29260-0 $5.25 U.S./$6.25 CAN.

- **BLISSFUL, TEXAS**
  by **Liz Ireland,** author of TROUBLE IN PARADISE
  Prim and proper Lacy Calhoun's world was turned upside
  down when she returned to her hometown and discovered that her
  mother was running the local bordello! And even more surprising
  were Lacy's *im*proper thoughts about the infuriating and oh-so-
  handsome Lucas Burns!

  HH #661 ISBN# 29261-9 $5.25 U.S./$6.25 CAN.

- **WINNING JENNA'S HEART**
  by **Charlene Sands,** author of CHASE WHEELER'S WOMAN
  Jenna Duncan was sure the handsome amnesiac found on her property
  was her longtime correspondent who had finally come to marry her.
  But when Jenna learned his true identity, would she be willing to risk
  her heart?

  HH #662 ISBN# 29262-7 $5.25 U.S./$6.25 CAN.

KEEP AN EYE OUT FOR ALL FOUR
OF THESE TERRIFIC NEW TITLES

HHCNM0503